DEACON

STONE SOCIETY BOOK 12

BY FAITH GIBSON

I0598270

Copyright © 2019 by Faith Gibson

Published by: Bramblerose Press LLC

Editor: Jagged Rose Wordsmithing

First edition: September 2019

Cover design: Jay Aheer, Simply Defined Art

Cover photography: Adobe Stock

ISBN: 978-1732864849

Dedication

For Laurann. You're the reason I fell in love with paranormal. The fact that you read my books is humbling. Thank you from the bottom of my heart.

Acknowledgements

First off, I need to thank my readers for waiting on Deacon's story. The Stone Clan is my heart and soul, and I can't tell you all how much I appreciate you loving them almost as much as I do. I always knew this book would be hard to write, and it was. I hope you read the words and remember how precious family is. Whether by blood or not, there are people who come into your life and you just know they are your tribe.

Speaking of tribes, I have to thank mine. It grows and changes, but at the core, there are a certain group of people who take my journey with me. Some daily, some every once in a while. I couldn't do it without you: Candy, Chris, Jennifer, Katie, Kendall, Kerstin, Nikki, and Riley – I love you all.

Thank you to the beta readers who take the time to read the unpolished version and offer feedback.

A special shout out goes out to Ana Martinez and Vernon Donbraska for choosing Sabrina's name back when I was writing Jonas.

Jay Aheer of Simply Defined Art, thanks for making Deacon and the Atlanta cityscape shine.

To the man - I love you will never be enough.

Prologue

2027

New Chicago

SABRINA WAS DESPERATE to find food. She opened all the cabinet doors again, praying she'd overlooked a can of soup or a container of noodles. She wasn't surprised to find nothing. She was surprised the utilities hadn't been turned off. It was the middle of the month, so hopefully they had a few more days until that happened. Because it would happen.

"Sabrina, I'm hungry," Jasmine whined for the tenth time in as many minutes. Sabrina was hungry too, but there just wasn't any food in the house. During the week, things weren't so bad since they could at least eat lunch at school. But it was Saturday. She had used the last of the rice for breakfast. Trying to keep four mouths fed without money was getting impossible. Their mother, Michelle, had gone to work on a Tuesday three weeks ago and never returned. Her mom worked two jobs to make ends meet, and sometimes she went on a date on the free night she had off from the diner where she waitressed. Sabrina called both the office and diner when she didn't come home, but both managers said her mom hadn't shown up for work that day. Every day, Sabrina called, and every day, she received the same

1

message. Nobody had seen nor heard from Michelle. When the manager at the office asked Sabrina who was looking after her and her siblings, she lied and told him their grandmother.

Being fifteen and the oldest, Sabrina took it upon herself to watch over her younger siblings, praying her mother would return, because if she didn't, they were going to starve. Or worse. Sabrina knew she couldn't get a job, not without quitting school. Even if she did that, she wasn't old enough to work the hours it would take to bring in enough money to put food on the table and keep the lights and water on.

Sabrina had no idea who her father was. Jasmine's had been killed in a drive-by shooting eight years ago, and Terrence and Jerrick's father was in jail and had been since before Jerrick, their youngest brother, was born. Sabrina had no idea who the man's parents were or if they were alive.

Sabrina's grandmother, Cynthia Woodard, had money, but Sabrina didn't think she'd be willing to help. When Sabrina had been born, her grandmother tried to get Michelle to give her up for adoption, but she'd refused. Grandmother had relented but vowed if Michelle didn't finish school and go to college, she would be cut off permanently. Michelle towed the line for a couple years, but when she met Jasmine's father, she'd fallen in love with the man who swore he'd take care of Michelle and her child. Both he and Cynthia were true to their word. Grandmother cut Michelle out of her life, and Maurice took care of them until he was gunned down.

"Bree!" Jasmine wailed.

"I know, Jas, but we just don't have anything." Sabrina blinked hard to keep the tears from falling. She had done the best she could for three weeks, but now it looked like it wasn't going to be enough. She knew if she asked anyone for help, the police would come, and they'd be separated. With no other recourse, she went to her mother's bedroom and found the notebook her mother kept with phone numbers, social security numbers, and insurance information. Sabrina took the book back into the kitchen where the landline hung on the wall. She didn't know any other kids who still had the old-fashioned type phone, but she didn't care if it wasn't a fancy cell phone.

When she removed the receiver from the hook, she held her breath, praying there would be a dial tone. When the normally annoying sound came through, she sighed before taking another deep breath and dialed her grandmother's number. After it rang five times, an automated voice spoke, saying the person she was trying to reach was unavailable. At the beep, she cleared her throat. "Uh, Grandmother, it's Sabrina. I'm sorry to bother you, but Momma's missing, and we're all hungry. I did the best I could, and I wouldn't call unless it was an emergency. We're out of food, so I guess, to us, that's an emergen—" Another beep sounded, and Sabrina stared at the receiver. She didn't know whether to call back or not.

Sabrina hung the phone up and stood staring at it. A small hand found hers, and Sabrina looked down to find Jerrick staring at her with his thumb in his mouth. It was something he'd grown out of a long time ago, but after their mother didn't return home, he'd reverted back to doing it and not only at night. She picked up his slight frame and hugged him close. Jasmine and Terrence were watching. "Did she answer? Is she going to help?" Jasmine asked.

"I left her a message, but yeah, she'll help us," Sabrina said, praying she wasn't lying. "We just have to wait a few hours for her to get here. Let's go play a game to get our minds off our bellies."

Terrence and Jasmine hated Candyland, but it was the only game they had that Jerrick could play as well. Sabrina did her best to concentrate on the game, but she couldn't stop wondering if she should try her grandmother again. If the woman didn't get the message for a day or two, all of them were going to be starving. A spoonful of rice between her younger siblings wouldn't last long in sating their hunger. Sabrina had given up her own portion and divided it between the others. It was a sacrifice she would make again if only they had something to share.

A knock at the door had all the kids freezing. "Stay here," Sabrina said while standing from where they were seated around the worn coffee table. She peered through the peephole. When she saw not only her grandmother but a policeman and a scowling, strange woman, Sabrina shoved her fist in her mouth to keep from crying out. Sure, Grandmother had come to the rescue, but she'd brought trouble with her. Sabrina turned to look at the hopeful faces of her siblings, and in that moment, she knew she had no choice but to open the door.

"Sabrina? It's your grandmother. Open up." She looked again through the peephole to see her grandmother motioning toward the door to the cop. When he took a step forward, Sabrina unlocked the deadbolt. She pulled open the door slowly, but her grandmother pushed her way inside. That was Cynthia Woodard – large and in charge. "Sabrina, this is Officer Kelly and Miss Higgins."

"Did you bring us some food?" Jerrick asked, still sitting on his knees by the coffee table.

"No. I thought we'd discuss your mother first."

"But we're hungry," Jerrick whined.

"I'll find something while you talk to your granddaughter," Miss Higgins said.

"You won't find anything. We ate the last of the rice this morning," Sabrina told her.

"Surely there's soup or something," her grandmother responded.

"When I said we're out of food, I meant completely out.

I stretched it as far as I could."

"I'll send my partner to the store," Officer Kelly offered. He stepped out of the room while pulling out his cell phone.

Miss Higgins asked, "Why don't we sit down?"

Sabrina sat on the sofa, and her siblings rushed to sit beside her. Jerrick crawled onto her lap, and Sabrina wrapped her arms around his waist. He stuck his thumb in his mouth, leaning his head against her shoulder. She didn't miss the frown on her grandmother's face. Grandmother took a look at the battered chair and remained standing. Miss Higgins either wasn't too good to sit on the worn-out furniture, or she was better at hiding her disgust. It wasn't that bad.

As soon as the policeman returned, Miss Higgins asked, "How long has your mother been missing?"

"Three weeks. She left for work on Tuesday, the twelfth. She didn't have to work at the diner that night, so she had a date. When she wasn't home the next morning, I got worried and called the office. She never showed up that day. There or the diner. I kept calling, but she never went back to either job."

"Who's been taking care of you?"

Sabrina ducked her head. She knew she couldn't lie, because she had no one to back her up. "I have."

"You've been getting the kids to school and feeding them? What about paying bills?"

"I make sure they get on the bus, and then I walk since my bus comes early. I guess Momma paid the bills before she left since nothing's been cut off yet."

"You're a very brave young lady, Sabrina. I understand wanting to take care of your brothers and sister, but that responsibility shouldn't fall on your shoulders. Your grandmother told me" — Miss Higgins looked at a notepad Sabrina hadn't noticed before then — "Jasmine's father is deceased, and the boys' dad is incarcerated. What can you

5

tell me about their grandparents?"

Sabrina shrugged. "Nothing. I don't really remember Jasmine's grandparents. We haven't seen them since the funeral. We never saw the boys' grandparents."

Sabrina looked at her own grandmother. "What's going to happen to us?"

Instead of Cynthia responding, Miss Higgins spoke up. "First thing we're going to do is have the police try to find your mother. While they're doing that, we're going to see if we can find your siblings' grandparents or some close relatives. You'll be going with Mrs. Woodard."

"No! You can't separate us. Grandmother! Do something. You can take them in. You can take us all in!"

"That's just not possible, Sabrina. You will come live with me, but I'm afraid your brothers and sister will have to find other accommodations."

"You mean like a foster home! No. Miss Higgins, please don't separate us. I can take care of them. At least until Momma comes home." The adults passed a look between themselves, and in that moment, she knew – her mother wasn't coming home.

"You've done a wonderful job looking out for your siblings, Sabrina. But you just aren't old enough to be given that responsibility full time, especially without the means to support them. I promise I'll do my best to place them with family first."

Another knock sounded at the door, and the officer opened it for his partner. A younger man was holding bags of food and a drink carrier. "I wasn't sure what you liked, but I figured burgers were a safe bet," he said as he carried it all toward the kitchen. Their apartment was small with the living room being separated from the kitchen by a six-person table. Her siblings, momentarily forgetting the conversation, ran to the officer.

"Thank you," Sabrina said as she pulled the food from

the bags and handed Jasmine and Terrence a burger and order of fries, then opened Jerrick's for him, getting him situated with ketchup before she passed out the drinks. Only then did she sit down to her own meal. "I know you're starving, but don't eat so fast you make yourselves sick." Sabrina didn't have the same problem. Even though she was hungry, she had trouble swallowing around the lump in her throat.

Yes, they needed help, but at what cost? They were going to be separated. She knew it, and it broke her heart. But was that worse than dying from starvation? At some point, the utilities would have been turned off, and then they'd have likely frozen in the coming months.

While they were eating, the adults whispered to each other. Grandmother's face was sad yet stern as always. The officers kept glancing at them with pity in their eyes, and Miss Higgins just looked tired. Sabrina knew how she felt. Instead of approaching them all, she had to try one more time. She stood and walked to her grandmother, taking the woman's hand and leading her down the short hallway to her bedroom. When she closed the door, she begged, "Grandmother, please. Take us all."

"Sabrina, I'm sorry. I just don't have the room. Things have changed since you were little." Her grandmother tried to smile, but she just couldn't seem to bring herself to do it. "I've been sick, child. I had to stop working a few years ago, and I don't have the money I used to. I sold my home, and now I live in a two-bedroom apartment. Granted, it's in a nice neighborhood, but I just can't take them all in. And now with your mother…" Grandmother lost the stoic façade she always wore, and tears leaked from her eyes. "Now that your mother's gone, I'll have to take care of any finances she left you with. I'm truly sorry. But I promise, we'll keep in touch with your brothers and sister, and I'll make sure you can see them as much as you want."

Sabrina nodded, refusing to cry. She had to stay strong for her siblings. Returning to the living room, she pulled them all to the couch and told them, "I promise you, no matter what, we'll always be a family. I'll come see you as often as I can." Jerrick didn't completely understand what was going on, but the older ones did. When Miss Higgins told them she'd contacted Jasmine's grandparents, Sabrina felt a little better, but it was her brothers she worried about. If they had no other family, they would be put into foster care, and Sabrina had seen enough kids in her class come out of the system with scars, both internal and external.

While they were packing, an older couple appeared in the living room. Jasmine's grandparents, Ezra and Delsie Wilson, welcomed their granddaughter with open arms, and when they heard about the boys' plight, they agreed then and there to take them into their home. Miss Higgins made a few calls and was happy to announce the three of them could remain together for the time being. Sabrina almost asked if she could go with them, but the four of them would be asking too much. They packed as many of their belongings as they could. Since the apartment was paid up until the end of the month, Grandmother assured them all they could come back for anything they couldn't take with them on their first trip.

After tight hugs and lots of tears, Sabrina watched as her siblings walked away with Jasmine's grandparents. She knew it was for the best, but it didn't make the heartache any less.

Chapter One

DEACON WAS DESPERATE to find relief. Visiting Jonathan and sitting with Priscilla was painful, but being around Sabrina was equally as tormenting. From the first time Dr. Bailey – Sabrina – walked into Jonathan's room while Deacon was there, he had fought the pull to drag his mate to the nearest closet and make her his. He couldn't, though. If she was anyone else, anyone besides a doctor, maybe he would. But Sabrina was smart. Beautiful. She was needed by those like Jonathan who depended on her to make them better. She would be a blessed addition to his life, but what could he offer her? Other than money, nothing.

From patrolling for Unholy, watching over the Pen, and hiding from his mate, he was exhausted. That was saying a lot considering he was a Gargoyle. It took a lot for them to get tired. On top of all that was the mental exhaustion from his empathic power. Or curse, as he usually called it. All Goyles felt emotions in others, but it was amplified in him for some reason. Deacon had been around the others when they found their mates, so he knew what to expect. Or so he thought. Staying away from Dr. Sabrina Bailey was equal parts necessary and excruciating. He had too much on his plate to get involved, but at the same time, he needed her like he needed air.

He watched her intently as she came in and out of

Jonathan's room without ever introducing himself. In fact, he did his best not to make eye contact and avoided being in the room at the same time if at all possible. Deacon wasn't ready for all that came with having a mate, especially one as important as his. What would someone like Sabrina see in one such as Deacon? She was an oncologist in one of the best hospitals in the South, and if Jonas had his way, she would be the next chief of staff. Deacon was a warden at a penitentiary. She deserved someone who had a high-profile job. Someone who was smart like she was. Someone whose looks matched hers. The only thing they had in common was the color of their skin. No, he had nothing to offer the stunning female, and he wouldn't tie her down with a mate bond. Besides that, whenever they were in the room together? She made it perfectly clear by the way her eyes narrowed she was not interested. If he didn't know better, Deacon would say the doctor was scared of him.

If Sabrina wasn't Jonathan's oncologist, Deacon wouldn't run into her as often as he did, but he couldn't stay away from the human male who'd come to mean so much to all the Clan. They all took turns sitting with the man when he felt like company, but each of them had important jobs to do. Lately, Gregor had been spending more time than usual at the Pen giving Deacon days off he didn't necessarily want.

Pulling the iron skillet of cornbread from the oven, Deacon didn't register the pain on his palm until he was opening the drawer to grab a knife. Deacon placed the skillet on the stove and held his hand out, watching as the reddened skin turned back to its normal shade of dark tan. He sighed, knowing his scattered thoughts needed to be corralled. He wasn't worried about himself, but if he wasn't paying attention when around humans, someone else might pay the price.

After buttering a couple slices of cornbread, Deacon added them to his plate of leftover roast, okra, and mashed

10

potatoes. Normally, he would have added fresh, sliced tomatoes to his meal, but he hadn't had time for a vegetable garden, and the ones from the store had no taste. Padding barefoot over to the table, he slumped down into one of the chairs. The pine table was large enough for ten people in a house just as spacious. He'd allowed Sixx to convince him to purchase the place in the middle of forty acres, telling him he might one day find his mate and start a family. Hope was an elusive beast most days, but on that day, he'd allowed it to seep in and agreed on purchasing the property.

Deacon couldn't call it a home, because he knew homes were built on love. Family. Mates and children. As he ate his food without really tasting it, Deacon imagined Sabrina coming home to him after a long shift at the hospital. He would have supper ready for her, and they would enjoy it along with a glass of wine before settling in to snuggle on the sofa while listening to her favorite music. Or curled up together on the screened-in porch while listening to the frogs and crickets fill the night with nature's music.

Scrubbing a hand over his face, Deacon pushed back the ache in his chest. He should be happy to know he had a mate. Eager to get to know her and let her know him. If he was a different kind of male, he would be. But Sabrina Bailey deserved better than someone as simple as him. If he was ever going to pursue her, and he knew it was inevitable, he needed to go shopping. His black fatigues, worn blue jeans, and T-shirts weren't going to cut it. He needed some button-ups and at least a couple pairs of nice jeans. The ones he owned were threadbare and had holes in the knees. Perfect for setting out on his Harley but nowhere the type of clothing to take a doctor out to dinner.

Pushing away from the table, Deacon grabbed the empty plate and placed it in the sink. He dumped the rest of the leftovers into the garbage and put the dishes in the sink with the plate. Much like cooking, washing up the dirty pots and

11

pans was soothing most of the time. When he'd dried and put everything away, he crumbled the rest of the cornbread then took it outside, scattering it over the ground for the birds. He checked the hummingbird feeders and watered the various plants and flowers in the small garden he'd designed just off the patio to attract the little birds that fascinated him. He had added this section of plants immediately after moving in, and they came back each year bigger and brighter than the last.

Deacon was on the schedule to patrol the city for Unholy that night, so he changed out of his knit shorts and into his battle gear. Opting to ride his Harley, he left the sanctuary he called home and headed toward downtown. Since he was going to be in the area, Deacon first stopped by the hospital. Hopefully, Sabrina would already be gone.

Jonathan was in a good mood considering all he was going through. He wasn't getting better. In fact, the cancer was spreading, and he had called Rafael that evening, asking him to stop by the hospital alone. While they waited, Jonathan talked about his family who had dedicated their lives to taking care of the Di Pietros. Rafael's family, which hailed from Italy, was one of the most well-loved and respected Gargoyle Clans in the world, and Jonathan considered it an honor to have been part of Rafe's life, as well as all the other members of his family.

When Rafael arrived, Deacon stepped outside the room to give them privacy, and that's how he found himself in a heated argument with his mate. He felt her before she came into view, and it didn't surprise him when she headed his direction.

"I need you to step aside." Sabrina stopped several feet away, tucking her hair behind one ear before shoving her hands in the pockets of her white lab coat.

Deacon crossed his arms over his chest, not to be imposing, but to keep from grabbing the stunning doctor and throwing her over his shoulder like a caveman. Dr. Bailey

12

was an exquisite African American who stood about six inches shorter than Deacon. The perfect height to rest against his shoulder. Her dark hair framed her face, and her eyes were an exquisite shade of light brown. Eyes that were currently lit with fire.

"Jonathan and Rafael are speaking privately. I'm sure you can give them a few minutes alone. Can I buy you a cup of coffee while we wait?"

The doctor took in Deacon, from his fitted black T-shirt, his black fatigues, all the way down to his black boots. "No, you can't buy me coffee. What you can do is get out of my way before I call someone to have you removed."

Deacon pulled his phone out of his back pocket and flipped through the contacts. "Here. Call Dr. Mooneyham."

"Why do you have the chief of staff's number on your speed dial?"

"He's family." Sabrina's eyebrows dipped, and he pulled the phone back when she didn't take it. "His daughter works with me, and his niece is my boss's wife. So, family."

"You work with Isabelle?" Sabrina's voice rose as if she didn't believe him. Deacon didn't think the doctor was a bad person, but here she stood, judging him without knowing him.

"I do. If you'd like, I can have her vouch for me."

"What I'd like is to see my patient. I'm a busy doctor, and—"

The door opened, and a grief-stricken Rafael stepped through. "Dr. Bailey, would you please join us?" He motioned toward the room. It didn't take an empath to know Rafael was reeling from Jonathan's announcement.

"Of course."

Deacon stepped aside so the doctor could enter the room. He inclined his head to Sabrina before placing his hand on Rafael's shoulder, giving it a squeeze. "I'm going to patrol, but call me if you need me." Rafael gave a barely

13

perceptible nod before ushering the doctor into Jonathan's room. He hated leaving Rafael, but Deacon had a job to do. He knew Rafael had a mate who would comfort him far better than Deacon could, so he exited the hospital, straddled his bike, and met the other Goyles who were patrolling the city with him.

Slade landed next to Deacon on the balcony outside Rafael's office. They'd been patrolling for hours and had yet to sight one Unholy. Deacon had been surprised to see Slade, but he didn't give voice to the question of why the Goyle wasn't with Matthew. Instead, he did question what was going on below. "Where are they?"

"I was wondering the same thing. It's not like them to hide several nights in a row."

"Deacon, you need to see this." Malakai's voice was strong through the comm in Deacon's ear. Ever since Julian had upgraded the small device, it had made their lives easier when flying over the city.

"Where are you?"

"Two blocks south of the hospital."

Deacon and Slade launched themselves into the sky and headed that direction. Rafael's office was a couple miles from the hospital, but using their shifter speed, it didn't take long to meet up with Kai and the others. When they landed atop one of the tallest buildings in downtown, Deacon noticed what had the other Gargoyle flustered. Around twenty Unholy were marching in formation down the street. But that was all they were doing. Where the beasts normally fought amongst themselves or wreaked havoc on human businesses, these were silently strolling down a dark alley in a quieter part of the city. The one walking in front of the others was talking on a cell phone.

"When did they start using phones?" Kai asked.

"And walking in formation?" Deacon used his shifter hearing to listen in on the conversation.

14

"...headed back now. Tell Drago the program was successful. All the men reacted positively."

"Okay, that's just strange. They look like Unholy, but...," Deacon mused aloud. He wondered at the program the man spoke of.

"They sure as hell aren't acting like it. Do you want to go question the guy with the phone?" Slade asked. "I'd like to know what kind of program he was referring to."

"So would I. Let me get Frey on the line first." Deacon stepped away from the edge of the building and pulled out his cell phone. When Frey answered, Deacon said, "Frey, we've encountered something strange." Deacon recounted the scene below as well as the partially overheard conversation.

"Have Kai's team follow them to see where they go. If you can, you and Slade grab an Unholy from the back and bring him to the Pen. We'll question him and find out what we can."

"We're on it." Deacon disconnected. He didn't have to relay the plan, because the others were able to clearly hear Frey's voice.

"As soon as the others round the corner, you grab his right arm, and I'll get his left," Deacon told Slade who nodded in affirmation. In perfect choreography, the two of them dove off the rooftop and used their wings to slow them when they reached the Unholy right before he rounded the corner. Using one hand to grip the Unholy's bicep and the other to cover his mouth, Deacon dug his claws in to keep a tight grip on the male. The Unholy didn't fight their hold while in flight, but as soon as they landed on the roof, he struggled to break free.

"Let me go! I wasn't causing trouble."

Deacon and Slade looked at one another when the male spoke coherently. Most of the Unholy they'd come across were mindless fighting machines. He continued struggling,

15

but he was no match for two mature Gargoyles. Slade wasted no time securing the male's arms behind his back while Deacon gagged him.

After making sure there were no humans in the area, Deacon and Slade dropped to the ground with the Unholy between them and met Kai at the tricked-out SUV the Clan used in transporting their "guests." After getting the male restrained in the back, they waited for Kai and his group to return to the vehicle.

"What the hell, Deke? When did Unholy learn how to talk in full sentences?"

"I don't know, Brother. Let's hope he's willing to give us that answer when we question him at the Pen."

It took a while for Kai's group to return. "They piled into a van, and we had to follow in the air. They drove to an old warehouse over off Industry Boulevard. They were alone, but the inside was set up like barracks with room for approximately one hundred males. Since we have the location, we didn't wait around to see what they did next." The male inside the SUV was staring straight ahead. "I guess we need to get this one to Frey. You coming with?"

Deacon and Slade both confirmed they were, and they silently walked back to where they'd parked, lost in their own thoughts.

Chapter Two

SABRINA MADE IT to the lounge before the tears fell. Her nerves had been on edge from facing the big man guarding Mr. Holt's door. His voice had been soft and placating. Hell, he even offered to get her a coffee, but his size had her trembling. On top of that, Mr. Holt had decided to halt all treatment. Sabrina hated when patients gave up, but it was their decision. She saw daily how much the chemo and radiation took out of her patients, but not having experienced it personally, she had no right to argue with them. Not when they were older and tired, like Jonathan.

His employer, Rafael Stone, had sat stoically while Jonathan told Sabrina of his decision. She didn't have to be empathic to know how badly Mr. Stone was hurting. The haunted eyes belied the calm outward façade. She was glad Mr. Holt's sister hadn't been in the room upon his announcement. Sabrina could only imagine how that conversation was going to go. On more than one occasion, Priscilla had been physically removed from her brother's room, and Dr. Mooneyham had even given her a mild sedative one of those times. Seeing the two siblings together made Sabrina think of her own brothers and sister.

Sabrina had no idea what it would be like to have a sibling hurt so badly on her behalf. Maybe Jasmine would be sad. Sabrina had kept in touch with her and her brothers as much as possible while they were growing up in different homes. They'd lost contact the years Sabrina was in college and then med school. By the time she was finished, Jasmine had gone to college as well, getting her degree in social work. Sabrina was proud of her sister, wanting to help children who had lost their parents or been kicked out of their homes.

Terrence had gone to college, and last Sabrina spoke with him, he was living in California working for a pharmaceutical company. Jerrick had joined the military, but Sabrina and the others lost touch with him once he enlisted. Both Jasmine's grandparents had passed away, but before they died, they hadn't heard from Jerrick in years. The four siblings had been lucky after their mother disappeared. Sabrina had been worried the boys would have to go into the foster care system, but the Wilsons had moved heaven and earth to keep the three siblings together. Sabrina often wished she'd been with them, but whenever she had that thought, she felt guilty. Her own grandmother had given Sabrina what she could monetarily, even if it was more out of familial obligation. Never once did her grandmother tell Sabrina she loved her.

The door to the lounge opened, and Sabrina swiped the tears off her face. Sabrina was surprised to find Dr. Mooneyham standing there. "Sabrina, my dear. Are you all right?"

"Yes. Just..." Sabrina sighed. "It never gets easier, but you probably know all about that."

"I do. Listen, I wanted to talk to you about something. When you have a few minutes, please come find me in my office."

"Of course. I'm finished with my rounds, so do you want to meet now or tomorrow?"

"That's up to you. If you aren't too drained, we can talk now. It might help take your mind off Jonathan."

"How did...? Never mind. Let me grab my things and

18

I'll meet you downstairs in, say, twenty minutes?"

"I'll be waiting." The chief of staff left her alone in the lounge, and Sabrina blew out a breath. She was curious as to what Joseph wanted to talk to her about, and if it would help take her mind off Mr. Holt, she was all for it. After making sure she didn't look like a raccoon, Sabrina retrieved her purse from her office after inputting some notes into her computer then headed downstairs.

It had been a couple years since she'd been inside Joseph's office, but it hadn't changed much. The only thing she noticed different was the addition of some photos. She took one of the plush, leather chairs opposite his desk and relaxed as much as she could. Sabrina had no reason to be nervous, but being called to the office without being told why was enough to give her pause.

"I'll make this quick to ease your worries. I will be retiring soon, and I'm hoping you'll be interested in taking my place."

Sabrina sat up, her hands on the arms of the chair. "You want me to be chief of staff?" Sabrina never would have imagined that was what he was going to discuss with her.

"Do you have a better candidate? Sabrina, you're one of the best doctors I have ever had the pleasure of working with. You're smart. You are dedicated. But above that, you care. I need to pass the hat to someone who has the patients' best interests at heart, not someone who's going to run the hospital like a business."

"Isn't it a business, though?" As chief of hematology and oncology, Sabrina knew what it took to oversee a department. For the last several years, she had run her group like a well-oiled machine, but did she want to be in charge of all departments?

"In a sense, yes. But the business end is for the CEO to handle. My job is to oversee the other chiefs and make sure the patients are taken care of first and foremost. You manage your department better than any of the chiefs we have on staff. You may treat it as a business, but you do it with care and compassion. If one of your doctors isn't available, you're always there to take up the slack. Your department is the only one which hasn't received a complaint filed since you've been head of your department. I know what it takes to run this hospital, and I believe you are the best doctor for the position. I don't need your answer right away. Take time to think about it. I'm not one to pry into my staff's personal life, but as far as I know, you don't have a partner at home to discuss your decision with."

"Is that part of your reasoning in choosing me? I don't have someone at home; therefore, I'm going to be here all the time like I am now? Because if so, I don't plan to stay single the rest of my life. If the position is going to require longer hours than I already have, that's not a selling point."

"No, you being single has nothing to do with my recommendation. Even though it wasn't what I meant, it was insensitive of me, and I apologize. If anything, I know once you find someone to share your life with, you'll be more than capable of managing a home and work life."

Sabrina was stunned. She'd always admired the doctor, but she never knew he held her in such high regard. "May I ask you a question? It has nothing to do with this, but I'm curious."

"About?"

Sabrina clasped her hands in her lap. "The men who come to visit Mr. Holt. Who are they, exactly?"

Joseph rested his elbows on the arms of his leather chair and steepled his fingers under his chin. "You know Rafael Stone is Jonathan's employer. The others are either members of Rafael's family or those he holds in high regard. The Stones are hugely responsible for reviving this city over the past thirty years, and they have many they consider family whether by blood or not. Those are the men coming to visit

Jonathan. They also consider him and Priscilla family. Is there someone in particular you're wondering about?"

Sabrina didn't want to delve into her personal life, not when Joseph was considering her to take his place, but it seemed he knew these men well. She didn't have to admit to what happened in her past. "They're all so... intimidating."

"Yes, they are, but they're protectors. I can assure you of one thing; Rafael would trust any of them with the life of his wife and unborn son. And now that you're part of Jonathan's life? You've automatically been added to the list of those under their protection."

Sabrina sat up taller, scooting to the front of her chair. "Protection? Why would I need protection? Are they some kind of mob? Am I in danger?"

"Oh, heavens no. I only meant you're one of theirs now. Let's say you're driving home after work one night and your car breaks down. You could call any of the men and they'd be there and have you home before Triple A even shows up. I can see by the incredulity on your face you don't believe me, but I have no reason to lie. These men consider me family since my daughter and niece are married to two of them. I know them, Sabrina. I know the kind of men they are. They're the good guys. The ones depicted in romance novels. The ones other men could only aspire to being."

Sabrina relaxed back into the seat and did her best not to roll her eyes. That would be both immature and unprofessional. "That's ridiculous. I'm nothing more to them than Mr. Holt's doctor."

"I promise you are much more to them than that. Don't let their size intimidate you. Surely you have seen Frey and Abbi?"

"Yes. I've met them a couple times."

"Have you noticed how Frey is with his wife? How he looks at her? Touches her constantly? He's one of the largest of their Clan, and he would rather die than let something

21

happen to Abigail or their children. All the men you've met are the same way. I promise you have nothing to fear from them. Especially Deacon."

"Deacon?"

"Yes, the black male who seems to fancy you."

At least now she had a name and could stop calling him "the man". "Wait. Did you say clan?"

Joseph grinned, shrugging one shoulder. "Eh. It sounds better than tribe. Let's just say there are a lot of people the Stones consider family, and whether you want to believe it or not, you are now one of them."

Sabrina needed to direct her boss away from the topic at hand before she laughed at him. "It sounds far-fetched, but I'll take your word for it. You haven't steered me wrong in all the years we've known each other."

"Excellent. Now, why don't you go on home and get some rest? I know today was trying for you with Jonathan's decision."

"I will. Thank you for the recommendation. It means the world to me."

"You're most welcome. I'll see you tomorrow."

Sabrina's head was spinning as she left her boss's office. She felt better about the man – Deacon – now that Joseph had vouched for him as well as all the others who visited Mr. Holt. But being considered one of their own? That was nonsense. As soon as the cancer took its final toll on the man's body, she would never see his family again. Unless...

No. Sabrina wasn't the type to ask a man out. But he had already offered to get her coffee. She could always take him up on his offer, just a day or two later. Couldn't she? There was something about Deacon that drew her to him, besides his good looks and soft demeanor. No. She shouldn't think about getting involved with a man now. Not when she had to consider Joseph's offer to take over as chief of staff. If she was even approved by the board. There would be multiple candidates, and some of her colleagues were more than ready to step into Joseph's shoes. Some who wouldn't be happy if Sabrina were to get the position. She wasn't going to worry about that now. Joseph didn't mention how long she had to decide, but since it wasn't immediately, she had time to give it some thought.

It was later than usual when she exited the elevator into the parking garage. Sabrina was one of the lucky ones who had a reserved spot. She'd long ago learned to wear sensible shoes, and her soft soles made no noise as she strode across the concrete. Cars on upper decks rolling over the metal joints echoed around her. Honking from the street met with doors closing and people talking. The air wasn't yet steamy in the New Atlanta early evening, but it would be getting that way soon.

Sabrina clicked the unlock button on her key fob, and the headlights blinked as the alarm sounded. When she was about ten feet from her car, an aluminum can skidded across the concrete. Having thought she was alone, the hair on Sabrina's arms stood on end as if she'd touched a raw electrical wire. She turned to see if someone was behind her, but there was no one there. There had to be, though. There was no wind blowing to have pushed the can along the ground. Hurrying, she got her door open, and she slid into the leather seat of her sedan. Once safely inside with the door locked, Sabrina looked in her rearview mirror.

Shivering, she started the engine and backed out of the spot. When she put the car in drive and accelerated forward, she took another glance in the mirror. In the corner, the shadow of a man slipped behind a concrete pillar. "It was another doctor. That's all." At least that's what she tried to convince herself.

DRAGO BIT THE end of an unlit cigar while staring out the passenger window of the SUV. He'd tossed Arden the keys, because if Drago got behind the wheel, he would have played demolition derby with the humans on the road. After finding his mate murdered, Drago spent a week hunting the Goyle responsible. When he finally caught up with the male, he'd been holed up in an abandoned warehouse. The other Gargoyle didn't have a sword with him, probably having rushed from the hotel where they'd been staying. It wasn't a fair fight, but killing Drago's mate hadn't been fair either. Before he took the male's head, Drago asked why he'd felt the need to kill to the human woman. The male, like an idiot, shrugged and said because he could. Drago shrugged his own shoulders and swung his sword with all the rage he held inside. He'd tasked a couple of his followers with cleanup. Even though the warehouse was abandoned, they didn't need some homeless human stumbling upon a decapitated Gargoyle.

Audrey had given Drago a purpose outside of defeating the American King, if only for a couple days. Now that purpose had been taken from him, and there was nothing left but rage. It simmered below the surface waiting to be unleashed. Arden drove silently, letting Drago stew in his turmoil. He only spoke when Drago gave him direction or asked yes or no questions. They needed money. He still had some of what Kallisto had sent, but assembling an army was costly. The Greek Goyles had pledged their loyalty to him. All except the one who was no longer with his head. If he asked them to do something illegal or immoral, they would.

If he was going to go up against the Stone Clan, they needed swords. They couldn't fight against other Gargoyles and win without them. Swords of the caliber they needed required cash. Finding someone to forge them wasn't impossible, but finding someone who could forge the

24

number of weapons they needed who wouldn't ask questions was. Most of the Greeks had managed to travel abroad with their own, but some had not. Those Unholy who were taking to the new drug well – the Reborn – also needed to be armed. Drago required funds for more of the serum as well as weapons. He'd received a call from Trexon only minutes before with the good news about the success of the latest experiment.

It was imperative the newly arrived Greeks had ways of making money outside of regular jobs, and Drago knew a way to accomplish that. Kavin and Burk, along with quite a few Gargoyles from Greece, were doing well in California. Kavin had managed to get in with a security firm who took jobs which weren't legal. Mercenaries for hire. It suited the Gargoyles perfectly for the time being, and those who had come from Greece who were willing to work were fitting in well.

Drugs were a messy business, one Drago wasn't interested in. People, however, were a different story. For whatever reason, most Gargoyles were not only naturally fit but handsome as well. With nothing more than a look, both women and men gave themselves over to a night with the males. At least that was what Drago had experienced in his long life. Human trafficking was a lucrative business. Even Alistair, with all his money, had been involved in the trade. Over the last thirty years, with governments focused on rebuilding, the fight against such things had fallen through the proverbial cracks. Drago was ready to take advantage of the less than stellar job the American police did in tracking down those who bought and sold humans.

It was another reason for having a base of operations on the Eastern seaboard. Moving humans quickly was imperative to success, and the man they were going to meet needed someone who could provide humans in a timely manner. Drago had to be successful for his ultimate plan to succeed. He glanced in the side mirror at the large, paneled truck following along. Instead of showing up at the meeting empty-handed, Drago was going to show Mr. Collins he and the Goyles were more than capable of delivering the merchandise.

Chapter Three

THE BASEMENT WAS the lowest level of the penitentiary. It was where the Unholy were locked away from the other inmates. Isabelle wasn't allowed in the Basement, so Dante was on hand to assist in interrogating the Unholy Deacon and Slade had brought in. Normally, Gregor or Deacon would take the lead in whatever was going on in the building since they were both wardens, but the male they had in custody was unlike any Unholy they'd ever encountered, so Frey was there in official Clan capacity. Deacon and Slade stood off to one side, while Dante stood next to the door.

"What's your name?" Frey asked the less-than-monstrous-looking Unholy who was secured to a chair in the middle of a large room that was otherwise empty.

"I want my lawyer."

All the Goyles looked at one another. They'd never heard one of the creatures speak much less with reason.

"You aren't under arrest, so there will be no lawyer. My name is Geoffrey Hartley. We only want to ask you some questions about the Unholy you live with."

"I know what you are, Mr. Hartley. Or should I call you Frey? Isn't that what your family and friends call you?"

"Are you saying you're my friend? Because if so, this will go a lot smoother."

"No, I don't reckon we are. But I do know you and all

27

your buddies here aren't any more human than I am. I've seen all of you when you're out hunting us."

"Then you should know what we're capable of."

"True, but you don't scare me. If I tell you what you want to hear, you'll either kill me or send me back, and they'll kill me. Either way, I'm dead. And I'm okay with that. I didn't ask to be turned into a monster."

"We aren't going to kill you, and if you help us, we won't send you back either. What's your name?"

The male blew out a breath and looked up at the ceiling. Frey waited patiently for the man to decide whether or not he was going to cooperate. After a couple minutes, he looked at Frey. "Evan Powell."

"Thank you, Evan. Can you tell us how you came to be an Unholy?"

Evan shifted in his seat and returned his stare to the far wall. "I got out of the military and couldn't find a job. I made a deal with the devil, and I lost a part of myself I didn't think was left. Turns out I was wrong."

"What part was that?"

"My humanity. I did things for my country. Saw things. It changed me. Then I agreed to work for Gordon Flanagan, but I didn't understand the consequences of what he was offering."

"But you're not the same as you were before, right? What happened to set you back to normal?"

"I guarantee I'm not normal. As for how I'm able to think for myself again, that's a blur. The past several years are nothing more than static, like when a radio is set between stations. One minute I'm a soldier without a platoon. I'm looking for a job that no one will give me. The government taught me how to hunt and kill, but they didn't teach me how to reacclimate to being back in society. You can't live without money, and you can't get money without a job. So, when I was approached with an offer that sounded too good to be true, I took it. A few days later, things went from bad to worse. I was nothing more than an animal in a cage following orders. The next thing I know, I'm being led out of a building, walking behind others like me. Until those two grabbed me." The male gestured to where Deacon and Slade were leaning against the wall.

"After you were turned, did you have the ability to think for yourself?"

"Yes? Maybe. I don't know. I think at some point, whatever was done began wearing off, but it was all I knew by that time. I had no one waiting for me. Nowhere to go, and no money to get there with."

"I thought Flanagan paid you."

"It was a lie. He promised the world, but that world was only a different kind of hell than the one I'd been living in. I guess I should have read the fine print."

"You signed a contract?"

He nodded. "For all the good it did."

"How many humans have you harmed since agreeing to join Flanagan?" In the thirty years since Flanagan raised the first Unholy, hundreds of humans had been injured, but less than twenty had died at their hands, as far as the Clan knew.

"None. Most of the time, we were told to fight each other."

"And the other times?"

"Until Flanagan disappeared, that was it. Now the new boss is building an army. One that can fight against you."

"How do you know this?"

"They think the Unholy are all mindless zombies. Most might be, but I could hear them talking."

"You said 'they'. Do you know the names of the men in charge now?"

"No last names, but the big boss is Drago. He had two helping for a while – Kavin and Burk – but I haven't seen them around lately. Two more showed up not too long ago.

29

Their names are weird too, like Ren and Trax. I'm not sure, though. Drago hasn't been around for a couple weeks or more that I know of."

Dante pushed off the wall. "Evan, do you know if any of the other Unholy are experiencing the effects wearing off?"

"We don't really talk to one another."

"What about those of you who have undergone treatment to counter the effects? How many are there?"

"There were twenty of us in my group. I've noticed a handful of others who were taken a couple at a time, but that's it."

"Can you tell us who administered the test?"

"I'm pretty sure it was a Dr. Craven."

Dante's demeanor went from stoic to contemplative. That name meant something to him. "Thank you, Evan. Frey, can I talk to you outside?"

Frey inclined his head and followed his cousin out the door. Deacon and Slade remained silent while waiting. Deacon almost felt bad for Evan. He'd heard of men and women returning from war without the means necessary to return to civilian life. He never understood why the government didn't take more care of their soldiers once their tours were up, after they'd given so much of themselves. He'd seen countless wars over the years, and although he hadn't fought in any of them, he knew Frey had. If the male wasn't Gargoyle and part of a huge Clan who had his back, he might have turned out like Evan.

Deacon didn't have to reach out with his shifter senses to know how Evan was feeling. The sadness and fatigue were like a small cyclone, circling the man and emanating outward.

When Frey and Dante returned, Evan said, "Please, just kill me now. I can't return to the others, and I don't want to be locked up in here for the rest of my life."

Frey walked over to stand in front of Evan. "We're not

30

going to kill you. With your permission, we'd like to take a blood sample."

"What for?"

Dante stepped up beside Frey. "We'd like to see if we can determine what you were given to counteract what made you an Unholy. We are going to put you in a cell for the time being. If you cooperate, you will be treated well."

"And if I don't?"

"You'll be treated like any other Unholy, with no privileges."

"I'd rather just die."

"Evan, do you not have family out there looking for you? Parents? A girlfriend or wife?" Slade asked. The male was naturally laid-back, but the concern for their captive was palpable.

Evan hesitated before answering. "No. They... I reached out to them when I got out of the service, but they're pacifists. They told me if I enlisted not to come back when I got out."

Dante placed his hand on the male's shoulder, and his tension eased somewhat. More than once, Dante had done the same to Deacon when the pain was too much to bear. "Will you let me draw your blood?"

"Yeah." Evan dropped his chin to his chest.

"Thank you, Evan. If you'll come with me to the infirmary, we'll get that taken care of, then we'll find you a room to rest in and some food if you're hungry." When the man nodded, Dante gripped Evan by his bicep and helped him stand him from the chair.

Frey motioned for Slade to go with Dante. Once the door was closed, Frey said, "For now, put him next to Gabriel where Kallisto is. Make sure he's comfortable. We'll have to talk to Rafe about our next steps, but I want to figure out if he's telling the truth about not hurting humans. I can't willfully keep him behind bars just for the choice he made to trust Flanagan."

"I agree. I wonder how many more were in Evan's same position when they agreed to the experiment. If we can figure out what the anti-serum is…" Deacon didn't finish his thought. His heart was leading him in a direction he didn't know if the others would agree with. "I'll go make sure the cell is set up." Frey clapped Deacon on the shoulder as he walked by but didn't argue. In all his years, Deacon had never killed another being, even an Unholy. He'd fought them plenty, but in the end, he'd used his fists to take them down and send them to the Pen. If he had his way, they would find the anti-serum and return every last Unholy to their former selves. Then they could weed through which ones were good and which were not. If that happened? Maybe their lives could see some peace for a while.

When Deacon arrived at the room next to Gabriel's, Isabelle was talking to her brother through the glass. The Gargoyle had been through hell when Gordon Flanagan's men caught him as he was going through his initial transition. Gabriel didn't remember much of what happened after that, and if it wasn't for the fact that he was Isabelle's brother, the male would have been taken out after he kidnapped Kaya. Over the months he'd been in the Pen, Gabriel had come a long way in recovering, but every once in a while, he had moments where Vincent Alexander, the cold-blooded killer Flanagan trained him to be, would try to push his way forth. It was those times Isabelle left her office and went straight to her brother. She was the only one who could calm him down. Isabelle wasn't allowed around her brother out of his cell unless there were two Gargoyles with her, but she would stand outside his door for hours on end talking to him, reminding him of the brother he'd been when she was a toddler.

It was also against the rules for Isabelle to give Gabriel cigarettes, but she did it when she thought she could get

32

away with it. Like now. Deacon didn't have to smell the smoke to know what was going on. The guilty expression on Dante's mate's face said it all.

"Isabelle."

"Deacon, I was just…" She thumbed over her shoulder toward the door and backed away.

"It's okay. I won't tell this time." He grinned at the doctor, shaking his head. He would never admit it, but he had snuck a few cigarettes to the male on more than one occasion, but it was always when Gabriel was allowed outside for his sunlight breaks. Isabelle had tried the stop-smoking patches, but with Gabriel having a Gargoyle's metabolism, they didn't work. Deacon didn't see anything wrong with giving the male the only thing he requested.

"Did Dante tell you why he's here?" Deacon asked.

"Just the basics. I thought I'd spend time with my brother while I waited on him."

"Dante has taken Evan, the male we're interrogating, to your clinic to draw blood. I'm getting this room ready for him until we figure out what to do with him."

"If you got a name out of him, that means he isn't Unholy, right?"

"He, along with several others, have been given something to counteract the effects. It's why Dante is taking blood samples. To see if you can figure out what it is that changes them back to being able to function somewhat normally."

"Yes!" Isabelle pumped her fist into the air. When Deacon stepped back at her outburst, Isabelle blushed. "Don't take this the wrong way, but not enough inmates get sick. You rarely call me, and I'm bored."

Deacon had a feeling there was more to it than her being bored. "What about Connor?" If Deacon had a child, he would be hard-pressed to spend any time away from him or her. He would want to make sure they were always safe and happy, but he knew that was an impossibility. It was one of the reasons he didn't want offspring.

"He is spending a lot of time with Amelia now that school's out. They play while Abbi's teaching her dance classes. As much as I miss him, it gives him time to just be a little boy. When he's around her, he focuses on her and not having a tutor for a while. Against his wishes, Dante and I decided to give him a summer break like other kids get."

Deacon knew Connor's special gifts had made it hard for the boy to thrive in school. On top of being able to see things in his mind, he was years ahead of his peers when it came to knowledge. The boy was a genius, and his parents were trying to give him a normal childhood instead of allowing him to skip grades just because he knew more than some of his teachers.

"Izzy," Gabriel called from inside his cell.

Isabelle turned her attention to her brother. "What is it, Gabriel?" She insisted everyone call him by his real name and not the one he'd gone by when he worked for Flanagan.

Gabriel didn't say anything else, and Deacon couldn't see inside his room, because the window in the door was small. Isabelle pushed open the slot where they passed his food tray to him and held out her hand. Deacon could smell the stench of extinguished cigarettes. When Isabelle pulled her hand back, she glanced up at Deacon. "I would apologize, but it's his one enjoyment in life."

"Like I said, I won't tell. Now, I need to get this room ready for Evan. You need to go throw those away and wash your hands."

Isabelle told her brother she'd see him later, and as Isabelle past by Deacon, she patted him on the arm. "You're a good male, Deacon Wright."

Deacon shook his head, grinning. He wondered what Dante thought of his mate breaking the rules for her brother. He had a feeling the medical examiner would chastise her

34

then pull her in for a long kiss. Thinking of kissing had Deacon thinking of his own mate. Would he get on to her if she broke the rules? Probably not. He'd rather get to kissing her. When his jeans started getting a little too tight, he did his best to push those kinds of thoughts from his mind and got back to the task at hand.

Chapter Four

SABRINA INCLINED HER head to the man standing inside Mr. Holt's room. She was equally relieved and disappointed it wasn't Deacon. He had been front and center in her dream, and in it, he was gentle and loving. Sabrina was pleased to find Kaya Stone sitting quietly with Jonathan when she went to check on him. It wasn't the first time she'd found the former police chief visiting with Jonathan, but knowing the man worked for Kaya and her husband, she wasn't surprised. He wasn't just an employee; he was family.

Sabrina approached the bed, and Kaya gave Sabrina a sad smile as she rose to her feet. Kaya's hand immediately cradled her large belly, and Sabrina was briefly hit with a wave of jealousy. She hadn't been lying when she told Joseph she didn't plan on being single the rest of her life. She wanted the husband and kids and dogs, and the chaotic life that went with having those things.

"How are you?" Kaya asked, pulling Sabrina's hands into her own, offering comfort. Sabrina almost lied, because it would have been easier and more professional to tell the other woman she was fine. When Kaya squeezed her hands, Sabrina found herself telling the truth.

"Not too well. I..." Sabrina looked to Jonathan to make sure the man was sleeping.

Kaya released her hands and put her arm around Sabrina's shoulder, ushering her out into the hallway. "You can talk to me, Dr. Bailey."

"Please, call me Sabrina." In that moment, she wanted nothing more than to be talking to Kaya as a friend and not a doctor. She didn't have any friends, only colleagues and acquaintances. Lately, she'd been realizing how lonely her life had become. All she had was work and her patients. When she first started out, that had been enough, but seeing Kaya and the other women who visited Jonathan with their husbands had been a wake-up call. The love between not only the couples but between all the visitors to Mr. Holt's room was both heartwarming and bittersweet. What would it be like to have a man look at her the way Rafael did Kaya? To know you had so many who considered you family? Sabrina had her siblings, but with them scattered across the country, they weren't close.

"Okay, Sabrina. If I had known the reason Rafael was coming to see Jonathan last night, I would have come with him. This can't be easy for you."

"No, it's not, but in my line of work, you either learn to compartmentalize the pain, or you go home every night and cry yourself to sleep. He's not the first patient to decline treatment, and he won't be the last. The only bright spot is knowing he has such a huge support system in place."

"That he does. I wanted to speak to you about that. Jonathan doesn't want Priscilla to know about his decision."

"But she's his sister."

"She is, but you've seen her when she thought he had a chance at getting better. If she knows he is no longer receiving treatment, we'll have to keep her sedated. Her brother is her whole world, and I can only hope this little one will be enough to help her through her loss." Kaya patted her stomach. "Oh, crap. Sebastian, calm down, kiddo." Kaya smiled. "That's better. Thank you."

That tinge of jealousy was back, but Sabrina did her best to hide it. "I like the way you talk to him like he can understand you."

Kaya's cheeks flushed, but she smiled and admitted, "I feel like he can. Do you have kids?"

"No, not yet."

"Well, when you do, you'll understand. I carry around this little person with me twenty-four seven. Sometimes, he's the only one I have to talk to, and I've always had regular conversations with him. I tell him how much his Papa and I love him. Tell him all the things we're looking forward to when he gets here. I try to keep my fears to myself, but I swear, he already knows my moods. Like now, when I mentioned Priscilla, he pushed at me so I'd know he heard me. Maybe I'm crazy, but..." Kaya shrugged, the pink in her cheeks returning.

"I don't think you're crazy. I think it's wonderful, and hopefully one day, I'll get to experience it for myself."

"Are you seeing anyone? Because I happen to know a certain someone who is quite smitten with you." Kaya cocked an eyebrow, grinning.

"Uh, no. I'm not seeing anyone."

"Good. That gives me hope."

Sabrina couldn't help her own grin. "And why is that?"

"Because the—"

"Kaya."

Sabrina shivered at the deep voice. She already knew who it belonged to, but when she turned to face him, she took a step backwards. Then Sabrina remembered Joseph's words from the night before about how all the men who visited Mr. Holt were kind despite how large they were.

"Hello, Dr. Bailey."

"I'm just going to go back and check on Jonathan." Kaya pressed her hand to Sabrina's, giving her a wink. Oh. *Oh.*

"Hello, Mister...?"

38

"WRIGHT. MY NAME'S Deacon Wright. I was hoping you'd take me up on my offer for coffee, and if you're too busy for coffee, maybe I could treat you to dinner sometime soon instead? How do you feel about Italian?" What in the name of all that was holy was he doing asking her to dinner?

Deacon had been around the others when they found their mates, so he knew what to expect. Or so he thought. Resisting Sabrina was an exercise in futility, but the way she was studying him didn't mean she felt the same. His beast was rumbling in the recesses of his mind, which meant it was butting in. *Stop pushing.*

It's inevitable.

He knew his beast was right, but he thought he was stronger than that.

There's nothing stronger than the pull to our mate. You know this.

He did know it, but he didn't have to act on it. When he stepped off the elevator, Deacon had reached out to see if he could sense Sabrina. Not only did he feel her, but he also heard her voice as she and Kaya spoke softly outside Jonathan's room. And it seemed his Queen was trying to play matchmaker.

Sabrina studied his face a few seconds before she sighed. Deacon braced himself for rejection, but the doctor surprised him. "Actually, Italian is my favorite, so yes. You may take me to dinner."

"Really?"

Sabrina cocked her head to the side, frowning. "Do you often ask women out expecting to be turned down?"

"No. I don't ask women out." When she raised her eyebrows, he continued, "I don't date." Deacon should really shut up, but her confusion was as tangible as her distrust. He knew the mate bond should have already kicked in, drawing her to him. There was an undercurrent of lust, but reluctance was shoving her desire out of the way. That made sense, because under normal circumstances, there was no way a smart, sophisticated woman like her would ever be interested in a commoner like him. "What I'm trying and failing to say is I'm a busy male without a lot of free time, but I would never forgive myself if I didn't take you out."

"May I ask you a question?"

"Of course."

"How do you know Mr. Holt? I assume you're close to him with as much time as you spend in his room."

"He's family." When Sabrina crossed her arms over her chest, he explained, "Long story short, he and his sister, Priscilla, are the caretakers for Rafael and Kaya. That part you already know. Rafael's brother, Gregor, is my boss, and over the years, all the Stones welcomed me into their homes as part of the family. I spend every Sunday at Rafael's manor with his extended family. I love Jonathan like a father. We all do."

"That explains why there are so many visitors. I asked Dr. Mooneyham about that, and he said you all were family but didn't go into detail."

"It's going to be a huge loss to all of us when Jonathan passes."

Sabrina saddened at Deacon's words. He wanted to pull her into his arms and offer comfort, but he didn't want her pushing him away. He used his words instead to help ease the pain. "Death is inevitable, Dr. Bailey. Especially when someone is as sick as Jonathan."

"We were hopeful the next round of treatment would make a difference. You knew Mr. Holt decided to stop treatment, didn't you?" Her tone wasn't accusing. Not exactly.

Deacon wouldn't lie to her. Not about that. He would do

40

his best to always tell his mate the truth, but until they were truly bonded – if they were ever bonded – he might have to omit things she couldn't be aware of. "Yes. It's why I wanted to give Rafael time alone with Jonathan."

"I don't understand. There are other options we haven't tried. I hate seeing any of my patients give up."

Deacon reached out, against his better judgement, and took her hand in his larger ones. The need to touch her was great, and as soon as she felt his skin against hers, her eyes widened. "The fact that you care so deeply about your patients is one of the things which makes you a great doctor, but sometimes, a person can only take so much before they need peace. You've already tried several regimens, and Jonathan is tired and has been for a long time. He's lived a good life, but he's ready for the peace that only death will bring." His mate stood there, staring at him. "I'm sorry. I didn't mean to upset you." Deacon took a step back, releasing her hand.

Sabrina shook her head. "No, you didn't. Not really. I understand what you're saying about wanting peace. There are times when a person comes to a point in their life when all hope is lost."

Deacon wanted to know at what point in Sabrina's life she'd lost hope, because he had no doubt she was speaking from experience. As her mate, it was his duty to protect her from anything that impacted her, whether it was keeping her safe physically or making sure she had the best life possible to ensure she was content mentally. His beast was right. It was inevitable, and he needed to get over his insecurities that he wasn't the best male for her. He couldn't let one thing from his past dictate his future. If the fates deemed him worthy, who was he to argue? They had their reasons even if he couldn't see them. The only way he was going to be able to give her that best life was to move forward instead of hiding from her.

"About that dinner. If I may have your phone number, please?" Deacon pulled his phone out of his back pocket, unlocked it, and handed it over.

Sabrina hesitated, but she eventually took it and added her contact information. "I'm free Thursday night," she said, handing his phone back.

"Excellent. How's six o'clock?"

"That works for me. I'll text you my address." Sabrina smiled, but it didn't reach her eyes. Deacon figured she was thinking about Jonathan. "Now, I'm going to go in and check on my patient."

Deacon pushed the door open, allowing Sabrina to enter ahead of him. While she walked over to the bed, he stopped to speak to Kai.

"I was on my way to the morgue and thought I'd stop and say hello." Deacon was using Trevor as an excuse to try and catch a glimpse of Sabrina. He had no business at the morgue, but he'd become fond of Jasper's mate. The human was funny as well as quirky, and the two of them had bonded over their love of video games, even if Trevor kicked his ass more often than not.

Deacon glanced over at Kaya who was grinning at him. He shook his head and rolled his eyes at her. He knew his Queen meant well, and he couldn't be mad at her for trying to put in a good word for him with Sabrina. He was glad he interrupted her, though. It wasn't her place to get him and Sabrina together. Deacon felt his mate's eyes on him, and when he turned to her, she had an amused look on her face. She'd no doubt caught the silent exchange between him and Kaya.

Malakai motioned toward the door. "Let's give them some privacy."

Deacon wanted to remain in the room with Sabrina, but he had work to do. He'd only stopped by to see how Jonathan was feeling, hoping to see his mate, and since he

42

had Kaya and Malakai keeping him company, Deacon didn't want to overwhelm the man. He took one last look at Sabrina before closing the door.

"Congrats, Brother." Kai clapped Deacon on the shoulder, squeezing.

"For?"

"Taking the first step with your mate." Kai took a few steps away from the door, but he didn't go so far that he couldn't see it. He shoved his hands in the back pockets of his jeans. "It gives me hope, you know? Watching all of you find your mates makes me think there's someone out there for me, too."

"It's something I've always longed for, but now that it's within my grasp, I'm scared, Brother. Scared I won't be able to keep her safe. I'm worried I'm not good enough for her. Terrified she'll find me lacking after our date and decide I'm not what she wants."

"What about the mate bond? That alone should assure you about being with her."

"It should, but I also believe our mates should have a choice. Just because the fates think we are perfect for one another, what if Sabrina only finds me attractive because of it? She's a doctor, and I'm... I'm just me."

"Do you think Gregor isn't good enough for Tessa? That Frey isn't good enough for Abbi? I could understand if you were comparing yourself to Rafael, who's King. Or Julian who is a genius. But Gregor has the same job you do, and Frey owns a gym."

"No, of course not. I guess I see what you're saying. And I'm not saying Sabrina is better than Tessa or Abbi because she's a doctor. I just don't want to ever feel like she's settling."

Kai crossed his arms over his chest. "I'm in the same boat. I don't even own a gym; I merely work at one. But let me remind you. Like me, you have more money than you'll

43

ever spend. You're smart, you're kind, and you're one of the good guys. We are so much more than our job title. I don't care if my mate turns out to be a princess or the next president or a maid. If I'm ever lucky enough to find my one, I'm going to grab her tight and never let go. I'll do everything in my power to protect her and make her happy. I'll give her every reason to see me for the male I am and not my job title."

Deacon admired his friend's determination. He knew Kai was right, but Deacon had never been all that confident, no matter that he was a Gargoyle. He needed to take a page out of Kai's book and think positively.

"You're right, Brother. Thursday night, I'm going to start showing Sabrina I'm the male for her."

"That's the spirit. Now, let's talk about Unholy."

44

Chapter Five

SABRINA COULDN'T THINK straight around Deacon, and when he touched her? Her brain momentarily short-circuited. He apologized for upsetting her, but it wasn't his words that had her staring at him without speaking. She'd never encountered such a visceral need to be around someone the way she did when she encountered Deacon Wright. Over the past few weeks, she'd been drawn to him whenever she entered Mr. Holt's room. Deacon attempted to blend into the background whenever she saw him, but that was impossible. At over six feet, the man was imposing in height as well as with his broad shoulders that seemed to carry the weight of the world on them. She'd never been intimidated by any man until her last boyfriend had used his mass to coerce Sabrina. And even though Deacon scared her with his size, there was something about him she couldn't ignore.

She didn't miss the silent conversation between him and Kaya. By the rolling of his eyes, Deacon found Kaya's interference in his personal life ridiculous, if the smirk on his face was any indication. She felt better about saying yes to dinner when she realized Kaya felt comfortable enough with the guy to butt in. Rafael Stone wasn't small by any stretch of the imagination, but Deacon was nearly as large as Frey Hartley, another one of Jonathan's "family." If Deacon was half as gentle with her as Frey was with his wife, she might get through dinner on Thursday without throwing up or running out the back door of the restaurant. Or both.

It had been several years since Sabrina had been in a relationship. At first, she was hopeful Garrison would be the one. She'd dated a couple guys in college, but her focus had been on studying. She always knew, once she decided to become a doctor, she would put her studies and career first. Then, once she was established in her profession, she could relax a little and begin dating. She met Garrison at a hospital fundraiser. He was charming and kind. Said the right words. Did the right things. Things that had Sabrina overlooking the little red flags she should have seen. Having not been around a healthy relationship since her mother had been married to Jasmine's father – and she'd been young back then – Sabrina had nothing to gauge her own relationship by.

In the beginning, Sabrina insisted they take things slowly, and Garrison agreed. When she first allowed him to keep a toothbrush and change of clothes at her house, it made sense. When her closet began filling up with more of his clothes, and her bathroom counter had as many of his toiletries as hers, Sabrina stepped back to assess the situation. She took a long look at whether or not she was in love with the man. She thought she was, but on those nights he went to his own home, she didn't miss him. She appreciated the quiet. Enjoyed being able to watch what she wanted on TV. Drink a glass of wine without his running commentary of how important he was at his job. Didn't have to worry about coming home from a long day of seeing patients and having to cook for him and do the dishes because he said that was her job.

It was then she realized he wasn't the one. She wanted someone who understood when she needed quiet time. A man who would cook dinner or at least order take-out when her heart was too heavy for the task. Someone who asked what she wanted rather than assumed he knew best. Sabrina knew he had to go after she told Garrison she needed a weekend to herself. When his large hand wrapped around her throat as he shoved her into the wall accusing her of cheating, she was done. After he'd released her and apologized, promising to never touch her in anger again, she'd told him to take his things and leave.

She tried not to dwell on what happened afterward. It only brought pain to her heart and induced a panic attack for months. Sabrina hadn't gone to the police, nor had she gone to the hospital to have her wounds tended. He'd left bruises on her face and ribs before pushing her to her knees. It could have been worse, but shoving his dick down her throat until she nearly passed out had been bad enough. Garrison had been smart in leaving no DNA evidence behind on her body, and she attributed that to the fact he was a cop. He stormed off without his clothes but not before he trashed most of her home. After giving herself a few days to deal, she packed all his things into boxes and took them to the nearest donation truck. She'd thought about texting him to come get them off her porch, but Sabrina didn't want him anywhere near her. She had never given him a key to her place, but she still had the locks changed and an alarm system installed. Briefly, Sabrina considered getting a dog, but her long hours at the hospital would have meant the animal was alone more than it wasn't.

It had taken more than a year for Sabrina to agree to another date, but she only said yes because the man was a doctor. Someone who swore an oath to heal. She drove her car to the restaurant so she could leave if she needed to. The man had asked if they could go back to her place, but she said she wasn't ready. He asked her out a few more times, and each time she declined anything more than dinner. He finally stopped calling. She still saw him around the hospital, and he was friendly with her without making her feel bad. After that, she'd been fine coming home after work and spending weekends alone. Until now. And as much as

Deacon's size intimidated her, Sabrina was trusting both Joseph's and Kaya's word about Deacon Wright being a good, kind man. God, she hoped they were right.

After spending a few minutes in Jonathan's room chatting with the older man and Kaya, Sabrina's heart felt lighter than it had the night before. It mainly had to do with the light that had returned to Mr. Holt's eyes. Deacon was right when he said sometimes peace could only come from death, and she believed Jonathan was ready for the suffering to end. If his friends and family were any indication, the man had lived a good, happy life. Who was she to deny him the serenity he sought in moving on to the next part of his journey?

Sabrina was leaving when Kaya stopped her. "It was good talking to you, Sabrina. I look forward to seeing you soon."

Sabrina smiled. "Me too." Somehow, she knew she'd made a new friend in the pretty blonde. When she stepped into the hallway, Dante Di Pietro, the medical examiner and another friend of Mr. Holt's, was walking down the hallway with a small boy.

When they were standing in front of her, Dante said, "Dr. Bailey, this is my son, Connor."

Sabrina held out her hand. "It's a pleasure, Connor."

"The pleasure is mi—" Connor froze, grasping Sabrina's hand. When he released it – after several long seconds – he looked at Dante and whispered, "Da."

Sabrina looked behind her to see what spooked the boy, but there was no one there. She waited for Connor to tell his father what was wrong, but they looked at each other, not speaking. "Dante? Is everything okay?" she asked.

"Connor hasn't been feeling well, that's all. If you'll excuse us, we want to check in with Jonathan for a few minutes."

"Of course." Sabrina stepped aside, and when the two of

48

them entered the room, Connor looked at Sabrina with an expression that could only be fear. But what reason did the boy have to fear her?

DEACON STEPPED INTO the morgue just as Trevor was rushing out. "Where's the fire?"

"Hey, Deke. Gotta get over to campus before I'm late for class. Dante's on his way if you wanna wait."

"Yeah, I can do that. See you later." Deacon hadn't expected Dante to come in to work today since he was helping Isabelle with the blood sample he'd taken from Evan the night before. The male had been cooperative, even going so far as telling them all about Drago's warehouses. The ones he knew about at least. They had called Rafael after talking to the male, and he agreed they should set him up in a cell much like Gabriel's.

Deacon had the day off, which in the past, had been few and far between. In the last several weeks, Gregor had been spending more time at the Pen. At first, Deacon chalked it up to Tessa being out of town with Tamian, but lately, he thought something might be going on with the couple. Deacon didn't want to pry, but it hurt him deeply whenever Gregor was near, and he wanted to help his boss. Not that he could give the male advise on what to do if something was wrong in his relationship with Tessa, considering Deacon had never been in one. It was one of the reasons he was scared shitless about taking Sabrina out to dinner.

He had considered asking Gregor for tips on dating, but he didn't want to make the male feel any worse than he already did. Dante and Connor entered the morgue a few minutes later, and Deacon blurted, "I need help."

Dante frowned, looking between his son and Deacon.

49

"Let me get Connor settled." He took the boy into his office and returned a few minutes later. "What's wrong, Brother?"

"I have a date with Sabrina." Since all the immediate members of the Clan knew who Jonathan's doctor was, he didn't need to expound on it being Dr. Bailey.

"That's good news, isn't it?" Dante glanced between Deacon and his office.

Deacon reached out with his mind, and he felt Connor deeply troubled about something. "I'm not sure," he answered, scrubbing a hand down his face.

"Tell me why you aren't sure."

"She's..." Deacon paused, remembering his conversation with Kai. "It's been twenty years since I took a woman on a date, and then it..." Deacon took a deep breath. "I have no idea what constitutes a good date with someone like Sabrina. I don't want to screw up the first time I take her out."

"What do you know about her?"

"Nothing, other than she's a doctor. And she doesn't like being in the presence of large males. I've felt her trepidation whenever she enters Jonathan's room, and it has nothing to do with him or his condition. If we leave the room, her tension recedes."

"Maybe something happened in her past. Have you spoken to Jonas about her? He is her boss and could probably give you more personal information."

"No, I don't want to put him in the position of betraying her trust. Just... I asked her out to dinner."

Dante leaned against the front of his desk. "Where are you taking her?"

"I thought about Chez Vaison, but I didn't want her to think I'm trying too hard to impress her. Giovanni's is more my speed, but I also don't want her to think I'm not trying hard enough. Where did you take Isabelle on your first date?"

50

Dante smirked. "Chez Vaison, and I *was* trying too hard. I didn't know her first husband had tried to buy her affection. I showed up in the Aston Martin with flowers and a diamond bracelet. I chalked her lack of enthusiasm up to her reluctance to go out with me in the first place. She'd only found out about Gargoyles and then transitioned into a half-blood a few weeks prior. Add to that the idea of fated mates. It was a lot to digest. What has you worried about Sabrina?"

"She's a doctor. Educated. Smart. Beautiful. I would say I'm only a warden, but that would sound like I was disrespecting your brother. I drive a truck and ride a Harley. I don't own any pants other than threadbare jeans or my work pants. I'm going to need to go shopping."

"My advice is let her see the real you. Don't take her to an expensive restaurant until your anniversary. Don't go out and buy a suit you'll never wear again until possibly on said anniversary. Nice jeans and a button-up should be okay for Giovanni's. The mate bond will do a lot of the work for you, but I understand not wanting a mate who hasn't chosen you for herself. Talk to her. Ask her questions about her family and her life. Listen to what she tells you, and listen to what she doesn't. Trust your abilities. I have a feeling your powers are even stronger than mine."

Deacon should have known Dante suspected there was more to Deacon's empathy. The older male was powerful in his own right, and he was observant. Other than Gregor, Deacon had never trusted anyone enough to tell them, but this was Dante. His family. "You're right. About my abilities. I'm more empathic than anyone I know of, and sometimes it gets to be too much. My beast does its best to shield me from the harshest of emotions, but sometimes…" Deacon blew out a breath.

Dante's smile was sympathetic. "I can't imagine. Well, I can, but my own abilities are nowhere near what you're describing. Is that why you've never been in a relationship?"

51

Deacon didn't want to divulge too much about himself, even if he considered Dante family. Deacon wasn't a virgin. Like most males, he had been with females when he was young. It didn't take him long to realize sleeping with random women wasn't for him. He hadn't been on a date in over twenty years. Not since the last one turned out to be more than he could handle. He couldn't think about that now. Not when he had his mate within his grasp. "That's part of it. Mostly, I've been holding out for my mate. Why start something with a female I knew would end in heartache? I get why Sin did it. Some males prefer having someone to go home to every day, even if they're not going to live as long as we do. I just couldn't do it."

"I understand. Before Isabelle, I was only with a handful of females, and those were simply to scratch an itch. For an alpha Gargoyle, I'm not the most assertive when it comes to those types of things," Dante said.

Deacon was surprised Dante admitted something so personal, but it went a long way in showing he had trusted the right male with his doubts. He felt better, but he still needed to go shopping. "I'm going to get out of here and let you get busy."

"I'll let you and the others know as soon as Isabelle and I figure out what Dr. Craven gave Evan. In the meantime, we have Julian and Lucy searching for the scientist."

"Let me know if they find him. I'll go after the man myself."

Dante grinned, and it was good to see the male smiling so often. It was something he rarely did before he met Isabelle. "You'll have to stand in line. Gregor's already called dibs, but I have a feeling he won't mind some company."

"I'll talk to him tomorrow when I get to the Pen. For now, I've got some shopping to do. I stopped by to see if Trevor wanted to go later, but he's busy with school."

"You should call Travis and Brynna. If anyone can choose the right clothes for you, it will be her."

Deacon smiled, thinking of Banyan's sister and Trevor's brother. Brynna still hadn't told Travis he was her mate, but whenever Deacon was around the couple, he knew it wouldn't be long. The love she felt for the human consumed Deacon and briefly overshadowed any sadness or turmoil he felt from the others around him. "That's an excellent idea. Thanks for the talk, Brother." He held out his hand for Dante to shake, but the male pulled him into an embrace. Calm instantly flooded Deacon, and he appreciated it more than he could ever say.

"Anytime."

DANTE ENTERED HIS office to find Connor sitting quietly, his hands folded in his lap. "I'm sorry, Da. That's the best I could do."

Dante placed his hand on his son's shoulder and squeezed gently. "Don't apologize, Son. You'll figure it out." Dante picked up the drawing. In it, Sabrina was being grabbed by a large, black man. Connor's visions were usually detailed, but in this one, the man's facial features were blurry. "Can you not see who the man is? Or did you not have time to finish?"

"I can't see him."

The child had only a regular lead pencil but had still managed to shade both Sabrina and the man so their skin tone was depicted correctly. His talent for drawing never ceased to amaze Dante. "You did well, Son. I need to make a call, and then we'll get you to the gym." Dante hoped he could get to Deacon before the male got too far away.

Chapter Six

DEACON EXITED THE hospital via the back door to the lower level where the morgue was located. He forced himself to leave and not go back upstairs in search of Sabrina. He called Travis about him and Brynna going shopping with Deacon, but Travis asked if he could call him back in a few minutes. Deacon was still leaning against his bike when his phone rang. He expected it to be the human returning his call. When he saw it was Dante, his beast nudged him.

Hurry. Something is wrong.

"Dante?"

"Can you return to the morgue? There's something you need to see."

"I'm still outside. I'll be right there." Deacon pushed off his bike and wasted no time getting back inside. "What is it?" he asked as soon as he strode through the door.

"We stopped by to see Jonathan earlier. I introduced Connor to Sabrina, and when he shook her hand, he had a vision."

"What did he see?"

Dante held out a piece of paper. When Deacon grasped what he was seeing, he had to steady himself. Connor's visions were legendary among the Clan, and he'd never known the child to be wrong. He'd also never seen one incomplete. Before he could comment on the man's lack of clear facial features, Dante explained, "He can't see the man's face."

"What does that mean?"

"I'm not sure, but regardless, we need to keep an eye on your mate."

"I need to warn her."

"And tell her what?" Dante glanced at Connor and sighed. "Until you claim Sabrina and she knows about us, we will keep an eye on her. Talk to Frey and explain what's going on, and he'll set up round-the-clock protection."

"I can watch her." Not that Deacon didn't trust the others of their Clan, but Sabrina was his responsibility.

"I understand you want to be the one protecting her, but you have a job. We'll talk to Frey and see who we can put on rotation. We can also let Jonas know what's going on. He will want to help as well, I'm sure."

"Gregor's spending more time at the Pen, and he's got Remy there shadowing, so if I asked, he'd probably be okay with me taking time off." Deacon's phone rang, but he didn't recognize the number. He almost let it go to voicemail, but his shifter nudged him to answer anyway. "Hello?"

"Deacon, it's Brynna. I hijacked Travis's phone and got your number."

"Oh, hello, Brynna. I'm going to have to cancel our shopping trip. Something has come up that needs my attention."

"Now you're just hurting my feelings. I'm all ready to hit the mall. Why don't you text me your sizes, and I'll grab some things for you?"

"You don't have to do that."

"I don't mind. I need a little retail therapy anyway, so if you trust me, I'll pick out several outfits. If there's something you don't like, I'll return it for you later."

Deacon hated shopping, so Brynna's offer was a godsend. "That would be much appreciated."

"It really is my pleasure. Text me those sizes, and I'll get back to you. We'll meet up sometime tomorrow." The female said goodbye and disconnected.

"I need to get Connor over to the gym. Abbi is taking him and Amelia to the aquarium. Why don't you follow me, and we will talk to Frey together? You call Gregor, and I'll call Jonas on the way. He and Paxton can keep an eye on Sabrina in the meantime."

Deacon agreed and followed Dante and his son outside. Once they arrived at Hartley's, Deacon parked next to Frey's Jeep and slid off his Harley. When they entered the gym, the whirlwind that was Amelia saw him and took off running. "Uncle Deke!"

"Hey, munchkin." Deacon bent down and scooped the girl up, tossing her into the air before catching her and settling her on his hip. She placed a kiss against his cheek, and Deacon absorbed her happiness.

"Momma's taking me and Connor to see the sharks. You should come with us."

Deacon fake shuddered. "Sharks? No, thank you."

"You're so silly. They can't hurt you, 'cause they're in a big tank."

"I'm not as brave as you and Connor. Maybe I'll go next time." He kissed her on the forehead before placing the child on her feet. Amelia ran to where Connor was silently watching. When Amelia got close, the boy's mouth curled in the smallest hint of a smile. Deacon didn't know how Dante dealt with having a son who was special. Or one who saw the horrible things he did in his mind. Deacon didn't think he'd be able to stand it, with or without his enhanced empathic abilities. He'd never had to worry about having a child of his own, but now that Sabrina was in the picture, he wondered if she wanted kids. Gods, he hoped not.

Before he could think on it more, Matthew brushed past him without speaking. Several emotions flushed over

Deacon, and none of them were good. If Slade didn't claim the teen soon, it might be too late when he did.

AN HOUR LATER, Sabrina was still shaken from Connor's behavior. Dante's explanation of why his child froze didn't match the look of trepidation on the boy's face or the way he'd whispered his father's name. His smaller hand had squeezed hers before he let go. Father and son had stared at one another for a few seconds, and if she didn't know better, she would have sworn they were communicating silently. Sabrina wondered what that would be like, to be close to your own child. Some questions were better left unanswered, she supposed.

Sabrina's hand stilled when she put the key in the lock. It turned too easily. When she pushed open the door to her office, she froze. A large vase filled with red roses sat on her desk. She paused, looking back at the door which should have been locked. She could have forgotten, but that wasn't like her. She approached the flowers and sorted through the stems looking for a card to see who sent them. Her first thought was Deacon. If they were from him, she needed to bring it to his attention how she detested that particular flower. The smell reminded her of a funeral home. When her grandmother passed away, roses of all colors had lined the small parlor where her body was held for viewing.

Garrison had given her a fresh bouquet of roses before every date. Sabrina informed him she would rather have something else, but he'd insisted she only deserved the best. She knew then, before everything else, he wasn't the man for her. If he couldn't abide that small request, what else would he ignore? Everything.

"How lovely."

Sabrina jumped at the voice. Abandoning the search for a card, she turned to find Paul Blankenship, Chief of Pediatrics, standing in her doorway.

"Paul, what brings you by?" The man had to want something, because he never set foot on the fifth floor otherwise.

"Can a colleague not drop by to see how you're doing?" Paul stepped farther into the room, and Sabrina moved to stand behind her desk, putting as much space between them as possible without running from her office. She hated the effect larger men had on her, but in that moment, there was nothing she could do about it.

"You could if we were friends or even friendly, but we're not. So, I'll ask you again, what brings you by?"

"You wound me, Sabrina." Paul reached out and stroked a rose petal. "I might have heard your name mentioned in regard to the chief of staff position. I just wanted to wish you luck. Possibly convince you to have dinner with me."

"I don't need luck. I have the necessary skills required to do the job, and should I decide I even want the position, it will be up to the board to choose the candidate best suited to the job. As for dinner, I'll have to pass. Now, if you'll excuse me, I have work to do."

Paul plucked the petal from the flower and let it float to the floor. His skin wasn't as dark as hers, so she didn't miss his neck flushing with either anger or embarrassment at having been turned down. He muttered something Sabrina didn't catch before turning and striding from her office. What if he had brought the flowers?

Sabrina dropped into her chair and gripped the armrests. She knew she was abrasive to certain people. Mostly those men who reminded her of how she didn't want to be treated. Sabrina had always wondered why someone as egotistical and rude worked with children every day. The few times she'd visited the third floor to see a new patient, he'd not been around, so she didn't know how his bedside manner was. He might be a teddy bear around the kids, and it could be Sabrina he had a problem with. Then why did he suggest dinner? Regardless, she put it out of her mind by returning her attention to the roses. There wasn't a card included, so she had no way of knowing who sent them. Usually, she was better about remembering to lock her door. If it had been locked, someone who had a key had entered her private area.

When a possum walked over her grave – what her grandmother called it when the hair on her nape stood on end – a shiver ran through Sabrina's body. She glanced out the door to see if someone was there. She thought briefly Paul could be hanging around watching her, but she'd heard his heavy footsteps when he retreated. Sabrina eased across the floor so she could look out into the hallway. No one was there.

The feeling of being watched had happened more than once, and it was really beginning to freak her out. She didn't understand why she attracted the same type of man she wanted to avoid. Where were the skinny, short men? Sabrina wasn't a large woman, but she guessed her position in the hospital could be intimidating to some. She never ventured outside home and work other than to get her hair done. She never went anywhere to attract a suitor, so what did she expect?

Trying to put the uneasiness out of her mind, Sabrina sat down and unlocked her computer. The scent of the roses were a distraction she didn't need, so after she'd tried and failed to keep busy for a good twenty minutes, she stood from her desk and carried the flowers down to the nurses' station where someone could enjoy them, making sure her door was locked on the way out. When she was almost back to her office, she caught sight of a large man hurrying around the corner, away from where her office was situated.

Sabrina took off at a sprint, but by the time she reached

the hallway, the stranger was pushing open the door to the stairs. He glanced back at her. His face was mostly hidden by his hooded sweatshirt, but there was something familiar about him. Before she could figure out what it was, he slammed the door open and took off.

When his hood slipped back, Sabrina thought... No, that was impossible. This man was tall, broad, with cropped hair, and dark skin. That could have been Garrison if he wasn't wearing his uniform. Or, it could be Deacon.

Someone grabbed her arm, and Sabrina jumped, a small shriek escaping her throat.

"Sabrina, are you okay, dear?" Dr. Mooneyham released his grip, but his face was still etched in concern.

"I don't... Yes, I'm fine."

"You don't seem fine. Did something happen?"

Sabrina didn't want to come across as some helpless female, especially not when Dr. Mooneyham was considering her to be responsible for the hospital.

"Sabrina, you can talk to me. If something has happened, please tell me. It's my responsibility to assure all my employees are safe."

"Someone let themselves into my office and left..." No, she would sound crazy if she told him she was upset over a bouquet of roses. "It's nothing really. Just my overtasked imagination."

"No." Her boss's voice was stern, and she took a step back. When he spoke again, it was softer. "No, Sabrina. Do not ever downplay something if it causes you even the slightest bit of alarm. Someone let themselves into your office. Let's start there. Are you certain your door was locked?"

"I could have forgotten, but..."

"But that's not like you. So, let's assume someone has a key. Did they take anything?"

"No, they left something. A vase of roses. There was no

note, so I have no idea who they were from."

"And where are the flowers now?"

"I took them to the nurses' station. I hate roses, so either someone was trying to impress me and had no idea, or they were looking to intimidate me, and it worked."

"Is there someone aware of your dislike of roses?"

Sabrina didn't want to delve into her personal life. Not like this, but her boss was asking all the right questions. "Yes, but I haven't seen him in quite a while. There's no reason for him to be anywhere near my office."

"I see. What else?"

"What do you mean?"

"When I startled you, you were staring around the corner. Did you see someone?"

"Yes, but I didn't get a good look at his face. I'm probably being paranoid for no good reason. Really, like I said, I'm fine. There's no need for you to worry."

Joseph scowled. "I happen to think of you as more than an employee, Sabrina. I consider you a friend, and if I want to worry, I will. Tell me, how many more patients do you have today?"

"Four. But—"

Joseph held up a hand to silence Sabrina. He retrieved his phone from the holder on his hip and frowned before putting it to his ear. "Dr. Mooneyham." Joseph listened for a bit before his gaze turned to Sabrina. "I see... Yes, absolutely. As a matter of fact, we may need to accelerate the schedule. I need to call Julian. I... Can I call you back? There's something I need to do. Excellent. I'll talk to you soon." When Joseph disconnected, he took a deep inhale. When he let it out, he was still staring at Sabrina.

"Joseph, what is it?"

"I'm not exactly sure, but for now, I want you to come with me to my office. I need to make a call, and then I'm going to accompany you on your rounds."

"What? Why? Joseph—"

"I don't like the fact that someone was in your office without your permission, or that some stranger was lurking around. Please, dear, for my peace of mind, allow me to shadow you for the rest of the day."

"Okay, but I really don't think it's necessary."

"I insist. Now, gather what you need, and we'll get started."

Sabrina couldn't help but feel like her boss was keeping something from her, but she did as he asked.

Chapter Seven

"WHAT DO YOU mean, he disappeared? Where the fuck did he go?" Drago had to rein in his anger lest he threw his phone against the wall.

"I'm sorry, Sir. No one noticed until we were already at the warehouse. I went back out and searched the area myself for over three hours, but there's no trace of him."

"Godsdamnit. Put Trexon on the phone." A Reborn wandering around the city with the ability to understand what the fuck was going on around him could ruin everything. The last thing he needed was for the male to be captured. Fucking Stone Society. Drago bet his left nut the male had been caught.

"Sir?" Trexon answered.

"I want you to keep all the Unholy separated from the Reborn. And those who have half a brain now? You need to instill the fear of the gods in them. Make sure they understand what will happen if they jump ship."

"Yes, Sir."

"Also, I'm sending a new guy in. His name's Hagen Rossum, and he's a computer specialist."

"I remember him. He's the kid Kallisto hired to hack for Alistair."

"That's the one. Set him up in my apartment for the time being. If everything goes as planned here, I'll be back within a week. Hagen knows what is required of him, so once he's settled, you shouldn't have to watch over him. Maybe have Renneck stay with him the first night, but after that, he can come back to the compound."

"We'll handle it."

Drago disconnected. Trexon had better handle it. Losing one of the Reborn could be detrimental in the hands of the Stones. If the male talked, Rafael had the resources to find Dr. Craven. Drago pulled up the scientist's number and called the man. Of course, it went to voicemail. "Call me as soon as you get this message. And Craven? You better not sell me out."

Arden entered the room without knocking. "The truck is loaded with the next shipment."

"Good. I'm needed back in New Atlanta, so I'm leaving you in charge of this part of our operation."

"What's going on?" Arden poured himself a tall glass of whiskey before leaning against the bar.

"One of the Reborn went walkabout, and the one in charge of overseeing that particular project failed to notice until it was too late."

"Could he have gone back to his family?"

"It's possible but not probable. The ones who've been turned the longest were promised money when Alistair was funding the project for Gordon Flanagan. The ones who joined the ranks later did so because they had nothing left. They're soldiers coming home from the military who have no family, or they have PTSD so severe they can't figure out how to become part of a society which no longer wants them. I have a feeling the American Clan took him. I need to get back to ensure Dr. Craven keeps his end of the bargain."

"I'll take care of things here. Like I said, we have a shipment ready, and there's plenty more where they came from."

"Very good. I'm going to call a meeting and announce to everyone you are in charge. If anyone steps out of line,

64

take their head. We don't have time to babysit our own males."

Drago lit the cigar he'd been chewing on, mesmerized by the smoke as it drifted up before dissipating into nothing. His plan had to work, or the Greeks as well as the Unholy would disappear like the smoke.

"COME WITH ME," Frey said. Deacon knew Frey wasn't mad at his son; he was worried. When they found Matthew, Frey said, "Matthew, would you like to apologize to Deacon?" Frey's voice was calm, but Deacon knew he was reining it in.

Matthew sighed and turned around. His shoulders dropped when he realized Deacon was standing next to Frey. "I'm sorry, Deacon. I don't know what's gotten into me. Can we chalk it all up to teenage hormones?"

Deacon and Frey looked at one another. They didn't have to speak out loud to know what the other was thinking. They'd had this conversation a couple times while out patrolling for Unholy. If Slade didn't claim Matthew soon, the teen was only going to get worse.

Before either one spoke, Matthew continued, "Do you think it's too late to enroll in summer classes at UGA?"

"I thought you wanted to take the summer to relax?" Frey stepped closer, leaning his hip against the table where Matthew was folding towels. Deacon remained where he was, not wanting to get in the way.

"I did, but if I get a couple classes in now, I won't have to worry about my schedule as much during the season."

"I'll have to get with Slade and see if he can get into his apartment earlier if that's what you really want to do."

"No!" Matthew took a deep breath. "About that. Can we

have someone else babysit me?"

That was it. Deacon couldn't stand by any longer while Matthew floundered without Slade. "I'm going to make a phone call," Deacon said, leaving Matthew and Frey alone.

"Deke," Frey called out, but Deacon kept going. He had vowed to stay out of the other male's business, but Matthew was important to Deacon, and he at least had to tell Slade what was going on so he could think about how his decisions were affecting his mate.

Deacon walked out of the gym and moved around the side of the building for privacy. He took a deep breath, pushing it out as he hit Slade's contact number.

"Deacon? What's up?"

"Your boy is getting ready to run."

"What the hell are you talking about?"

Deacon relayed the conversation. "He's upset, Slade, and you're the only one who can do anything about it."

"You know I can't," Slade groaned.

"I don't know anything of the sort. Frey has given his blessing, so anything else holding you back is just an excuse. Are you going to be okay with another male following him to Athens to watch over him? Spend time with him?"

"No, I'm not, but... Fuck. I'll be there in twenty." Slade disconnected, and Deacon returned inside. Frey was hugging Abbi, and Kai was holding Amelia's hand. Dante had Connor off to the side. The Goyle was kneeling in front of his son, talking to him in hushed tones. Of all the emotions Deacon was getting hit with, Connor's were the strongest. Even more so than Matthew's. When Deacon looked around for the teen, he didn't see him. Doing his best to close off everyone else around him, he reached out, searching. By the time Deacon got a lock on Matthew, the others were gathered together as Abbi readied the kids for the aquarium.

Lorenzo entered the building, and Amelia pulled away from Kai. "Uncle Zo!" she yelled as she launched herself at the newcomer. Deacon loved how the girl greeted all the Goyles enthusiastically, giving some of them cute nicknames. And by the look on Lorenzo's face, he did as well.

"How's the princess today?" Lor asked.

"We're going to the aquarium. Uncle Deke's afraid of sharks, so he's not gonna go. Are you afraid of sharks?"

Lor winked at Deacon before answering. "Yes, I am. Have you seen the teeth on those things?" He did a full-body shiver, causing Amelia to laugh.

Amelia cupped her hand around her mouth and whispered into Lorenzo's ear. Deacon didn't want to intrude on her secret, so he turned and went in search of Matthew. The teen was in the men's locker room, holding a bottle of cleaner and a rag. Instead of wiping down the counter, he was staring at nothing.

"I really am sorry for being rude," Matt said when he noticed Deacon.

"Apology accepted. Would you like some help cleaning?" Deacon needed to get to the hospital to check on Sabrina, but he wasn't going to leave Matthew until Slade showed up.

"Nah, but thanks. I've got most of it done. I just need to clean the showers, and then I'll be finished."

"If you're su—"

"Matthew?" Slade rushed into the locker room, sliding to a stop when he saw the teen.

"I'll just…" Deacon thumbed over his shoulder, leaving the two to talk. He clapped Slade on the shoulder when he passed by, squeezing hard. Deacon could hear Frey and Dante talking in the office, so he headed that way. When he entered the small room, he opened his mouth to tell them Slade was there, but when he noticed Lorenzo, he kept that to himself.

"I took the liberty of telling Frey and Lor about

67

Connor's drawing," Dante said.

"Thanks. I'm sorry he had to see that in his mind. I don't know how you do it. Either one of you. Kids are…" Deacon closed his eyes briefly. "Kids are great, but I can't imagine being responsible for their well-being."

"You don't want kids with Sabrina?" Frey asked.

"If she wants them, I'll deal with it, but I hope I can convince her to wait a while. First, we need to talk about that drawing and what it means. If something were to happen to her before we're mated, it won't matter if we want kids or not."

"I talked to Gregor, and he's good with you taking time away from the Pen. I've also asked Lorenzo to help cover your mate when you need to rest. For the time being, I've taken you both off Unholy patrol." Frey stood and walked around to the front of his desk, leaning against it. "I know how it feels to have someone after your mate, and I also understand wanting to be the one guarding her. But you need to stay sharp. If you wear yourself down, you won't be any good to her."

"I'm not going to turn down help. Lor, I appreciate you stepping in. Between the two of us guarding her outside the hospital and Jonas and Paxton on the inside, we should be able to stop whatever it is Connor saw." At least Deacon hoped they could. "The only thing that bothers me is he couldn't see a face."

"I've been thinking about that," Dante said. "I don't know for sure, but I'm thinking the face was obscure because there's only the possibility of what his vision showed happening. Most of the things he's drawn perfectly have come to pass exactly the way he depicted."

"What if it's something that already happened? Could it be she's blocking something from her past?" Lorenzo asked.

"That's a valid point. That would be the less evil of the two scenarios. But until Deacon mates with her or at least finds out more about Sabrina, we need to be vigilant in her safety," Dante said. "Jonas has agreed to shadow her at the hospital, as will Paxton. Jonathon doesn't need a guard twenty-four seven, so Paxton can help Jonas when he has duties which pull him away from Sabrina."

"I have a date with her Thursday night. If that goes well, I should be able to get closer to her sooner rather than later. I don't want to drive her away by delving into her past too quickly, though." Deacon was already nervous about the date. He didn't need the added stress of pushing her away by saying the wrong thing.

"I'll be glad to take the overnight shift at her home. If you'll give me her address, I'll go by and scope it out. Find the best vantage point to watch her from," Lor offered. "Also, it might be prudent to have Julian run a basic background check on Sabrina. Nothing too invasive, but one deep enough to see if there's something from her past that made its way into the news."

"That's not a bad idea. I wouldn't look at it as an invasion of privacy but more of gathering intel for security purposes," Frey added. "You won't be the first Goyle to have checked into his mate. While you're at it, why don't you have him monitor the security cameras in the hospital? He has Lucy there to help, so it isn't like he would be short-handed at the moment."

"I'll call him before I head to the hospital. Speaking of short-handed, what did Rafael decide about Lachlan? Did he ever get in touch with Hunter?"

Frey pushed off his desk and shoved his hands into his pockets. "Hunter told Rafe he would come to New Atlanta if it was absolutely necessary, but he still hasn't forgiven his mate. Since Lucy is here training with Julian, Rafael put Lachlan's release on hold. Lucy's good, from what Jules says, and that gives them time to look for a replacement for when she and Tamian head to New York."

Deacon ran a hand over his short hair. He didn't want to have Julian dive too deep into Sabrina's background, but he told himself it was necessary. "Okay. I'm out of here. Lorenzo, I'll text you Sabrina's address. If you'll do midnight to six, that'll give me plenty of downtime, and Jonas and Paxton will have eyes on her at the hospital."

"You got it, Brother. And I'm always a phone call away if you need me during the day."

Deacon gripped Lor's hand and pulled him into a hug. Lorenzo left the office, and Deacon let out a deep breath. "Slade's here. I haven't felt Matthew's turmoil in the last few minutes, so maybe the two of them are going to work things out."

"I think I'll go see how things are going. He is my son, after all." Frey squeezed Deacon's shoulder on his way out of the door.

"And I have blood samples to help my mate with. If you need us, don't hesitate to call." Dante patted Deacon's arm and followed his cousin out of the office, leaving Deacon alone.

Deacon closed the door to Frey's office so he could call Julian in private. He'd just pulled his phone out of his pocket when a text came through. When he opened it, Deacon barked out a laugh at the photo of Brynna holding several pairs of jeans and at least half a dozen shirts, her face smiling like she'd hit the lottery. If shopping made her happy, he was glad to have needed her assistance. Thinking of his date with Sabrina, he wondered if his mate liked the mall. That was a question he would ask on Thursday. He sent a return text to Brynna telling her to buy everything she was holding before he dialed Julian's number.

Chapter Eight

HAVING HER BOSS shadow Sabrina shouldn't have made her nervous, but she felt like there was more going on than him being cautious. She couldn't be the first employee to have flowers delivered anonymously. And that shouldn't have freaked her out as much as it had. After the phone call, Joseph had stuck to Sabrina every step she made with the exception of going into the restroom, and then he'd made her use the private one in his office.

When it was time for lunch, Joseph finally excused himself to take care of some business, but before he walked off, he told her a man named Paxton, one of the men who visited Jonathan Holt, would be guarding her.

"Joseph, I don't think a guard is necessary."

"Do this for my peace of mind. Paxton won't follow you as closely as I did. As a matter of fact, you won't even know he's there."

Sabrina had doubted she wouldn't be able to find Paxton, especially if he was walking around in his uniform. Like the others who stood outside Jonathan's hospital room, the man was large and impossible to miss. While she went about her day, Sabrina searched for the man, but either Joseph had been correct and the man was stealthy, or he'd given up on following her around the hospital. That was fine with her if he had. She didn't need to take someone away from their job just because she was being foolish.

Although Mr. Holt had decided to stop treatment, Sabrina still stopped by to see him before she left for the day. Her breath caught when she walked in. Deacon's head was tossed back, his throat vibrating as he laughed at something the older man had said. When he turned her way, Deacon's eyes sparkled, and his smile was blinding. This one encounter was enough to have her defenses evaporate, so she didn't know how she was going to make it through a date with the man.

Deacon stood and gently patted Jonathan on the leg. "Do you need anything before I go?"

Jonathan started to say something, but he choked on a cough before he could get the words out. Deacon rushed forward, pulling the older man up to a seated position, wrapping his massive arms around his friend so quickly Sabrina barely registered him moving. When the coughing spell was over, Jonathan patted Deacon's hand, and Deacon slowly lowered the patient back to the bed. "Thank you, Deacon," Jonathan whispered. Deacon brushed the man's hair back off his forehead with such tenderness, Sabrina could only stare in wonderment. She knew not all large men were abusive, but to see the way Deacon tended to his friend chipped away another piece of her armor.

Maybe, just maybe, going on a date with Deacon would help tip the scales away from thoughts of all larger men being bad news. Heck, he was already doing that. As was the man she noticed leaning against the wall just inside the door. Paxton inclined his head to her before pushing away from the wall and stepping up to the other side of Jonathan's bed. Deacon looked at Paxton, and the man nodded. Whatever the silent question had been, Deacon must have liked the answer, because he squeezed Jonathan's hand and said he'd see him the next day.

Sabrina caught Deacon's eye as he was walking out of the room. She didn't say anything, only gave him a sad smile. After spending a few minutes with the patient, Sabrina left the room to make her way to her office so she could gather her things to head home. She should have been surprised to find Deacon waiting on her, but she wasn't.

"Leaving for the day?" he asked.

"Yes. I just need to grab my things."

"I'll walk you out." The way he said it left no room for argument, and if she was being honest, Sabrina was thankful her boss and these other men were watching out for her. *You're under their protection.* Joseph's words came back to her in that moment. As they walked the hallways, Deacon didn't try to engage in conversation. He silently followed her while she retrieved her purse, shut down her computer, and locked the door. When they made it to her car in the parking garage, Deacon opened her door after she hit the fob to unlock it. Once she was seated, Deacon said, "Drive safe." He closed the door for her, and Sabrina watched in her mirror as Deacon strode to a motorcycle parked a couple spots over. She'd never thought much about bikes, but damn if he didn't make his look sexy. Oh yeah. She was in trouble with this one.

Sabrina blew out a breath and started her car. Deacon spoke very little after leaving Mr. Holt's room, and he didn't touch her. She wanted him to. Badly. Several times she felt the urge to reach out and touch his arm or hold his hand. Each time, she had to forcibly resist. What was it about him that drew her to him? After dating Garrison, Sabrina could appreciate a man who didn't have much to say as long as he wasn't always quiet. It would make for a long dinner if she had to carry the whole conversation.

Deacon followed her out of the garage and turned right onto the street behind her. He followed her all the way home, but when she pulled into her driveway, he didn't stop. She had already texted her address to him for their date, so him knowing where she lived didn't bother her. What did make her take pause was the fact that she wished he'd pulled in the driveway behind her and asked to come inside.

She was used to being alone for the most part, but she was at the point in her life where she was ready for companionship. At least on the weekends and maybe a couple nights during the week, if not more. She'd tried it with Garrison, but he had been the wrong man. Maybe Deacon would be the right one. When she stepped inside, Sabrina paused, trying to picture Deacon in her home. Would he sit in the recliner and expect her to wait on him? Or would he join her in the kitchen and help her with supper? Maybe he'd be the one to cook for her.

Sabrina laughed out loud imagining someone like Deacon donning an apron and puttering around the kitchen. She'd never thought of herself dating a biker. Or a warden at the penitentiary. Would he expect her to ride on the back of his motorcycle when he took her out Thursday? Surely the man had a car. But if he didn't, she would gladly climb behind him and wrap her arms around his tight body. Sabrina laughed again. "Girl, you are getting way ahead of yourself." Shaking her head, she went into her bedroom to change into her comfy clothes. Since she was alone, she took off her bra and breathed a sigh of relief as she did every day at this time.

After slipping into some yoga pants and a T-shirt, she padded back to the kitchen to find something to eat. As much as she'd hated the way Garrison treated her, Sabrina was looking forward to her date and what happened after. If things went well, she would enjoy asking Deacon over so she could cook for him. It was something she loved doing. It was one of the things that let her mind drift away from the patients and their diseases. Cooking for one wasn't nearly as fun as whipping up a large meal to share with someone else. She opened the fridge so she could see what she had on hand. If their date went well, she was going to ask Deacon over on Saturday, and she wanted to be prepared ahead of time.

"Getting ahead of yourself again," she said aloud. But after talking with Joseph, Sabrina had a good feeling about Deacon. She already felt safe with him. Well, maybe not safe from the way she was drawn to him. She would need to be on guard if they were alone, because she didn't trust herself not to jump him as soon as they were behind closed doors. Maybe it had been too long since she'd had a man in her bed. Or maybe Deacon was just that sexy.

Thinking about what she would like to cook and seeing what she needed from the store, Sabrina made a grocery list. She had plenty of time to get to the store before the weekend. And maybe while she was out, she would stop at the mall and find some new lingerie. Just in case.

DEACON MET LORENZO and Mason at an elementary school not far from Sabrina's house so one of them could take his bike back to his house. He didn't trust leaving his baby out where it could get trashed by teenagers with nothing better to do, or worse, stolen. Lorenzo had already scoped out the neighborhood and found the perfect spot to watch her home where they wouldn't be seen. After making his way to a vacant house behind Sabrina's, Deacon climbed to the roof and settled in.

While keeping his senses alert for anything amiss around Sabrina's home, Deacon opened his phone to read the document Julian had sent. It tore at Deacon's heart reading about Sabrina's less than stellar childhood. Being an only child, he didn't know what it was like having a sibling, much less three. And to be separated from them? That had to have hurt. It didn't surprise him that Sabrina had accumulated debt from college and medical school. According to Julian's findings, Sabrina's grandmother had left a small sum of money in the bank upon her death, but it hadn't been enough to pay for much of Sabrina's education. Deacon felt guilty for prying into her personal information, but he wanted to help her any way he could. He should've waited until they completed the bond and handled it then, but he wanted his mate to have every advantage, and that included not being bogged down worrying about finances. Besides, who knew when they'd actually get around to completing the bond? They had yet to go on a date or spend any amount of time together.

Sabrina also had payments on the house she lived in, but if they were going to have a future together, Deacon planned for them to live at his house. Maybe all that extra room would get some use. Except... Why had he let Sixx convince him to buy something so large? Oh yes. So he could fill it with a family. A mate and children. Only Deacon didn't think he could handle the children part of that equation.

Deacon finished reading over Sabrina's information. There was nothing which stood out. After she graduated high school, she immediately started college. Her grandmother had died soon after, but Sabrina didn't miss any time away. She continued on to medical school in New Chicago where she had lived all her life. Only when she'd been offered an internship in New Atlanta had she moved, and she'd been there ever since. What Julian hadn't unearthed was whether or not Sabrina had ever been in a relationship. Deacon couldn't see someone as attractive and successful as his mate being alone all these years. That was something he'd have to find out from her.

The rest of his time watching her house went by slowly. When midnight came around, Lor handed off his bike keys. "I've stashed my truck close by, so I'll follow Sabrina to the hospital in the morning."

"Thanks, Brother." Deacon made his way to his bike,

which was parked a few houses down on the next street over. As he wound his way through the backroads home, Deacon did his best to keep his mind clear. He trusted his Clan to watch over his mate while he went into work. He was looking forward to getting back and talking to Gregor. He wanted to know if Evan had told them anything more after the initial interrogation.

When he walked into the back door of the Pen after a few hours of sleep, Deacon was surprised to hear Tessa's voice coming from Gregor's office. Her laughter was like a ray of sunshine after a dismal storm. Instead of the turmoil he'd been feeling from Gregor these last few weeks, he was met with happiness. Relief. Whatever the two had been going through had either been hashed out, or at the least, put on hold. He hoped it was the former, because that would be two less people he had to deal with when it came to their emotions.

It had been too long since he'd seen the feisty redhead, and when Deacon stepped into Gregor's office, Tessa jumped up and wrapped her arms around his waist. Gregor growled, and Tessa said, "Shut it, Stone." Gregor winked at Deacon over Tessa's head. Not only was Gregor his boss but one of his closest friends. Gregor knew Deacon would die for Tessa, so the little show of jealousy was just that – a show. Probably for Tessa's benefit.

"All right, Red. Let the man go. We have work to do."

Tessa released Deacon, patting his face.

"Welcome home," he whispered.

Tessa smiled before looking at Gregor. "It's good to be home. Really good."

And that was Deacon's cue to leave the two of them alone. When he made it to the door, he said, "I'll be downstairs with Evan when you're ready," raising the bag of fast food he'd brought their prisoner. Closing the door behind him, Deacon locked it for good measure.

Chapter Nine

DEACON PEAKED INTO Gabriel's cell as he walked past it to get to Evan's. The albino-looking male was doing handstand push-ups without his feet against the wall. Deacon was impressed at the level of control it took. When he reached the next room, he paused at the window and observed the "Reborn," as Drago had named those who were undergoing the reversal from Unholy. As far as monikers went, Deacon could think of worse. Evan was seated on his bed with his back against the wall, reading a paperback. When Deacon knocked on the door, Evan looked up, his eyebrows raised.

"May I come in?" Deacon asked.

Evan nodded, and Deacon unlocked the door. "Good morning."

"Morning."

Deacon held out the paper sack. "I come bearing breakfast. It's not much, but I thought you might enjoy it."

Evan placed the book face down on the bed. "I could eat." When he didn't make a move to get up, Deacon closed the door behind him before moving farther into the room. He wasn't scared to be alone with the male. He, like the rest of the Clan, had gone up against Unholy numerous times and always came out the victor. Deacon handed the bag over then moved to the small desk and pulled out the chair. He studied the male while he ate, letting him get through his breakfast before asking any questions. Evan had just taken the last bite when Gregor entered the room. They called it a cell, but it was set up with a few comforts like the desk and a small loveseat. The room also had an attached bathroom. They had remodeled this cell when they did Gabriel's, and it was where Kallisto had been held up until they wanted it for Evan.

Isabelle had been present when they moved Kallisto to a smaller, less accommodating room. Alistair's daughter had remained silent throughout the move, much to Isabelle's chagrin. The woman had kidnapped Connor, and Isabelle had no trouble roughing her up if she got out of line.

Gregor leaned against the wall, crossing his legs at the ankle. "Evan, we'd like to ask you a few questions about the reversal procedure."

"What do you want to know?"

"As much as you can tell us, like where you were taken. By whom. How long were you there? Those kinds of things."

Evan described the building where the experiments had taken place. "And that's what they were doing – experimenting. I've seen others come and go, and not all of them came back any different than when they left. But that was months ago. I guess they figured out the right concoction, because instead of taking a couple at a time, they took twenty of us."

"Tell us about the doctor performing the experiment," Gregor said.

"His name is Dr. Craven, but I think he's more mad-scientist than doctor. He's older, like in his sixties, and he has five others helping. Two are older, like him, but the other three are all younger, and I don't think they're doctors or scientists at all. I think he keeps them around in case any of the Unholy get out of hand."

"What makes you think that?"

"Because they were dressed in all black and carried big

79

weapons."

"Did they talk about anything other than what they were doing to you?"

"Yeah. I guess they thought since we were Unholy we wouldn't pay attention to what they were saying. While I was being prepped, I overheard them talking about how things had changed since Gordon Flanagan was no longer in the picture."

In the next room over, Gabriel yelled, "No! No! No! Izzy! No! Izzy!" The turmoil within the male hit Deacon hard, bringing him to his knees.

"Deacon?" Gregor knelt beside him.

"I need to…" Deacon grabbed the sides of his head with his hands. "I've… got to… get out of here."

Gregor helped him to his feet, and Deacon stumbled to the door and wrenched it open. Gabriel was still muttering when Deacon passed his cell door. The farther away Deacon got, the less pain he felt from the male, but the pain was still close to debilitating. His shifter pushed out with as much comfort as it could, but it still wasn't enough.

Deacon made his way up the back steps, leading farther away from Gabriel and whatever hell the male was going through, not stopping until he reached his office. When he shut the door behind him, Deacon slid to the floor, landing hard on his ass. Pulling his feet closer, he rested his head on his bent knees, pushing his fingertips into his temples. He knew he didn't have long until someone came to check on him.

What the hell happened to set Gabriel off? Deacon had been around the male every day since he'd been captured, and although Gabriel didn't talk much other than to ask for a cigarette, he seemed to be okay with his situation. If he was hurting – which he shouldn't be since he was a Gargoyle – it would make sense that he called out for Isabelle. Deacon thought back, and when he replayed the conversation, he

80

wondered if it was talk of Gordon Flanagan that upset Gabriel. Whatever it was, Deacon would have to let Gregor and Isabelle deal with it, because there was no way he could be around the male while he was so emotional. Deacon's head felt like it was splitting in two, even with a couple levels between him and the tormented male.

During the first three centuries, Deacon had wandered the world, staying as far away from large cities as possible. Being black, he was subjected to the threat of slavery. His parents had managed to remain safe because of their wealth. When Deacon left home, he took a small part of that money with him as he looked for his place in the world. As a Gargoyle, he had his strength to keep from being captured, and he'd done his best to only harm those who attempted to trap him. He spent most of his time as a nomad, seeking out small villages on remote islands. The fewer people he encountered, the easier it was to deal with his empathic ability.

It wasn't until Deacon met an old woman who told him he needed to head west to the Americas that he set out for a place where he would need to shield himself from the myriad of people he encountered. She told him that's where his destiny lie. Over the course of his travels, Deacon had met enough people with special abilities to know she believed what she told him. Some were gypsies, some witches, some merely humans with gifts of sight. Tessa's cousin, Lilly, was one of those witches.

Deacon had done as the old woman suggested, and when he landed in the United States, he started in Rhode Island where there weren't as many people. As he became accustomed to living around humans and getting a grip on his abilities, Deacon branched out to larger areas, and he eventually settled in Chicago. He was there when the world fell apart. While reading over Sabrina's background, he wondered if he could have encountered her at some point when she was a child. Thinking back on the way his life had gone sideways, had it been because his mate had been close by and he didn't know it?

Deacon was still sitting on the floor when Gregor entered his office.

"Are you okay, Brother?"

"I will be. Gabriel's pain hit me hard. What the hell happened?" Deacon had admitted his empathic abilities to Gregor when he first came to work at the Pen. His boss needed to know in case he had an episode like the one earlier. Deacon had become accustomed to all the inmates' emotions, and for the most part, those who were behind bars were resigned to being in a cell. They were guilty, and they knew it was what they deserved. It was only when he had to visit The Basement where they kept the Unholy that his beast had to help shield him from the outbursts, both physically and mentally.

"Gabriel heard Evan talking about Craven and Flanagan. It took his mind back to when he was captured and tortured. Isabelle arrived and was able to get him settled, but any further conversations with Evan are going to need to be done somewhere other than his cell."

"I want to be there when you talk to him." Deacon pushed up from the wall, and he took Gregor's hand when he offered it.

"Do you need time to regroup?"

"No. I'm better now. The worst of the pain has dulled to its usual hum." Deacon had explained to Gregor as best he could how the emotions of so many was a constant buzz in his brain.

"If you're sure. We moved Evan to the holding room we first had him in. I want to know everything he does about Drago and everyone they have amassed for their army. When he comes for us, we need to know what we're up against."

"I agree. Let me grab some water, and I'll meet you

82

down there."

Gregor inclined his head and left Deacon's office. Deacon poured a tall glass of water from the cooler and downed it. He did that several times before making his way to the bathroom, where he splashed water from the tap on his face. He took stock of his appearance in the mirror while he dried off with a handful of paper towels. His eyes were still a little bloodshot as they got when his pain was the worst, but other than that, there was no indication there was anything wrong. Tossing the towels into the garbage can on the way out, he headed down the hallway to the stairs which led to the Basement.

IT TOOK A few hours once he reached Audrey's hometown, but Drago found her human piece-of-shit husband and disposed of him. He didn't bother telling the man why he was going to die. Audrey was gone, and the man already knew it. Drago couldn't bear to speak her name, but even if he could have, Burt Hughes didn't deserve to hear it. Afterward, he'd driven to the small cemetery where his mate was buried. Had he not been hellbent on going after the one who killed her, Drago would have taken her body and had her cremated so he could keep her ashes with him. Arden had remained at the hotel to keep an eye on Audrey's friend. Lacy had passed out while the male had been choking her as he fucked her. A maid had found an unconscious Lacy and a deceased Audrey. Lacy had described what happened to the local police and then gone home to tell Audrey's family their daughter wasn't coming home.

With the first payment for the women in his bank account, Drago put in a call to Dr. Craven. The serum he'd come up with to reverse some of the effects of the Unholy was expensive, but Drago needed more of the Reborn to help in the war against the Stone Society. Craven had another serum he'd used before when Gordon Flanagan was alive. One that created a type of super-soldier. When Drago first took over the Unholy, he'd met a couple of the humans, but with nothing for them to do other than sit around babysitting the Unholy, they had taken off in the middle of the night. Drago needed males he could control. So, that particular serum was sitting on a shelf somewhere in Craven's possession. Drago had no doubt the man would sell it to the highest bidder, but that wasn't Drago's problem.

Drago had convinced the doctor to come up with a reversal of sorts. It had taken several attempts, but the latest batch seemed to be working. He wasn't going to use it on all the Unholy. He needed some of the mindless for collateral damage when it came time to take on Rafael. Once Drago was King, he might revisit the super-soldier need, but for now, he could only focus on the Gargoyles.

His phone rang, and Drago pushed the Bluetooth button on the steering wheel. "Craven," he said as his greeting. "I have your money for the next batch of counteragent. As a matter of fact, I have enough to double the amount you made last time."

"You have my account number. As soon as I receive notice the funds have been transferred, I'll get started."

"Very good. How long until it's ready?"

"A couple days at most. I'll call you when it's ready." Craven disconnected without another word. Drago was fine with that. He took the next exit where he could find somewhere to park and make the transfer. Forty more reversals with this batch would give him a nice number of Reborn. Another double batch after that would put them at one hundred. Now, he needed Arden to take care of getting more women to Mr. Collins. He had no doubt his second-in-command wouldn't let him down.

Chapter Ten

SABRINA WAS SURPRISED to see Paxton waiting for her when she parked her car. He was leaning against the concrete wall, but when she turned the ignition off, he strode to the door and opened it for her. Unlike most days, he wasn't dressed in his policeman's uniform. Today, he had on faded jeans, a T-shirt that stretched over his fit chest and arms, and black cowboy boots. If Sabrina wasn't so caught up in Deacon, she might have given Paxton a second look.

"Good morning, Dr. Bailey."

"Please, call me Sabrina. And good morning to you too. I hope you're not wasting your off day babysitting me."

"We are taking your safety seriously, so I don't consider watching over you a waste of time."

Well, didn't she feel properly chastised? "I apologize. I only meant I hate that you have to spend your day off working. So, tell me; what do you like to do on your off days?"

"Most days, I volunteer at a local LGBTQ center. And before you ask, I'm bisexual, if you want to put a label on my preferences. Even if I weren't, I would still help out. It amazes me how many parents disown their kids. I'm doing what I can to make them feel less abandoned."

Sabrina had to wonder if Paxton was speaking from experience. "Who you date is your business, but I think it's wonderful that you volunteer."

85

"It's the least I can do. I've been blessed in my life, and I want to pay it forward however I can. Whether that's by spending time with kids or making sure you're safe."

Sabrina was blessed, as well. She'd had a rough start, but things had turned out okay. Now, if she and Deacon were to be compatible? That'd make her life even better.

"How many patients do you have today?" Paxton asked.

"Seven. I need to do some computer work first, and then I'll start my rounds. If you need to do something else, I can lock myself in my office for the first hour or so."

"I wouldn't mind stopping by to check on Jonathan. But you have to promise to stay in your office. If I'm not back before you're ready to do your rounds, call my cell phone, and I'll be right up."

While Sabrina was unlocking her office, Paxton pulled out his phone, hit a few buttons, and Sabrina's phone rang inside her purse. "That's just me," Paxton said.

"How did you get my number?" Sabrina pressed the "ignore" button and moved to put her things on her desk.

"Joseph gave it to me yesterday. I should have told you."

"No, *he* should have. But I guess it's better you have it, just in case." Sabrina was going to let Joseph know she didn't appreciate his high-handedness. Yes, he was offering her a bodyguard, but she would like to at least have some say in what was going on in her life.

"Do you need anything before I go downstairs?"

"No, thank you. I should be ready to make my rounds in an hour."

"Okay, I'll be back, but call if you need to get out before then."

Sabrina nodded and followed Paxton to the door. Once he was through, she closed and locked it. She hated being boxed in. Her office wasn't small, but with the door closed, it felt smaller than usual. The reason she had it locked was what had her losing sleep the night before. She tried to keep her mind on Deacon and their date, but she kept going back to the roses and the stranger in the hallway. Needing the extra caffeine, Sabrina popped a pod into her coffee maker and hit the start button. While it was heating, she picked up her phone and opened the call from Paxton so she could add his name to the contacts list. She placed her phone on the corner of her desk where she kept it while she was working.

After she had her coffee mixed with some caramel creamer, she took a sip before sitting. Sabrina lowered herself into her chair and reached out to place the mug on her coaster. Sabrina gasped, jerking her hand away from a picture which had been taped to the top of the ceramic square. Coffee splashed over her desk and her hand, tears welling up in her eyes. Instead of grabbing something to wipe up the spill or clean her hand, Sabrina picked up the photo. When she got a closer look, it was actually three photos that had been taped together. One was her standing on her porch. One was Jasmine smiling at someone out of the frame. And the third was of Terrence in what looked like a professional headshot. Why had they only chosen those three? Why not include Jerrick? Unless it was because he was somewhere on the other side of the world in the military. And how had they gotten the picture into her office? The door had been locked.

Sabrina's doorknob rattled, and she jerked to her feet, her chair rolling back into the filing cabinets. A firm hand banged on the door, but Sabrina ignored it. She grabbed her phone and dialed Paxton. He answered before it rang once.

"Sabrina?" She couldn't find her voice as whoever was at her door continued knocking without saying anything. "Sabrina? Fuck! I'm on my way."

Tears continued to roll down her face as Sabrina stood frozen. Paxton announced himself as he knocked, so she knew it was him and not whoever had been trying to get in.

He must have been right down the hallway, because he was there within seconds. When she unlocked the door, he took one look at her and cursed under his breath. She wanted him to hold her and tell her everything was going to be okay, but the man did the opposite. Paxton took a step back and blew out a breath.

"Did you see who it was at my door?" she asked.

"There was no one there. Did they not announce themselves?"

Sabrina shook her head. "There's something else." She picked up the photo and held it out to him. "This was on my desk. I locked my door last night. Deacon watched me."

"And I watched you unlock it." Instead of taking it from her, Paxton pointed. "That's you, but who are the other two?"

"My sister, Jasmine, and my brother Terrence. I have another brother, but last I knew he was in the military."

"Do you have an envelope? I need to take the photo in and have it tested." Sabrina found an envelope, and Paxton told her to drop the photo inside. "Is there anyone who can take over your patients today?"

"I'm not letting whoever this is run me from my job. My patients need me, and I have you following me."

"Fair enough. Do you have napkins or something I can use to clean the coffee off your desk?"

Sabrina waved him off. "I made the mess." She opened the credenza door and pulled out a roll of paper towels, ripping off several sheets. As she dabbed them over the liquid, the tears returned. She did her best to blink them back, but one escaped.

"Shit," Paxton muttered. Sabrina glanced up at him to see he was texting someone.

"What's wrong?"

"I… Well, it's—"

"Sabrina!" Joseph rushed into the room and pulled

88

Sabrina into his arms. "Are you hurt?"

"No, just splashed coffee on my hand." Sabrina rested her cheek against Joseph's shoulder and sighed. "Why is someone after me? I don't have enemies. Well, except maybe Paul, but he wouldn't do something like this."

"Paul? Blankenship?" Joseph slid his hands down to Sabrina's and held her so he could look at her face. "Why would you think of Paul?"

"He stopped by right after I got the roses and mentioned the chief of staff position."

Joseph released her hands, stepping back. "That prick. Let me make one thing clear. He's not in the running, and even if he were to be nominated, there's no way I'd allow him to run my hospital."

Sabrina grinned at her boss. She loved when Joseph called it *his* hospital. If she took over as chief, would she think of it as hers? Heck, she already did for the most part.

"Can you stay with Sabrina while I run this to the lab?" Paxton asked.

"Of course, and besides, Deacon is on his way."

"Deacon? Why is he coming?" Sabrina asked.

"Because I care about what happens to you," Deacon said as he stalked into the room. There was no other way to describe the way the man made his way to her. When he reached her, Deacon pulled her to him and wrapped his large arms around her. A low rumble vibrated beneath Sabrina's cheek. "Why does my mate smell like you, Joseph?"

His mate?

Paxton laughed, and Joseph shook his head. "Sabrina's like a daughter to me. She was upset, and I gave her a hug until you could get here and do your job."

His job?

Something was going on, and Sabrina wanted to know what it was, but she didn't have time to find out. She had patients to see, and she still needed to get her computer work

89

done. But being held by Deacon was frying her brain. And causing her belly to do flips. And getting her panties wet. Another vibration rose up from inside the man.

"I'm just going to go." Paxton left, taking Joseph with him.

"Sabrina," Deacon husked.

"Huh?" Yep, brain fried.

"Look at me," he commanded. So, she did.

Deacon dipped his head and ghosted his lips against hers. *Oh, hell no.* If he was going to kiss her, he was going to do it right. Sabrina pulled Deacon's head down and showed him the proper way to kiss a woman.

DEACON LOST ALL thought of keeping Sabrina safe when she kissed him deeper. He'd only wanted to get her mind off the photo and whoever was stalking her, because he was convinced whoever was leaving items for her was doing just that. Now that he had her in his arms with their tongues dancing the sultriest of tangos, all Deacon wanted was to strip her down so he could feel her silky skin against his. Bury his cock deep within her body and claim her as his mate. But he couldn't. When Deacon broke the kiss, Sabrina sighed and pressed her forehead to his chest.

"Sorry," she muttered.

Deacon tipped her chin up so he could see her eyes. "I'm not." He wasn't sorry for the kiss, but he was sorry they were in her office at the hospital where they weren't really alone. "There'll be plenty of time for more of that later. Right now, I want you to concentrate on your job."

"What about your job? Why did Joseph say I was your job?"

Deacon couldn't tell her the truth, so he got as close to

possible. "I feel a strong connection to you, and as such, it is my job to protect you."

"Why did you call me your mate?"

"Because of that connection I mentioned. I know we've only just met, but I'm drawn to you, and I want us to have a chance to see if this connection might lead to something deeper. More permanent. It's fast, and we don't know each other, but I want us to get there."

"I feel it too. Is that weird? I've dated, sure. And I have to be honest. When I first met you, I was scared of you, but now I feel safe."

"Good. I want you to feel safe. These items that are being left for you mean someone is getting into your locked office. My boss's cousin is a security expert, and he's going to figure out who is doing this. In the meantime, you will have someone watching you twenty-four seven. I wish it could be me with you at all times, but that isn't feasible, so I have friends like Paxton helping me until whoever is doing this is caught."

"Do you think that's really necessary?"

"Absolutely. Your safety is the most important thing to me. Now, are you ready to make your rounds?"

"Not yet. I still need to make some notes in my computer, and I'm running behind."

"I'll wait in the hallway if you'd like."

"That would probably be for the best. If you sit in here, I won't be able to concentrate." Sabrina moved her hand from behind his neck down his chest and left it over his heart. Deacon clasped her hand in his and brought it to his mouth where he placed soft kisses on her knuckles.

"I'll be right outside." Leaving his mate was hard, but it had to be done. She needed to work, and he needed to call Julian.

When he closed the door behind him, Jonas was waiting. "Paxton left to take the photo to Julian. He's going to talk to him about added security around Sabrina's office."

"I'm sorry about earlier," Deacon said. "I know you have no designs on my female."

"I may have growled at someone getting close to my own mate a time or two hundred. Truth be told, I still do it, after all these years. I would say it gets easier, but it really doesn't. Our connection to our mate is deep and everlasting, especially after you complete the bond. Your mate is as much of you as your shifter is."

Deacon couldn't imagine how Sabrina could become any more ingrained in him than she already was, but he'd been around the others enough to know the connection would get stronger. That scared the shit out of him.

"Gregor has given me time away from the Pen until we figure out who's behind this. I told Sabrina she'd have someone guarding her at all times, and I plan on introducing her to Lorenzo later so she's not surprised to see him watching her home."

"I'm surprised you aren't moving in with her," Jonas said.

"Don't think it hasn't crossed my mind. But we haven't even had our first date."

"Then you better make it a doozy." Jonas winked, and Deacon groaned.

"I'm not the world's most experienced dater. It's been a long time, and even then, it wasn't anything serious. I said yes because the female wore me down. It was dinner and nothing more. I've waited on my mate to come along, and after four hundred years, here she is."

"Trust in the mate pull. Sabrina won't be able to stay away from you, especially now that you've kissed."

"How...? Never mind. I got so caught up in it, I forgot anyone was around. But I think you're right. What I felt from Sabrina was promising. I'm taking her to dinner tomorrow night, and if all goes well, that will be the end of it. Or the beginning, I should say."

The door opened, and Sabrina said, "I'm ready."

Deacon knew she meant she was ready to make her rounds, but he prayed she was ready to give them a chance. The smile on her face told him she was.

Chapter Eleven

DEACON GOT A text from Brynna while Sabrina was in with her fourth patient of the morning. Deacon wasn't going to leave his mate alone at the hospital, so he told Brynna he would stop by later to pick up the clothes she'd gotten for him. Paxton had returned after spending time with Julian and Lucy at the lab, but instead of shadowing Sabrina, the male had gone to see Jonathan since Deacon wasn't going to leave his mate's side. The elevator doors opened, and a wave of grief hit Deacon hard. When he saw who was walking down the hall, he understood.

Priscilla was moving slowly toward him with Rafael and Kaya on either side. Both looked grim, but he wasn't getting the same pain from them as he was the older human. They stopped in front of Deacon, and he pulled Priscilla into his arms. "Hey, Beautiful," he whispered against her gray hair. Sabrina stepped out of her patient's room, pausing until he turned Priscilla loose.

When Priscilla saw Sabrina, she choked back a sob. "Dr. Bailey, can't you do something? Please? You have to save him. I can't lose my brother." Priscilla's body shook as the tears poured down her face. Deacon was doing his best not to cringe, but the woman's pain was close to bringing him to his knees.

"Let's go somewhere and talk," Sabrina suggested. Priscilla allowed herself to be ushered into a small family room. Deacon remained in the hallway, while Rafael and Kaya went inside to support their housekeeper. Deacon closed the door to give them some privacy, but being Gargoyle, he had no trouble hearing Sabrina. He stood sentry, watching the four of them through the window.

"Miss Holt, I know how much you love your brother, and I understand wanting him to be around longer, but have you stopped to think what he's going through? At Jonathan's age, the treatment he's undergone has taken just as much a toll on his body as the disease itself. I talked to him at length about his decision. He's tired, and he's ready for the pain to go away, but he knows how badly this is hurting you, and it's tearing him up inside. He's not afraid to die, but he is afraid of how this will affect you when he does."

"He's been my whole life. Him and all my boys." Priscilla reached out for Rafael's hand.

"And you've been his. You've been his rock, Priscilla, and he needs you to continue doing that for him. He's not strong enough to do it for both of you." Rafael slid an arm around Priscilla's shoulders and kissed her on the temple. "If I've not said it enough, you and Jonathan have been the parents we all needed when ours left us. Kaya and I are going to need a mother's love and guidance as we welcome Sebastian into the world."

Deacon felt the second Priscilla's heart shifted. The sharp pain in his head and chest eased. "I can be strong. Just give me a minute to get my face together, and then I want to see him."

The four of them stood, and Sabrina handed the older woman a box of tissues. After blowing her nose and wiping her eyes, Priscilla stood taller than Deacon could remember. "I'm ready."

Deacon opened the door for them and remained where he was standing as Rafael led Kaya and Priscilla into Jonathan's room. He turned to Sabrina, who had her arms wrapped around her waist. Not caring who was watching, Deacon pulled her to his chest, offering what little support he could. "Thank you," he murmured against her hair.

"For what?"

"Your words. No one else had the courage to tell Priscilla she was hurting Jonathan."

"How do you know what I said? You were out here."

"I have exceptional hearing. Now, do you want to go to the cafeteria for lunch? Or should I call and have something brought in?" Deacon hoped the change of subject would be enough to keep Sabrina from questioning him.

"I don't know if I can eat right now. After the photo this morning and that conversation… I'm not…"

"You need to keep your strength up. How about I order soup or a salad? Something light?"

"Okay, but can we go somewhere? I'd like to get out of the building for a while."

"Anywhere you want to go." Deacon would take her to her favorite restaurant or on a long vacation if she asked it of him.

"Anywhere?" she asked, pulling away from his embrace. When she looked around and noticed another doctor staring at them, she frowned. "Let's go." Sabrina didn't wait on Deacon to follow as she headed away from the man who was staring at Deacon. Deacon glanced down at the man's badge, taking note of his name. Paul Blankenship was a handsome man. Almost as tall as Deacon but not as built. As he caught up with his mate, Deacon made a mental note to ask her about the doctor as well as having Julian run a thorough check on the man.

As they stood waiting for the elevator, Deacon placed his hand on Sabrina's back, rubbing small circles between her shoulders. He held his breath to see if she'd move away from him, but his heart warmed when she leaned in closer. Whether it was the mate pull or the need for comfort, he didn't care. His female was getting used to his touch. Welcoming it.

Once inside the elevator, Deacon asked, "Where would you like to go for lunch?"

"New Orleans," Sabrina deadpanned.

"Okay, but we'll need to stop and get my truck and some clothes. I don't think your first time on the back of a bike should be a five-hundred-mile trip. I'll also need to get a backrest for you."

"Who says it'll be my first time on a bike?" The elevator doors opened, and Sabrina stepped out. When she noticed he wasn't by her side, she turned around. "Deacon?"

"You've ridden with someone?" He wanted to find out who with and kill the man. Well, kill was a strong word. Maybe just maim him so he couldn't ride anymore. Sabrina grinned, and he realized she'd been goading him. "Not funny," he muttered, stepping out of the elevator. She hooked her arm through his.

As they walked, she bumped his arm with her shoulder and laughed softly. Her demeanor changed when she noticed a man squatting down outside her office. Sabrina drew up short, and Deacon placed his free hand on the one she was using to hold his bicep. "It's okay, Pretty Lady."

Julian turned and smiled. "Hey, Brother. I was going to wait until later to do this, but I thought it best to get to it sooner rather than later." He stood from where he was installing a new security panel on Sabrina's door. Julian fisted his heart and bowed his head slightly before holding out his hand to Sabrina. "It's lovely to meet you. I'm Julian Stone."

"Stone, as in Rafael and the benefactors to the hospital?" When Julian nodded, she asked, "Why would you be working on the door? Don't you have people for that?"

Julian laughed. "Yes, and I'm those people." He looked around before whispering, "I don't trust your safety to just

97

anyone. Let's go inside your office." Julian punched in a six-digit code, and when it beeped, he opened the door, allowing Sabrina to enter first. When they were safely inside, he said, "I've been monitoring the security feed for the hospital. Whoever is getting in knows where all the cameras are and keeps his head covered. This guy is good, but I'm hoping we'll get a match to the fingerprints we found on the photo. The new lock has a biometric scan as well as a six-digit code that I'll show you how to change or add access to for others who you allow in your office."

"Biometric?"

"Yes. It will only unlock with your fingerprint or anyone else's you feel safe enough to allow access."

"Wow, that's... I don't know what to say."

"You don't have to say anything other than tell me where you want to go for lunch," Deacon said.

Sabrina grinned up at him. "I already told you – New Orleans."

Julian said, "Hey, you should hit up Tessa. She'll probably let you stay in her house in the Garden District while you're there. I bet she can tell you the best places to eat, too." Sabrina gaped at Julian, and he asked, "What?"

"I was joking about lunch, but now that you've mentioned her, who's Tessa?"

"My boss's wife. She's also Joseph's niece. You've probably seen her around before. About your height, long red hair. Smart mouth. Anyway, if you're serious about New Orleans, we'll look at dates when we can both take some time off, and I'll talk to her about staying in her house."

Sabrina opened her mouth then closed it. Shaking her head, she said, "I only have another hour before my next patient, so let's go get something to eat that doesn't require a road trip. How about the little deli a couple blocks over? They have a wonderful roast beef sandwich."

"I bet it isn't as good as Deacon's roast," Julian said.

"You cook?" Sabrina asked.

"Don't look so shocked. Yes, I cook. I'm a single male, and I learned to take care of myself a long time ago."

"I'm sorry. You're right, I shouldn't assume anything." Sabrina shoved her hands in her smock pockets, looking at her feet.

Deacon tipped her chin up. "I'm not mad," he assured her. When she smiled, he turned his attention to Julian. "Jules, you want something from the deli?"

"Do you mind if Kat and I tag along? She's downstairs with Sophia for her checkup."

Deacon looked to Sabrina, his eyebrows raised in question. "Katherine is Julian's wife, and Sophia is their sister-in-law as well as Joseph's granddaughter."

"I have no problem with that. What about the lock?"

Julian clapped his hands together. "I'll work on the biometrics when we get back. For now, the code will suffice."

Deacon helped Sabrina remove her lab coat and hung it on the hook by the door while she grabbed her purse. Deacon and Sabrina headed on to the deli to save seats while Julian headed over to the other wing to walk with Kat. As they were walking, Sabrina said, "It's nice to see all the people in your circle."

"Yeah? Do you have a circle?" Deacon asked as he threaded their fingers together. The farther away from the hospital he got, the lighter his soul. There were plenty of people milling about on the sidewalk, but no one was dealing with the same types of trauma he encountered in the hospital.

"Not really. I have three siblings. I talk to my sister every once in a while. She's still in New Chicago, where I'm from. My brother Terrence lives in California, and we might speak on Christmas and birthdays. My youngest brother Jerrick joined the military, and none of us have spoken to him in years. I don't even know if he's still alive or not."

"Do you want me to have Julian look for him?"

"Julian? I thought he was a securities guy."

"He is, which means he has access to databases even the cops don't. Please keep that little tidbit to yourself, though."

"Is what he does illegal?" Sabrina glanced up at Deacon as they stopped for a red light.

"No. Julian Stone is one of the most honorable males you'll ever meet. I won't say he's never broken the law, because he did when Katherine was falsely accused of selling US secrets and sent to a maximum-security facility in Texas."

"I remember reading about her. She was that reporter, right?"

"Yes. Long story short, Julian found out where the Feds were keeping her, and he, Tessa, and Tessa's brother, Tamian, broke her out. Jules hid her away while he worked to prove her innocence."

"Wow. That's some story. I'd love to hear the long version someday."

"Hang around, and I'm sure you will. Here we are," Deacon said and opened the door for Sabrina. The deli was large, and the smells had Deacon's stomach rumbling. As they waited in line for the hostess to seat them, his phone pinged. He checked the message to see Julian letting him know both Sophia and Nik would be joining them. When the hostess asked how many, Deacon replied, "Six. The others are coming down the street now."

Deacon pulled out Sabrina's chair, and when she was seated, she asked, "Six? Who else is joining us?"

"Julian's brother Nikolas was with Sophia at her appointment, and they wanted to join us. I hope that's okay. They can be a little much when they're together. Most of the time, they're well-behaved, but sometimes they act like teenagers instead of adults."

Sabrina's smile didn't reach her eyes. "I wish my

brothers could have been that way."

Before Deacon could ask Sabrina to explain, the others came in the door. All four of them were smiling like it was Christmas morning. The love and joy radiating from the group overrode all other emotions Deacon was picking up from those eating around him.

"I'm gonna be a dad!" Julian yelled, picking Kat up and swinging her legs back and forth. Everyone in the deli clapped and some offered congratulations. The four of them sat down, and Deacon made the introductions.

Sabrina sat quietly as Sophia, who was six-months pregnant, gushed to Katherine about how great expecting a child was. He didn't know his mate well, but he could read her body language, and it told Deacon she wasn't as excited about the conversation as the other two females. Maybe it was because she was new to their group, but Deacon felt it was something deeper. Maybe she'd lost a baby at some point? Or it was possible she couldn't conceive? There were too many things he didn't know about his mate, but he vowed to start finding out all about her after their date.

As if sensing Sabrina's unease, Sophia and Kat turned the conversation away from babies and asked Sabrina questions about her and what it was like being a doctor. When Sophia mentioned her grandfather, Sabrina perked up. It seemed Joseph Mooneyham, a.k.a. Jonas Montague, was one of her favorite people, and she enjoyed hearing about him from someone who knew him well. It had taken Deacon a while to reconcile the young-looking Gargoyle with the older looking doctor. The prosthetic Jonas wore was something of his own making. He'd passed his secret along to a makeup artist in Hollywood many years prior, so all the masks used in the movies had been invented first by Jonas.

Deacon couldn't wait to tell Sabrina all about her boss. The real man behind the mask. He was ready for her to get to know Deacon as well as all the other Goyles. Seeing her at the table with Julian, Nikolas, and their mates, he wanted to have that same level of love and commitment they had. He wanted to celebrate with his family the small things as well as the big. Like babies. No, he still didn't want kids, but he could celebrate when the others had them.

The hour came to an end too quickly, and Sabrina was given hugs by the women as they left with Nikolas. Deacon and Julian walked Sabrina back to the hospital, with Julian telling anyone who would listen about his impending fatherhood. Deacon shook his head at the male, and Sabrina laughed at his antics. Deacon couldn't blame him for being happy. If Deacon didn't have his empathic abilities, he would probably want a houseful of kids. And depending on what Sabrina wanted, he might still get them. Instead of worrying about that far into the future, he laced their fingers together and enjoyed getting to know his mate.

Chapter Twelve

SABRINA COULDN'T REMEMBER enjoying herself more. Sure, she'd had to listen to the other two women go on about babies, but that wasn't their fault. The closer to forty she got, the less she felt she'd ever have children. At thirty-six, she wasn't too old, but she didn't want to put herself or a baby at risk if she waited too much longer. She had to wonder if Deacon wanted kids. Not that they were anywhere close to discussing those things. Then again, maybe they were. Before they got too serious, they should get all the heavy stuff out into the open. If there were things that would be considered deal breakers, it was better to find out about them in the beginning before hearts were too invested.

She wasn't going to kid herself; she was already invested in Deacon Wright, and the more time she spent around him, the harder she was falling. Sabrina had heard others talk about love at first sight. Even her boss had admitted to falling for his wife the second he saw her. After Garrison, Sabrina promised herself she'd be more careful who she gave her heart to. But what she was feeling for Deacon was already so much more than she ever felt for her ex.

Deacon was proving to be a gentle giant. One who surrounded himself with good people. The Stone brothers and their wives had accepted Sabrina immediately. Had made her feel at ease and welcome in their conversations.

Sophia and Nikolas joked and barbed at each other, but it was clear they were the be-all, end-all for the other. Katherine, the former outspoken newscaster, had been much quieter but no less a part of their little family. Julian couldn't keep his eyes off his wife nor his hand off her flat stomach as if he could already feel the life growing inside.

Once back at the hospital, Julian got the door panel set up with Sabrina's fingerprint. He showed Deacon how to program it so he could add whoever Sabrina approved. Several doctors and nurses walked by, but none commented on the fact that Sabrina was having a security panel installed on her door. If they wanted to know why, she'd tell them. Maybe the more people who knew what was going on, the sooner whoever was harassing her would stop. And she did consider it harassment. Sure, it had been flowers and a photo, but she hated roses, and the photo was of her siblings. That was the part she couldn't figure out. There were only a handful of people who knew about her life before New Atlanta, and of those, Garrison was at the top of the list.

Sabrina only had one more day before her date with Deacon. After that, if all went well, she hoped they spent more time together, and not just him following her around to keep her safe. Now that she knew he could cook, Sabrina wanted nights spent together in the kitchen followed by snuggles and glasses of wine on the sofa. Walks in the park. Many more heated kisses. And sex. Sabrina had a feeling sex with Deacon would ruin her for all other men. And that was her plan. She wanted Deacon, too soon or not. She wanted theirs to be the same connection she'd witnessed at lunch. She wanted someone jealous of the way Deacon looked at her like she hung the moon.

"You okay, Pretty Lady?"

Sabrina placed her hand on Deacon's chest. For some reason, she cherished feeling the strong heartbeat beneath the tight shirt. "I am. I need to get upstairs so my patients aren't waiting around. Not that they can go anywhere, but I try to be respectful of their feelings. I know other doctors do things on their own time, but I've never worked that way."

"Just another thing that makes you so wonderful," Deacon said softly against her lips. "Let's get going."

As they were walking to the elevator, Sabrina was aware of the eyes that watched them. She knew people were talking about Deacon following her everywhere, but she wasn't going to be bothered about it. She'd ignore the whispers if it meant she was safe. She hadn't missed the way Paul had leered at them earlier, but she wasn't worried about him either. If anyone had a problem with Sabrina having a bodyguard, they could take it up with Joseph, since he was the one who insisted on it.

The rest of the day flew by, and when it was time for her to leave, Sabrina wasn't ready to part with Deacon. "I know we're supposed to go out tomorrow night, but unless you have something else to do, what do you say we go tonight?"

Deacon hesitated, and Sabrina said, "It's okay. I can wait."

"I absolutely want to spend time with you, but I have another idea. How about we keep our date for tomorrow night, but tonight, you come home with me and let me cook for you?"

"I'd love to. I would like to stop home first and change clothes. If you'll give me your address, I can meet you there."

"I am not letting you out of my sight for one second. I'll follow you home, and then we'll head to my house."

"You're so bossy, but okay." Sabrina locked up her office for the night, and Deacon walked her to her car. When she was tucked safely inside, he strode to his Harley and climbed on. As she drove home with Deacon right behind her, she imagined herself astride his motorcycle, arms tightly wrapped around his body. Sabrina had never done anything exciting, and she thought it might be time to start living a little. Her childhood had consisted of watching her siblings while her mother worked two jobs between husbands. When she went to live with her grandmother, the most fun thing she did was go see a movie a few times a year. She'd had to leave her friends behind when she moved, and the few she made at her new school were into things like the band or sports, while Sabrina had been into reading.

After high school, it was college then medical school then work. Sabrina had never been on vacation. Never been to an amusement park or the beach. Garrison had offered to take her away for a weekend, but for some reason, Sabrina wouldn't say yes. Now, she wanted to say yes to Deacon. Yes to New Orleans. Yes to riding his motorcycle. Yes to whatever adventure he was up for.

When they got to her house, Deacon followed her inside. "Make yourself at home. There's wine in the fridge, but I don't have any beer or liquor."

"I'm fine for now," he said as he settled down onto her sofa. It was all Sabrina could do not to join him. Wanting to see where the warden lived won out over her libido. There would be time for kissing and other stuff later. Because, she had no doubt, alone with Deacon? There would definitely be other stuff. She padded to her bedroom and changed into jeans and her favorite lavender top. She didn't know whether or not Deacon would ask her to spend the night, and she didn't want to seem too forward, so she decided against packing a bag. When she walked into the living room emptyhanded, he frowned.

"What? Do I need to change into something else?"

Deacon stood and rounded the sofa to meet her. "No, you look beautiful as always. I thought you might take some clothes for tomorrow. You know, just in case we fall asleep on the sofa or something."

Sabrina shivered thinking about the *or something*. If

they didn't leave soon, she was going to show him *or something* in her bedroom. "I can do that. I didn't know what you had in mind, and I didn't want to be presumptuous."

Deacon moved until he was in her space, crowding her against the arm of the sofa. Leaning over, he whispered, "Where I'm concerned, you can presume all you want." His breath was warm on her ear, and her whole body tingled. Deacon's phone rang, interrupting the moment. "Damnit," he muttered. "Sorry. I'll take this if you want to grab a bag." Sabrina righted herself, and as she was walking away, Deacon said, "Hey, Brynna. Change of plans. I can't meet you tonight."

Brynna? Who the hell was Brynna? Was Deacon canceling a date? Granted, they'd just met, and Sabrina didn't have any right to be jealous, but she was. Had she read their interactions wrong? Read Deacon wrong? Instead of picking out work clothes for the next day, she sat down on the edge of the bed.

"Sabrina?" Deacon stopped in the doorway. "If you're having second thoughts, we can go eat and then I'll bring you back home. Either way, we need to leave soon. My friend Brynna and her boyfriend are stopping by the house to drop off... Well, it's kind of embarrassing, but I can tell you about it while I cook."

"Your friend?" Sabrina felt like an idiot.

"Yes. Actually, I met Brynna through her brother, Banyan. Her boyfriend, Travis, is the brother of Dante's assistant, Trevor. So, in a roundabout way, we're all friends and family."

"I'm sorry. I heard you on the phone, and I assumed... Well, let's say it wasn't pretty."

"Oh, love. I promise you now, there is no one else. Nor will there ever be. Not as long as you want to give us a chance."

"You're too good to be true," Sabrina told him. "I'll just

107

be packing that bag now, unless you've changed your mind."

"No, ma'am. I haven't." Deacon looked around her room, and when his eyes took in her bed, something crossed his face. It was heated, but then it was gone because so was Deacon. "I'll just wait in the living room," he called out as he walked away.

Sabrina quickly gathered everything she would need for the next day as well as a gown to sleep in. Just in case they didn't get into *or something.*

DEACON HAD TO get out of Sabrina's bedroom before his beast took over. Being so close to her with no one else around was too tempting. They had plenty of time before Brynna and Travis arrived at Deacon's place, but he didn't want to linger any longer than necessary. The sooner he got out of her house where everything smelled like her, the better.

His beast not only wanted to bed her, but when she admitted her jealousy over him talking to another woman, it was ready to claim her then and there. He'd quietly explained to Brynna the clothes were for his date the next night with Sabrina, and that she would be at his house. Brynna promised she and Travis would drop the packages and make themselves scarce. The two of them would be alone after that, but he would feel more in control at home. At least he hoped so.

Sabrina returned to the living room with a small duffel as well as a hanging bag. He took both from her, and they left her house. He had already seen the outside the day before, but the inside, while clean and neat, didn't feel very homey. Sabrina had little in the way of decorations other than some bright pillows on the sofa and a couple of random paintings on the walls. There were no pictures of family. Nothing to show Sabrina had those she loved and missed. Deacon's walls weren't much different, but he had been waiting to let a mate fill the home with their own touch. Maybe they'd been waiting for each other.

Since he was on his bike, Sabrina stowed her things in the trunk of her car and followed Deacon out of the subdivision where she lived to the outskirts of town where his home was. While he navigated the backroads, Deacon wondered how Sabrina would react to his home. It was farther out than hers, and it was nestled in the woods with no neighbors in sight. That was for his peace of mind as well as it allowed him to phase and take to the skies with no one able to see him under cover of a dark sky.

After stopping and speaking into the security box, the gate swung open, and Deacon drove the rest of the way down the drive. He pushed the remote on his bike that opened the garage and rolled in to park beside his truck. His four-wheel-drive was a newer model, so he wasn't embarrassed by it.

Sabrina pulled her fairly new sedan to a stop and got out, looking wide-eyed at his home. Deacon held his breath as he waited for her to say something. When she did, he exhaled and smiled inwardly.

"Wow. Deacon, this is stunning." She turned in a circle, taking in the trees and plants that had been growing for many years. Wildflowers edged the woods, creating a colorful barrier. His home was a two-story mixture of stone and dark wood. He loved it, and he hoped she did as well.

Deacon walked over to her and grabbed her hand, because he couldn't not touch her in some way. "Let me get your things, and then I'll give you the tour." After retrieving her bags from the trunk, Deacon led her through the garage and into the house via a hallway just past the mudroom.

"Your house is amazing." Sabrina took in the kitchen

before moving on to the living area. Deacon tried to imagine it through her eyes. Did she see a home? Or was she seeing the same thing he had at her place – somewhere to sleep at night with no real ties? When Sabrina caught sight of the double French doors leading to the backyard, she took a step in that direction then paused.

"Let's take a look," Deacon suggested. He dropped her bags on the table before holding open the door for her. "I sometimes have a large vegetable garden, but I've been busy this year. I didn't plant one only to have it wither from lack of care."

"You're full of surprises," Sabrina whispered, but Deacon caught the words. Several hummingbirds were hovering around the feeders, and Sabrina stood silently as they buzzed back and forth. "If I lived here, I would never want to leave." Her words were music to Deacon's ears. He wanted her to love his place, because if he had his way, she'd be living there with him soon.

"It's peaceful. I prefer it to a busier area. I have forty acres, and the nearest neighbors are half a mile on either side." He didn't tell her who his neighbors were, but several of the Stone Clan lived close by.

A car engine sounded in the distance, and when it slowed, he waited until it moved closer, coming down the driveway. "Travis and Brynna are here. Let's go say hello." Deacon held out his hand, and Sabrina took it. He slotted their fingers together as they walked side by side. He knew he should take things slow, but he couldn't help wanting to touch her every chance he got. Just as they reached the living room, the doorbell rang. Sabrina dropped his hand and remained by the sofa. Deacon opened the door to a grinning Viking princess and a shy Travis who was laden with shopping bags. Brynna bypassed Deacon, going straight to Sabrina.

"Hello, Dr. Bailey. I'm Brynna, and it's a pleasure to

110

meet you."

"Please, call me Sabrina. It's nice to meet you as well." Sabrina's greeting as well as her smile were genuine. Any jealousy from earlier was no longer present.

Deacon took the bags from Travis. "I'm just going to..." He hurried up the stairs and tossed the packages into his closet, then rushed back downstairs. He didn't know Brynna well enough to leave her alone with Sabrina, but when he found them in the kitchen, he relaxed. Travis was explaining some of the projects he was working on with Rafael while Sabrina and Brynna listened. All three had a glass of tea.

"I hope you don't mind," Brynna said, holding up her glass, "but I've grown quite fond of sweet tea."

"Not at all. I'm quite partial to it myself. It took a while, because up north they don't sweeten it." Deacon poured himself a glass, taking the last of it. While they stood around making small talk, he pulled several tea bags out of the pantry and put them in a boiler on the stove.

Brynna drained her glass. "I hate to drink and run, but Travis and I need to go. We're meeting Urijah and Banyan before we all head out."

"Are you going to Norway?"

"Yes. Now that their new house is finished, and spectacular I might add, they have asked Travis to get started on the new one there as well as the remodel." Travis blushed at Brynna's praise. "And I'm tagging along because I want to show Travis my homeland." Brynna was careful about how she phrased everything.

"Thank you again for the packages."

Brynna took both hers and Travis's empty glasses and put them in the dishwasher. "Don't thank me. I love shopping. Travis is the brave soul who put up with hours of me dragging him around the mall."

"I didn't mind," Travis replied softly, the love evident on his face and in his voice. Deacon had a feeling it wouldn't

111

be much longer before the two of them made the bond complete.

"Then I thank you both. When you return, we'll have you over for dinner."

The four of them said goodbye, leaving Deacon alone with Sabrina. "Let me see to the tea and then I'll get started on our meal." Sabrina watched everything he did, and it felt right having his mate in his home.

Chapter Thirteen

SABRINA FOLLOWED DEACON to the kitchen. "You said you'd explain the packages," she said, curious as to why the exquisite blonde had gone shopping for him. Sabrina had never met anyone as stunning as Brynna. If her boyfriend hadn't been with her, Sabrina would probably have still been a little jealous. Deacon was all male, and he had to find the woman attractive. Hell, Sabrina did, and she didn't swing that way.

Deacon glanced at her before pouring a cup of sugar into the tea container. "It's embarrassing, but I figure you should get to know the real me." Instead of turning to look at her while speaking, he stirred the sugar into the steaming liquid. "I haven't been on a date in a long time. I go to work and come home. If I do go anywhere, it's usually to Rafael's or one of the other male's houses. I don't exactly have anything to wear other than what you see here." He indicated his T-shirt and threadbare jeans. "So, I asked Brynna to go shopping with me, you know, to give an opinion on what would look okay for our date tomorrow. Then I got the call from Dante about someone stalking you, and Brynna offered to go shopping for me so I could watch after you."

Sabrina was touched he wanted to look nice for their date, but she didn't need him spending lots of money on new clothes. "I'm not that shallow," she blurted before she thought better of it.

"I don't think you are, but that doesn't mean I don't want to look nice for you. You could do so much better than me, but I don't want you to. That might sound selfish, but I'm deeply attracted to you, and I have a feeling we could be good together. I'm a simple male. That's not to say I'm poor or don't like nice things. It's just that I've never had anyone I wanted to impress."

"You do impress me. And judging by your home and the new truck in the garage, I don't doubt you do well for yourself. You've seen my house. I'm not materialistic. I may be a doctor, by I don't live extravagantly. I'm not one to spend tons on clothes or shoes or new purses. I came from nothing, and I learned at an early age how to be frugal. As long as we had food on the table, my brothers and sister and I were happy. We had each other when our mom was working two jobs."

"I'm sorry you had it rough. I'm an only child, and it's been a long time since I've seen my parents." Deacon finished the tea, adding a scoop of ice to help cool it off quicker.

"Do they live around here?"

"No. Last I heard, they were in South Africa." Deacon didn't elaborate on his parents, so she let the subject drop as he put the pitcher of tea in the refrigerator. After rummaging around, he gathered several items and placed them on the counter.

"What are you making?" Sabrina was intrigued. She'd never had a man cook for her, and it was sexy watching Deacon move so effortlessly around his kitchen.

"Since we're having Italian tomorrow, I thought I'd throw some fajitas together, if that's okay."

"Sounds perfect." Sabrina didn't know whether to help or just sit. "Do you want help?"

"No, thanks. It's easy, so why don't you have a seat and tell me more about you?"

114

"What do you want to know?"

Deacon bent over, pulling an iron skillet from the cabinet. Sabrina admired the way his jeans fit his firm butt and thick thighs. When he stood up, he was smirking at her. Instead of being embarrassed, she shrugged. "You have a nice butt," she admitted.

Deacon's mocha skin tinged a shade darker, and his eyes crinkled at the edges. "What do you like to do in your down time?"

"I clean house, do the laundry, mow, and run the weed eater." The housework wasn't necessarily the things she liked doing, but she didn't mind the outside work. Her yard wasn't that big, and she enjoyed being outside. She would be in heaven in Deacon's backyard among all the plants, flowers, and trees.

"I know those things are necessary, but what do you do for fun?" Deacon asked as he dropped strips of steak into the hot oil.

"Yard work is fun. At least for me. I lived in an apartment growing up and another one when I moved in with my grandmother. I love being outside, and there's something peaceful about the yard work. It's as if the universe gives us this wonderful thing, but it's up to us to maintain it and help it grow and thrive. If you ever need help with your gardens, just let me know."

"That was beautiful." Deacon looked at Sabrina thoughtfully before turning back to the stove. "And I may just take you up on that. Now, tell me your guilty pleasure."

"What?" Sabrina laughed. "Who says I have one?" Of course, she had one, but did she really want him to know what it was?

"Everyone has that one thing they think people will laugh about if they know."

"If you're going to laugh, why would I tell you?"

"I'm not going to laugh," Deacon promised.

"Oh yeah? Then tell me yours." There was no way his was as embarrassing as hers.

"I like to dance," Deacon said, again his face was turning that adorable shade of peach when he blushed.

"There's nothing wrong with that. Everyone dances."

"Not like I do," he muttered. Sabrina loved to dance. She did it all the time. Whenever she was getting ready in the morning or waiting on her food to cook, Sabrina would turn on some music and dance around the house. Why not? Nobody could see her. So what if he didn't dance well?

"Now this I have to hear. Are you that bad? Not everyone has good coordination." She didn't add in the fact that he was so large it would surprise her if he was able to move smoothly.

"Oh, I have plenty of coordination. If you're good, I may show you later. But now you have to tell me yours."

She could do this. Sabrina could admit what she liked to do in the privacy of her own home. If he judged her, then he wasn't that man for her. "I watch cartoons." Sabrina shrugged, and continued, "We didn't always have a TV growing up, but when we did, the four of us would snuggle up on the sofa and watch cartoons on Saturday morning. It was the only time I could watch television. I was usually too busy cooking or helping with homework and baths. It's probably silly, but it makes me happy thinking about those few days we were all together not worrying about anything."

"I don't think it's silly. Other than cartoons, do you watch television?"

"When I have time. During the week, I come home, fix something to eat, grab a glass of wine, and open a book. On the weekends, I'll watch a movie if there's a good one on. Mostly action films or superheroes. I'm not really the Hallmark channel type."

"That's surprising. I guess I was assuming you were like most women who liked roses and chocolates."

116

"I love chocolate, but I hate roses. They remind me of the funeral home when my grandmother died. Other than dancing, what do you like to do?" Sabrina wanted the focus off her. So, while Deacon cooked and then while they ate the best fajitas she'd ever tasted, they talked about anything and everything. All the simple questions you found out on a first date.

Sabrina helped Deacon clean up the kitchen, and she found herself daydreaming several times. Was this what it was like having a partner who took on the responsibilities with you? Not like Garrison, who expected to be waited on all the time. Sabrina could get used to having someone cook for her. She enjoyed cooking for someone else, but since it was just her at home, it was something she did as a necessity. Cooking for one person was hard, so she usually fixed something like spaghetti and froze what she didn't eat. Reheated food wasn't the best, but it kept from being wasteful or having to eat out so much.

"How about a tour?" Deacon asked when they finished.

"I'd like that." Sabrina had only seen part of the first floor. Deacon's home was larger than she thought, with room for plenty of kids. There were several bedrooms upstairs, a game room and office downstairs. "Do you want kids?" she blurted.

Deacon hesitated outside the master bedroom. He had saved it for last, and instead of going in, he let her get a good look while he remained in the doorway. The bathroom was luxurious with a whirlpool tub large enough for the both of them as well as a shower that had no door, it was so spacious. When he didn't answer her, Sabrina stuck her head out the bathroom door to make sure he was still there.

"I love kids." Deacon was rubbing the back of his neck, studying the floor.

"I'm sensing a but in there," she prodded.

"Let's grab a drink and sit outside." Deacon held out his

117

hand, and Sabrina walked to him. Instead of leading her down the stairs, Deacon pulled her into an embrace. "You look good in my bedroom," he whispered against her ear. Goosebumps rose on her flesh, and the need to make love intensified by a million. Throughout dinner, she'd had to physically make herself remain in her chair. Her hands itched to touch him. Her lips tingled in anticipation of kissing him. Her core throbbed with a longing she'd never encountered. Ever. What was it about Deacon that set her off yet set her at ease at the same time? She'd sworn off men who were so much larger than her, yet she knew in her soul this man would never hurt her.

Deacon pulled away from the embrace but entwined their fingers together as they made their way downstairs. "Would you like wine or something else?"

"Wine, please." They'd stuck to tea with dinner, and now she was ready to relax.

"Red or white? Dry or sweet? I have a large selection."

"I prefer whites over reds and dry over sweet." That's what she preferred, but she also wasn't that picky. If it was wet and made from grapes, she'd drink it.

"I'll be right back." Deacon disappeared into the garage, and less than a minute later he returned with a chilled bottle in hand. "I don't have a wine cellar, but I do have a room off the back of the garage. I think you'll like this. It's a Viognier." Deacon pulled down two wine glasses after releasing the cork. "Are you okay with drinking it now? I know we're supposed to let it breathe."

"I'm not a wine snob or connoisseur. I've been known to drink mine from a box. Don't judge," Sabrina added with an arch of her eyebrow.

Deacon laughed and set to pouring the wine. "I like how down to earth you are. It's refreshing." He handed her a glass, took one for himself, and placed his hand at the small of her back, ushering her toward the back doors. When they were outside, the sun was making its way out of sight, casting gorgeous lines through the trees. He motioned for Sabrina to take a seat, so she sat down on one of the larger pieces. It was either a small sofa or an overgrown loveseat, but either way, she chose it in hopes he'd sit next to her. He did.

Deacon slid his arm across the back of the seat, letting his fingers brush softly over her arm. "You asked if I want kids, and the answer isn't a simple yes or no." He paused to take a sip of wine. "I need to ask you something before we get too deep into those types of questions."

Sabrina eased closer, and Deacon's hand continued its slow caress. "Go ahead."

"It's been a long time since I've been on a date. Of those dates I did have, rarely did they turn into a second one, and that was of my own choosing. I never found anyone interesting enough to want to get to know. Until you. I really like you, but if you don't feel the same…"

"I do. I'll admit, I've shied away from larger men. I don't want to talk about past experiences, but I will say my last boyfriend didn't take it well when I broke things off. I haven't been on many dates since, and none of those amounted to anything more than dinner. Having said that, I like you too. I feel safe with you, and not because you've been assigned to be my bodyguard. My heart feels safe with you. Maybe that's too much too soon. I'm a practical woman, but I have learned to trust my instincts. I would like to see where this leads."

Deacon pressed his lips to the side of her head before letting his temple rest against her hair. "I love kids. I bought this house thinking I'd fill it up eventually. But as much as I love them, they scare me. As a parent, it's your job to make sure they're happy. Taken care of. Safe. I have the financial means to give them a good life. But the world is a dark place. It's full of evil, and I'm not only talking about kidnappers and molesters and traffickers. I'm talking about other kids. We can't shield them from everything life is going to throw at them. There's something you need to know about me." Deacon moved away so he could turn and look at her. "I'm empathic. I feel emotions from others, and I feel them deeply."

Sabrina was shocked at his admission, and she searched his face for any sign he was joking. She knew in her heart he wasn't. He had no reason to lie to her.

"One reason I live in the middle of the woods is to give my head a break. Being around so many inmates is tough, but for the most part, they're resigned to their fate. We get a few who are constantly screaming their innocence, and I have to let my co-workers deal with them. The hospital is a hard place for me. The patients are sick or dying. The families are hopeful until they're not. The only spaces in the building I feel at ease are the nursery and the morgue. Even the babies who are crying can have their needs met quickly. The morgue is self-explanatory. So, back to kids. I love kids, but I'm scared of the pain. I'm scared of not being able to meet their emotional needs and feel the backlash. Does that make sense?"

"It does. And the fact that you're so worried about their emotional support tells me you'd be a wonderful father. But I get what you're saying. Not that we're anywhere close to talking about a family, but just so you know, that's not a deal breaker for me. Yes, I would like to have kids, but I'm not getting any younger. I'll be thirty-seven in August. I know lots of women have babies in their forties, but I'm not sure I want to be closing in on retirement age and have a child just starting college."

Sabrina could feel Deacon's relief at her words. Could see in his eyes the hope for a future with her. Maybe it had been a deal breaker for him. She took a sip of wine and leaned back into his side. "This is nice," she said. "You were

120

right: it is peaceful here. My neighborhood isn't loud, but there's always some noise like a car door slamming. A dog barking. Sirens in the distance." Sabrina listened for any type of noise, and other than the rustling of the trees when a breeze blew and the hummingbirds arguing, there was nothing.

They sat in companionable silence, sipping wine and just being. But there was something she needed from him. "I want to see you dance."

Chapter Fourteen

DRAGO ROLLED INTO town just as the sun was setting. He bypassed the warehouses, already assured everything was under control. Hagen Rossum was sitting at the dining room table, laptop open, and fingers flying across the keyboard.

"We have a problem, sir," he said as soon as Drago closed the door. Drago liked that about the human. No need for formalities. Kallisto had taught him well.

"What is it?" Drago crossed the room and entered the kitchen to grab a beer out of the refrigerator. He was hungry but in no mood to cook.

"If you're hungry, I left a plate in the oven."

"What's the problem, Rossum?" Drago set the bottle down and opened the oven to find a covered plate of chicken parmesan. He stuck it in the microwave then turned to give the human his attention.

"The one you had Renneck keeping an eye on has left town. From what I can gather, it was sudden. Do you want me to track him for you? Find out where he went?"

"Yes. I already have something set in motion, and he's a vital part of that." The microwave dinged. "Did you make this?" Drago asked, taking the plate and setting it on the island.

"Oh, yeah. Sorry if it's not very good, but I like to cook. I'm just not as good at it as I am computers." The kid kept his eyes down, and Drago didn't like that, which was odd.

Normally, he was all about intimidation, compliance, and subordination. The same way Alistair had been. For whatever reason, he wanted the human to be at ease around him. Drago had plans for Hagen. Ones that would carry him far within their Clan if he was useful.

"I appreciate the effort." Drago took a bite and found it to his liking. "This is really good, Hagen. Feel free to cook any time you like as long as it doesn't interfere with your work."

"Thank you, sir." The kid beamed from those few words.

Drago served under Alistair Gianopoulos for hundreds of years. He watched how his King treated not only those under him but his children as well. Few of the Greek Gargoyles were loyal to Alistair because they respected him. They served Alistair out of fear. Not the way the Stone Society followed Rafael. Those males, whether family or not, lived and breathed everything Di Pietro-related, because Rafael was solid. He ruled his Clan with honor, stepping in and doing what needed to be done, right alongside the other Goyles. His Clan would fight to the death to keep Rafael King of the Americas. Drago would have one hell of a battle going up against the entire Society. He needed his own males to be loyal to him, so maybe he would take a lesson from the American King.

DEACON NEVER SHOULD have mentioned dancing. Now, he either had to pretend he couldn't dance well and embarrass himself, or show his mate what he could do and deal with how it made her feel. Hell, he wasn't sure if she was the same as the women from the movies. Sabrina might watch him with a critical eye and nothing more. Screw it. He took her free hand and pulled her to her feet.

"We'll need to go inside where I can turn on some music." Deacon led Sabrina to the living room and guided her down to the sofa. If he wanted to play it up, he could move a dining chair to the center of the room and really give her a show. Deciding against it, he left her where she was and pulled out his phone. He opened the music app and scrolled until he found the perfect song. It was the same one from the movie where he'd learned his moves. The only reason he'd seen the movie in the first place was because Matthew had been watching it one night while Deacon had been guarding the teen. Abbi and Amelia had already gone to bed, and Matthew had dared Deacon to dance, so he did. He enjoyed it so much he went home and it became an obsession of sorts. Practicing until he had every step, every move, down.

After pushing the coffee table out of the way, Deacon hit play and let the music take over. As soon as he began rolling his hips, Sabrina's eyes widened. When he pulled his tee up exposing his abs, she swallowed hard. This was so unlike Deacon – this seduction – but he knew he was getting it right when Sabrina's arousal hit his nose. Deacon called on his beast to keep his erection under control while he continued to move his hips. Ripping his shirt over his head, he tossed it across the room. Deacon ran his hands down his torso and back up, biting his bottom lip while looking at Sabrina through hooded eyes. He didn't have the props needed to do the dance exactly as the character from the movie, and honestly, he wouldn't have been as crass to pretend to orgasm while spewing water into the air. This dance was nowhere near as provocative as the one the guys did in the club, but it was steamy enough. He dropped to the floor, following the choreography for a few more steps, rolling his hips seductively, and then he flipped onto his feet.

Deacon pumped his hips, and Sabrina gasped. "Oh, my,"

she muttered, squirming against the sofa. He never intended to continue through the whole routine, but he was enjoying himself. Given his mate hadn't laughed at him, he took that as a good sign. Before the song was over, Deacon pulled Sabrina to her feet and into his arms. At that point, he was going to dance with her, but she had other ideas. Sabrina ran her hands down his chest, over his abs, and unbuttoned his jeans. When she paused at his zipper, she glanced up at him. For permission maybe. There was no way he would stop her if she wanted to take things further.

"You don't have to," he told her.

"I want you," Sabrina whispered.

As much as he wanted his mate's mouth around his cock, their first time wasn't going to be with her on her knees in the living room. Deacon picked her up, cradling her like a bride on her wedding day, and carried her upstairs to his bedroom. It had been hundreds of years since he'd bedded a female, and it was going to take every ounce of strength he could muster to get through this without coming too quickly. Not only that, but he was already fighting his beast for control.

She is ours. Claim her.

I won't. Not until she knows the truth.

Then tell her.

Not yet.

Deacon laid Sabrina in the middle of the bed. She was perfection, and she was his. "We don't have to do this yet."

"I want to. Unless you don't." Sabrina's breathing was harsh, and he knew she wanted him. She was transmitting want and need as clearly as the words she spoke aloud.

"Oh, I do. I have wanted you since the first time I saw you." Deacon removed Sabrina's shoes, tossing them to the floor. He moved to her blouse and unbuttoned it. Slowly, he unwrapped this flawless present that was his mate. Next came her bra, a lavender lace number which matched the shirt she had on. Deacon bit back a groan when her breasts were revealed. They weren't overly full, but they were more than enough for his large hands to enjoy. Next, he removed her jeans, leaving the lace panties that matched the bra. He would buy her sets of lingerie in every color under the sun if he was the one who got to see them on her luscious body. The one who got to remove them and cherish the treasures hidden within.

"Deacon, please," she begged, her hands on her thighs, close to her juncture.

Deacon removed his boots and socks so he could get his jeans and underwear off. When he stood naked in front of her, Sabrina raked his body with her eyes from his head down, stopping at his erection. His cock was leaking as it jutted toward her. "Deacon..." Sabrina pushed her panties down her toned legs. She held her hand out to him, and he took it, allowing her to pull him down on top of her. His dick was pressed between their bodies, and that little bit of friction was almost enough to have him shooting his load. He didn't want that. He wanted to give his mate what she needed.

"Do you have a condom?" Sabrina asked, taking care of his impending orgasm. He couldn't make love to her. Not without protection.

"No. Like I said, it's been a long time. Don't worry. I'll take care of you." Deacon leaned down, pressing their lips together. He had never gone down on a female, but he'd seen it done in porn, and he knew the mechanics. He could make her come with his tongue and fingers. That would have to be enough for now. Deacon knew he couldn't give her diseases, but she was his mate, and she could get pregnant if the fates willed it so without protection. What started off as a brush of lips turned into a feast. Sabrina took control of the kiss the same way she had in her office. His mate wasn't a meek lamb. She was fire and passion.

126

Deacon licked inside her mouth, tasting wine and Sabrina's own essence. It was a heady mixture, one that could get him drunk when nothing else could. He nipped at her bottom lip, sucking it into his mouth with just enough pressure to have her gasping into his mouth. Wanting more, he licked a path from her neck down to her breasts where he laved her right nipple. Teasing, biting softly, blowing on it, Deacon leaned on his forearm so he could use his free hand to squeeze her other breast, twisting her nipple. Sabrina writhed beneath him, wrapping one leg around his hips, arching into him.

Take her. She wants to be with us.

"I can't."

"Can't what?" Sabrina asked.

Shit. He'd spoken to his beast out loud. "Can't stop tasting you. You're exquisite."

"Please, Deacon. I need…" Sabrina grabbed hold of his ears, pushing his head, urging him lower. Not being able to deny her, Deacon slid down on the bed, pressing kisses to her soft skin as he went. He had seen nude females before, but never had he gazed upon his mate. The way her folds glistened with moisture. Her scent called to him, and he spread her lips with his fingers and fastened his mouth to her, sucking, licking, teasing. Deacon's cock was harder than it had ever been before, and he rubbed against the mattress, needing release before the beast overtook him.

Sabrina's breaths were coming in shallow pants as she pushed her core against his mouth. Deacon flicked his tongue over her nub and pushed a couple fingers inside her slick passage. Fisting her hands into the bedding, Sabrina arched and yelled out as her orgasm flowed through her body. Deacon lapped at her release, his own not far behind. Turning his head sideways, he squeezed his eyes tightly, begging his fangs and claws to remain where they were. Embarrassment flowed through Deacon at having come

127

against the bed like a virgin. He rested his cheek on Sabrina's thigh, willing his heart to stop racing. If this was how his body reacted without making love, he surely wouldn't be able to withstand it when he sank deep inside her. How did the others do it?

"First appointment I can get with my doctor, I'm getting on the pill."

Deacon popped his head up, taking in Sabrina's flushed face. The sated expression and smile she gave him rocked his world. "Does that mean...?"

"That I want to continue this? Oh, yes. If you make me explode like that with your mouth, I can't imagine what you'll be able to do with your... you know."

Deacon grinned. "My 'you know' is happy to hear that." He kissed her inner thigh before working his way up until they were face to face. "*I'm* happy to hear that." Deacon ghosted his lips across hers. "I'll be right back." He climbed off the bed and retreated into the bathroom to clean himself. He took his time, thinking about everything that happened. Deacon wasn't a seducer. He wasn't a suave, experienced male, but Sabrina brought out his inner tiger. Well, Gargoyle. He shouldn't be surprised, though. She was his chosen mate. He should have known everything with her would be easier than he'd ever found it before. After cleaning the release from his body, he wrapped a towel around his waist and returned to the bedroom. Sabrina was exactly where he left her.

"I think you broke me," she joked.

"Nah. Maybe bent you just a bit." He leaned over, kissing her again. When he tried to rise up, Sabrina snaked her arms around his neck, keeping his lips where she wanted them. His mate wasn't shy. Except she couldn't bring herself to say cock or dick. Deacon found that charming. Everything about her was charming, and he just knew everything would be okay. They would get to know one another, and when the time was right, he would tell her the truth of himself and the Gargoyles. She would accept the mate bond, and they'd live out the rest of their lives together. Maybe alone, maybe with children. But always together.

"Where did you learn to dance like that?" Sabrina asked when they came up for air.

Deacon pulled away and turned in search of his briefs. "Have you met Frey and Abbi's son, Matthew?" Sabrina nodded. "I was staying with him one night and that *Magic Mike* movie was on. He bet me I couldn't dance the way they could, so I got up and tried it. I wasn't bad, but I definitely didn't have the same moves the actors did. This is embarrassing, but I enjoyed it. I've always liked to dance, but that takes it to a whole different level. I came home the next day and spent some time watching the videos and practicing."

"Color me impressed. Have you ever danced like that in a club?"

Deacon sat down on the bed next to her thigh and picked up Sabrina's hand. He kissed her knuckles. "No way. First off, I don't go to clubs, and second, that kind of dancing is meant to do one thing: seduce. Not that I was trying to seduce you exactly, but I'm not the kind of male to shake my ass for just anybody."

"Only for me?" Sabrina played with the band around his underwear.

"Only for you. Now, what do you say we go grab another glass of wine and find a movie to watch?"

"Do you mind if I put on something more comfortable?"

"Not at all. Wait here and I'll get your bags."

"Or I could wear one of your T-shirts."

"Or you could wear one of my T-shirts." Deacon crowed on the inside, and his beast might have roared a bit. Okay, a lot. He opened a dresser drawer and pulled out one of his older tees. It was well-worn and soft as butter. Sabrina pulled her panties on then slid the shirt over her body. "Perfect," he muttered before picking her up and carrying her back downstairs.

Chapter Fifteen

SABRINA WAS IN heaven. She was snuggled up against Deacon's chest, her legs bent behind her on the sofa. His arm was securely around her where he was once again rubbing lazy circles on her skin. She should be freaking out. Things were moving way too fast, but then again, they weren't moving fast enough. Why had she gotten off the pill? Because she had sworn off sex and didn't need the chemicals in her body. And what man didn't keep condoms? Someone who hadn't dated in a long time. That was another plus in the Team Deacon column. There were so many checks in that column Sabrina needed a new sheet of paper. Not that she'd actually written anything down. The checklist was in her mind, and it was filled with nothing but good.

She hadn't had many lovers in her life, but of those she had, they didn't hold a candle to Deacon, and they hadn't even had sex yet. She knew when they did, she would combust. Her body was still tingling from the orgasm he'd given her with his mouth and fingers. Just thinking about his impressive cock had her struggling to remain still. She couldn't wait until one of them had protection and he could fill her up. Since they had another date tomorrow, they could stop at the drugstore and get condoms, since it would probably take too long to get in with the doctor. *Damn, girl.* Sabrina chuckled to herself. She'd never been this brazen when it came to having sex, but she'd never had a man like

Deacon Wright.

Being with him was so different than being with Garrison. Deacon asked for nothing. He gave everything. "Why hasn't someone snatched you up already?"

Deacon chuckled, the sound in his chest music to her ear. "I could ask you the same thing. But I think we were both waiting on the right one, and here we are."

Sabrina leaned up. "You really think so?"

Deacon bit his bottom lip, grinning. One dimple threatened to pop out of his left cheek, and Sabrina reached up to touch the skin there. "Yeah. I do. I know how I feel, so we'll take this as slow as you wanna go. Or as fast. Either way, I want you in my life, any way I can have you and as often. This right here? Sitting, relaxing together, is heaven to me. I'm a homebody. I love the peacefulness my place brings, and you feel right being here with me."

Sabrina lifted her face, and Deacon met her for a sweet kiss. She could kiss him for hours and never get tired of it. Whether it was the soft brushes of their lips or the more passionate mating of their mouths and tongues, she'd never get enough. Already, he had ruined her for other men, and she was okay with that. Sabrina knew in her heart this was it. He was her one.

When the movie credits played, Deacon kissed her temple. "You ready to turn in?"

Sabrina was excited. It had been years since she'd slept in the same bed with a man, and Garrison hadn't been one to hold her during the night. Would Deacon be the same way? Turning his back to her? Or would he wrap her in his arms? "Yes. I need to brush my teeth."

"I put your bags in the spare bedroom across the hall from my room."

Did that mean he didn't want them to sleep together? "Okay."

"I'm going to lock up. I'll be upstairs to check on you in

a few."

Sabrina didn't respond. Instead, she silently padded barefoot up to the second floor. She found her things in the bedroom like Deacon said. Grabbing her toiletries, she closed herself into the attached bathroom and sat down on the closed toilet lid. After a few minutes of thinking back on their day together, she made herself get up and get ready to turn in. If he didn't want to share a bed, that was fine. First, she brushed out her hair and wrapped it in her favorite silk scarf. Once that was done, she brushed her teeth. When she was rinsing the foam from her mouth, Deacon knocked.

"Everything okay?"

"Yes. I'll be out in a second."

She wiped her mouth with the hand towel and hung it back up. When she opened the door, Deacon was sitting on the edge of the bed. "I didn't want to assume or pressure you, but you're welcome to sleep with me."

Yes! She'd read the situation wrong. And that was okay. She should have known better, but instead of communicating, she had assumed the worst. Again. "I'd like that."

Deacon stood and reached for her hand. He touched her scarf and whispered, "Beautiful." Sabrina's heart melted a little. When they reached his room, he asked, "Which side do you sleep on?"

"The right, but if that's your side, I don't mind taking the left."

"I don't think it's going to matter, because I plan on holding you all night, and we'll probably end up in the middle." And her heart melted a little more. Deacon pulled the covers back for her. "Go ahead and climb in. I need to brush my teeth."

Sabrina did as he said, and she scooted toward the middle. That way he could choose whichever side he wanted.

133

DEACON LEANED AGAINST the bathroom counter, breathing deep to get his beast under control. His mate was in his bed, but he couldn't take her the way he needed. If he did, the fangs would come out, and she deserved to know what he was. Sabrina should know the truth and make the choice of whether they mated or not. She wasn't dressed to seduce him. She had gotten ready to sleep, and that's what they were going to do if it killed him.

Taking one last breath, he turned off the bathroom light and stopped at the door. Sabrina was in the middle of the bed. Deacon grinned. She was giving him the choice of which side of the bed to sleep on, so he chose the side closest to the hallway. Sliding under the covers, he rolled to his back, trying not to crowd her. Sabrina has other ideas as she turned on her side and wrapped an arm over his stomach, placing her silk covered head to his chest. Deacon pulled her closer, kissing her temple. "Goodnight, Pretty Lady."

"Night," she whispered. Sabrina's thigh snaked over his, too close to his dick. He held his breath, praying she settled in to sleep. After a few minutes, she said, "Deacon?"

"Hmm?"

Instead of speaking, she rolled until she was on top of him and kissed his jaw. Deacon grabbed her hips to keep her from squirming.

"I don't think I can do this," he admitted. Her mood changed from turned on to embarrassed, and she tried to climb off the bed. He didn't let her go far. "You misunderstood. I want you more than I've ever wanted anything in my life, but there are things you don't know. I'm not just a man, Sabrina. I'm not someone who wants you for a night. If you and I are together, to me, it's not random or temporary. With you on top of me, I want to make love to you. If you and I make love, that will be it for me. But you don't know the truth of what I am, and until you know, we can't do this."

"Then tell me." Sabrina ran a fingertip down his jaw. "Unless you're some psychopath or murderer..."

Deacon sat up so he could prop against the headboard, juggling Sabrina off his lap. "Nothing like that, but what I am is not to be taken lightly. It's not just my secret to tell, either. If you know the truth, I will be exposing all of my kind."

Sabrina sat up next to him and laced their fingers together. "What do you mean 'your kind'? I know from talking to Joseph you belong to a Clan of sorts. He assured me you are one of the good guys."

"That we are. We are good, for the most part. Just like humans, there are good and bad in every species, but my Clan – my family – we are the good of our kind."

Sabrina laughed, but it wasn't from humor. "Human? Species? You make it sound like you're some type of creature." She turned to face him. "Are you trying to tell me you aren't human? I'm a doctor. I think I would recognize if you were something else. Wouldn't I?"

"Not unless I wanted you to. My kind was made to look human so we blend in. We were created to protect humans without being detected. Are you sure you want to hear this? Because if you know the truth, you will be holding our safety in your hands. If you think what I tell you will be too much, you can walk away now. I will still keep you safe, because as your mate, that's my job."

"So, I'm a job to you?" Sabrina tried to pull her hand away, but Deacon held tighter.

"I'm not explaining this correctly. You are more than a job to me. You are my intended. My mate. Our kind has one being chosen for them by the fates, and I will never love another. I will never take someone else into my bed now that

135

I've found you. You, however, aren't bound the same way. If you decide all this is too much, I will release you and let you live your life without interference. Yes, I will still watch over you, because to me, you're everything. But I'll do it from a distance once your stalker is found and dealt with."

"I'm your mate. Is that why I felt drawn to you the first time I saw you in Jonathan's room?"

"Yes. Our bond is strong, but if you aren't ready for all it entails, you can walk away. Or if you would like to figure out if I'm someone you could see spending your life with, we can take it slow. Go on dates. Spend time together getting to know each other."

"I think I would like to know what you are, if not human, before making that decision."

Deacon couldn't believe how calm she was. He hadn't said the word Gargoyle or mentioned fangs, wings, or claws. How calm would she be the first time he phased in front of her?

"I promise whatever you tell me will be our secret. For whatever reason, I do trust you're a good man. Wait... male. You and Joseph used that term, so I'm assuming either my boss is one of your kind, or he at least knows the truth. I have known Joseph for years, and I trust him. He trusts you, so... tell me."

Deacon searched Sabrina's eyes, reaching out with his senses for any distrust or trepidation. When he found none, he decided he would trust her with the truth. He wouldn't admit to anyone else in the Clan being Goyle. That way, if she happened to tell someone, she would sound crazy.

"I'm what is now known as a Gargoyle. We were created by the gods to protect humans. Our kind has been around for millennia, living among you. In the past, we had females of our kind as mates, but they weren't given the same structure as the males, and most of them have died off. It has only been in the past couple hundred years that we

136

have been given humans for mates. Our mate is the other part of us. We have our shifter inside, but that's what we are at our core. I look human, but if the beast comes out, my body transforms into something else. My face will look the same, but... I don't want to scare you."

"I thought Gargoyles were those stone creatures on buildings."

"Those were created by humans many years ago as a symbol for our kind. Humans who know about us have lived among us, offering sanctuary when we need it. The symbols were to make us aware of the humans who would work with us. With our numbers being a fraction of that of humans, it was necessary to share our existence with a handful of humankind."

"And you have to trust who knows. I get that. So, you tell me your secret, and I decide what to do with the knowledge?"

"Pretty much. It's a huge responsibility. Not only do you discover there are nonhumans, but you find out one of them wants you for an eternity. And that's what it would be. If you were to decide you want me, there would be no divorce later. Mating with me isn't like dating or marrying a human. It's an unbreakable bond which lasts forever. There's another thing you need to consider. If you were to mate with me, you will stop aging. At whatever age a human bonds with their Gargoyle, that is the age they look for the rest of their life."

"You say that like it's a bad thing."

"It can be. If you remain in New Atlanta, how will you explain to your colleagues ten, fifteen years down the road why you still look like you're in your mid-thirties? We manage it by moving around and reinventing ourselves or hiding from the public. I've met humans who age more gracefully because of good genetics and how they take care of themselves. So, it wouldn't be a stretch for you to remain here for twenty years or so."

"And how do Gargoyles age? You don't look any older than I do."

Deacon grinned and gripped her hand tighter. "We transform into our shifter in our early teens and we stop aging in our mid-thirties. I'm four hundred years old."

"Get out of town. Really?"

"Really. Male Gargoyles can live to be over a thousand. If we aren't killed – and there's only one sure-fire way to kill males, and that's by taking our head – we are virtually indestructible."

"But if I'm your mate, won't you get lonely when I pass on in fifty years should my health hold out?"

"If you accept the mate bond, your body becomes less susceptible to human disease. You could die from say a plane crash or a stray bullet. Those are hypothetical situations, of course. But I do know a human mate who is over two hundred."

"Do I know any human mates?"

Deacon hesitated. If he told her the truth, he was putting his Clan at risk even more than he already had.

"Deacon, your secret is safe with me. What do you think would happen if I told someone what you've shared? They'd think I lost my marbles."

She had a point, and he did trust her, so he admitted, "Yes. As a matter of fact, you've met several of them."

Chapter Sixteen

SABRINA COULDN'T BELIEVE the conversation they were having. Well, she could, and she did. As far-fetched as it all sounded, she knew in her soul Deacon was telling the truth. "I'm going to venture a guess that all the men coming and going from Jonathan's room are part of your Clan. You said they were family, so that would make sense. And their women have accepted this bond? Joseph said I was already considered part of the family. That's why, isn't it?"

"Yes. Once we find our mate, they automatically become part of the Clan as do their family. You will find the men and women who are mates are a tight-knit group, and you'll have a new set of friends whether you want one or not."

"Men too?"

"Yes. There are gay Gargoyles. Is that a problem?"

"Not at all. I believe everyone should be able to love whom they choose without prejudice. And having a group of friends sounds nice. Especially if they're who I think they are. Kaya, if she's one of them, has already sang your praises and offered her friendship. It's been a long time since I've had that type of closeness, and I've missed it. My life has been filled with work and not much else." Sabrina was excited at the prospect of having people in her life who were more than colleagues. She was nervous about Deacon being something other than human, but it also gave her hope for the future if what he said was true. Did she believe in the whole fated-mate concept? She wasn't sure, but she really had nothing to lose by giving their relationship a chance and everything to gain. He was handsome and kind. He had shown her nothing but goodness so far. Both Kaya and Joseph had put in a good word for him. Kaya, the former chief of police, had to be a good judge of character, and Joseph... it was probable her boss was also a Gargoyle, and Sabrina held him in the highest regard. First, though, she wanted to see Deacon in his true form.

"Will you show me?"

Deacon frowned. "Are you sure you're ready?"

"As I'll ever be."

Deacon slid off the bed. "First, I'll start with my hands." He held his hands out in front of him, and razor-sharp claws extended from his fingertips. As quickly as the appeared, they were gone. "Now, my teeth." Deacon opened his mouth and fangs protruded over his bottom lip. "Just so you know, if we complete the bond, I will bite your shoulder with these." He tapped one of them with his finger. "It will happen during sex, and I've heard it only makes the orgasm that much stronger." He retracted the sharp canines. "Now for my wings."

"You have wings?" Holy crap. Those she had to see.

Grinning, Deacon rolled his shoulders, and a pair of leathery wings spread out behind him. Sabrina scooted to the end of the bed on her knees, wanting to get a closer look. She stretched out a hand, but Deacon took a step back, his wings disappearing. "Sorry, but we need to be mated first before you touch them. Let's just say that's more intimate than having sex."

"No one else has ever touched them?"

"Besides my Clanmates, no one has seen them."

"You said you protect humans. From themselves? Or what? Who?"

140

"I know you've heard of the Unholy." Sabrina nodded, staring at Deacon in his human form. "We patrol the city, making sure the Unholy keep to themselves. If we can, we arrest them and take them to the penitentiary. We have a special area we call The Basement where they are kept away from human inmates."

"And if you can't?"

Deacon looked at his feet. He didn't have to tell her what happened to the rest of them. As a doctor, she'd taken an oath to save lives, but she'd seen the Unholy on the news. They looked like a science experiment gone wrong. Not wanting Deacon to have to admit to killing, she changed the subject. "I can't imagine it's easy to fly without being seen."

"It's not. But living out in the middle of forty acres gives me the opportunity to do so."

That made sense. If Sabrina decided to become his mate, this house and all that came with it would become her home. It was farther away from the hospital than her own house, but living here with this exquisite male would be worth the extra drive time. Sabrina reached out her hand, and Deacon took it. "Nothing you've told me or shown me has scared me off. I'd like the chance to get to know you better before I let you bite me, if that's okay."

"It's more than okay. It's not a decision to be made lightly."

"Then let's get some sleep. If you need me to go back to the other room, I understand."

"I would love to hold you all night, but I'll leave that decision up to you."

Sabrina patted the space next to her. She trusted Deacon to not bite her in her sleep. He said he would only bite her during sex, so she had to keep her libido in check and not give him a reason to attack her. Why was the thought of him doing so more exciting than it should be? Deacon returned to his original position. Instead of draping herself across his

141

body like she wanted, she pressed her lips to his softly before rolling over away from him. He turned the lamp off and scooted so they were almost spooning. He didn't touch her, but she could feel the heat from his large body. She should have been scared at having this creature at her back, but Sabrina felt safer than she ever had. Sleep didn't come quickly. She replayed their conversation over and over. Images of his fangs, claws, and wings played out on repeat. Sabrina never would have believed he was something other than human had she not seen proof.

She thought about the other couples she'd met in Jonathan's room. Those women had accepted their males weren't human. At some point, they'd all had this same conversation, or probably one close to it. Deacon explained how his kind couldn't be killed easily. Jonathan was an older man. One who was dying, so that meant he must be one of the humans who knew about Gargoyles. She had so many questions, but they could wait.

Deacon's voice woke Sabrina the next morning. When she opened her eyes, he was standing beside the bed with his phone to his ear and a cup of coffee in his other hand. The smile he gave her warmed her inside. Garrison had never brought her coffee. He had expected her to wait on him, but here was Deacon. Their first morning together, and he was proving how different he was. Sabrina sat up and took the mug. "Thank you," she mouthed, not wanting to interrupt.

"Was there a card with your flowers?" he asked her.

"Not that I could find." Deacon relayed her answer to whoever was on the phone. She took a sip of coffee and found it was fixed exactly the way she liked. How had he managed that?

Deacon stared at Sabrina while he listened, his face etched in concern. "I'll check when I drop her off and let you know. Okay, thanks, Brother." Deacon disconnected the call. "That was Julian. He's our expert on anything to do with computers and forensics. Paxton took the photo you found to him. He's running the prints he got off it, but so far there hasn't been a match. Did you notice the words on the back?"

"Words? No. I kind of freaked out. What did they say?"

"Find Crave." Deacon ran a hand over his short hair. "There was another letter at the end, but it was smeared. It could have been an R, but he's not sure. Julian thought if the same person who left the picture was the one who left the flowers, there might have been a message on the card as well."

"The flowers should still be at the nurses' station. We can check when we get there."

"I'm going to fix breakfast while you get ready. Anything you don't particularly care for?"

"You're cooking for me. I'll eat whatever you make."

Deacon closed the distance and kissed her softly. She hated that she had both morning and coffee breath, but he didn't seem to mind. When he pulled away, Deacon ran a finger down her cheek. "I could get used to seeing you in my bed." Deacon didn't give her a chance to respond. He quickly left the room, and his footsteps were loud on the stairs. She could get used to it, too. Did she really need time to decide whether or not she wanted a life with him?

Thirty minutes later, Sabrina, dressed for work, walked into the kitchen to find the table set with a full breakfast laid out for them. "Biscuits and gravy? Will you marry me?"

"Any day. Any time."

Sabrina had said it as a joke, but the tone of Deacon's voice was serious. He rounded the table and pulled her chair out. Taking her empty cup, he placed a fresh coffee in front of her before sitting next to her. She couldn't remember the last time someone cooked for her. Probably when she was a teen living with her grandmother, and then it had never been anything as elaborate as what Deacon had whipped together in half an hour.

Sabrina felt a bit self-conscious about devouring so much food, but it was the best breakfast she could ever remember eating. Deacon continued to surprise her, and she was having a hard time keeping her hands to herself. Asking him to make the bond official then and there. Not only was he handsome and sweet, but he cooked for her. Brought her coffee in bed. Did things Garrison never thought of doing. It sucked that she continually compared Deacon to her ex, but she couldn't help it.

Deacon offered to drive her to the hospital, but she turned him down so she would have time to think without being tempted to touch him. He parked his truck in the employee lot close to her reserved space and walked with her to her office. She wanted to hold his hand but decided against it. They stopped by the nurses' station where she'd left the roses. Deacon pulled the flowers out, looking for a card. There was one in the bottom of the vase, but it was soaked from sitting in the water. He replaced the flowers all while the nurses stared at him. Sabrina fought the urge to yell at them for ogling her man. She needn't have worried, because Deacon only had eyes for her. When he placed his hand on her back as they turned toward her office, she heard more than one sigh. Deacon was that handsome, and if what he said was true, he was all hers.

"I need some paper towels," he said when she entered the code at her door before pressing her fingertip to the scanner.

"I'll get those for you," she offered, pulling a roll from her credenza.

Deacon dried the card as best he could. The words were smeared, but there was definitely a note in sloppy handwriting. "I'll get this over to Julian and see if there's any way he can clean it up. Lorenzo will be here in a few minutes to watch over you while I check in at work."

"Do you really think that's necessary?" Sabrina hated

144

taking Deacon and his friends away from their jobs.

"Until we find who's watching you, yes." Deacon closed the door and pulled Sabrina into his arms. "You're my mate, and the Clan will always have our backs. I've watched over other mates and their kids when help was needed. That's what we do." Deacon bent his head and nudged Sabrina's neck. "Gods, you smell so good."

Sabrina suppressed a moan. Being close to Deacon and not stripping him out of his clothes was harder than it should have been. She'd never been a wanton woman, but then she'd never encountered a man as sexy as Deacon. Male. Deacon was a male, not a man, and that made him all the more alluring. How many women could say they were in a relationship with a shifter? "Are we in a relationship?" she blurted. "What I mean is we only started seeing each other. We haven't had our first date, but it feels like I've known you forever."

"That's the mate bond. We belong together. The fates don't give us someone random to be with. They choose our perfect partner. Whether we just met or are together years, it will always be this way. And yes, we are in a relationship. One which will transcend time."

Deacon brushed his lips against Sabrina's, and she snaked her arms around his neck, pulling him closer. A knock on the door had them separating, but not before Deacon pressed his hand to her cheek. "You're mine, Pretty Lady, and I'm yours. I promise on everything holy I will make you happy."

Deacon released her to open the door. Sabrina's heart was still hammering double-time when a man almost as large as Deacon entered the room. Lorenzo, she presumed, made a fist, placed it over his heart, and bowed his head. "Sabrina, on my honor."

She wasn't sure what to make of his words, but she'd seen the chest-thumping before. She chalked it up to a

Gargoyle thing.

"You must be Lorenzo. I hope I'm not keeping you from something important."

"I assure you, there is nothing more important than your safety."

In that moment, Sabrina felt like she belonged. She had her work, which was life-changing and fulfilling when her patients beat the dreaded diseases they were struck with. She was important in the lives of those she helped, but it was short-lived. The patients went about their lives, forgetting their doctors and nurses. She was fine with that. But she was excited at the prospect of belonging to Deacon, and in turn, his family. She wanted the spontaneous lunches with his friends and their mates. Sabrina could see herself living in the woods with Deacon. Opening their home to the others for get-togethers. Adding her things to his and blending their lives. She looked forward to nights cooking together. Sitting wrapped in his arms drinking wine and sharing about their days.

"You okay?" Deacon asked.

"Sorry. Just lost in thought."

"Good thoughts, I hope."

Sabrina winked at him. "Yes. Very good thoughts."

Lorenzo chuckled. "Do I need to wait in the hallway?"

Deacon grinned and clapped Lorenzo on the shoulder. "No. I need to get going. I'll be back later." He kissed Sabrina again and left her wanting more.

"Later," she muttered, turning her face so Lorenzo couldn't see how Deacon affected her.

Chapter Seventeen

DEACON HAD ERRANDS to run that included stopping at the pharmacy for condoms. He didn't want to use them with his mate, but until she was on the pill, he wasn't going to risk getting her pregnant. He had no doubt they would be mated soon, but that didn't mean he was in a hurry to start a family if she wanted children. Even though he wasn't sure he could handle being a father, Deacon would give his mate anything she wanted. He'd lived with his empathic curse four hundred years. It wasn't going away, so he would deal with it for Sabrina and any children they brought into the world.

Deacon headed to Jonathan's room, but when he heard Priscilla's voice, he turned and went the other way. His beast was in an uproar from having their mate in their bed without claiming her. Deacon wasn't about to ask it to help shield him from the turmoil going on inside the older human or any of the pain he felt coming from family members of the other patients.

Something is...

What? Something is what?

I'm not sure. Do you not feel the... strangeness?

Deacon reached out with his senses, trying to lock down what his beast was referring to. Aside from the heartache and pain, he encountered confusion, annoyance, and urgency, but he couldn't pinpoint where it was coming from or if it was only one person. Hospitals were one of the worst places for an empath. When he compartmentalized as many emotions as possible, he finally figured out the off sensation was coming from the stairwell. Taking off at a fast clip, he opened the door. Heavy footsteps sounded a couple floors up, then a door opened and closed. Using his shifter speed, Deacon was at the same door within seconds. He slowed his steps, not wanting to bring attention to himself, while at the same time stopping to connect with whomever was sending out waves of stress. Those waves were overcome by all the other emotions rolling from the many patients and visitors.

Shaking his head, Deacon turned toward the elevator. Sure, the emotions had been so much harsher than all the others, but Deacon chalked it up to the person being overwrought with heartbreak. They had probably lost a loved one. He continued on with his plan to run errands and get to work.

Stopping by the lab first, Julian had news for him. "I figured out the message. It said, 'Find Craven.' Now I don't know about you, but I don't believe in coincidences. I think whoever is leaving Sabrina these notes knows what's going on with the Unholy."

"What would Sabrina be able to do if she found the doctor?" Deacon retrieved the note which had been left with the flowers. "Here. It's probably too saturated to do anything about, but if anyone can, it's you."

Julian took the card and studied it. "It will take a while, but I don't believe it's impossible. Let me get to work on this, and I'll call you if I get anything usable off it."

Deacon held out his fist, and Julian tapped his knuckles. As he was leaving, Lucy and Tamian entered the lab. "Good morning," he said.

"Good morning, Deacon. Did you find another note?" Lucy asked, rubbing her hands together. The few times he'd met the Gryphon, Deacon got the feeling she was as adventurous as Tessa.

148

"I did. It was at the bottom of the vase, submerged in water. I just dropped it off with Jules. Hopefully, you two will be able to figure out what was written on it."

"I do love a good puzzle." Lucy told him she'd see him later and rushed away to get started.

The love coming from Tamian for his mate washed over Deacon like a warm blanket on a cold night. That went a long way in calming him. Even with the miles he'd driven to get to the lab, Deacon had still been dealing with whatever it was he'd encountered at the hospital. He wished he could remain there, letting Tamian and Lucy shield him, but he had things to do.

"Is there anything I can do to help?" Tamian asked.

Deacon knew the male wasn't talking about the note. Tamian was a clone, made up of both Tessa's and Jonas's DNA. He had abilities most of the Clan didn't know about, but working with Gregor meant being around Tessa, and she had mentioned her brother's abilities on more than one occasion when Deacon was within earshot.

"I'm not sure. The vision Connor had showed a black man, but he couldn't see the man's face. Whoever is leaving things for Sabrina doesn't seem to be out to harm her. Instead, he's leaving these notes. Why her? Who is he to her, and why can't Connor see his face? Is it even the same person?" Deacon tilted his head back and sighed. "I want to protect her, but who do I protect her from?"

"What if it's someone who knows Sabrina but doesn't feel confident in talking to her in person? Maybe someone from her past? They did leave a photo of her siblings. What do we know about them?"

"Her sister is a psychologist in New Chicago. One of her brothers lives in California and works for a pharmaceutical company. Her other brother, the youngest, joined the military and hasn't been heard from in years."

"Have you had Julian run a search on them? The note in

the photo said to find Craven. If this is the same Craven experimenting on Unholy, any of the three could have reason to be connected. The sister could have encountered one of the test subjects. The one in California could have caught wind of the drugs being used, and the soldier... Gods, what if he came home and got mixed up in Flanagan's bullshit?"

Deacon prayed that wasn't the case. It would kill Sabrina if her baby brother had been turned into a monster. "No, I haven't, but I think it's time I ask him to."

Instead of leaving, Deacon returned to the lab and asked Tamian to repeat his suppositions. Since Jules was working on the note, Lucy offered to begin the search for information on Sabrina's siblings. He gave her what little information he knew about them before thanking them all for their help and taking his leave.

The theory which made the most sense was Terrence. Connor had seen a man, so that ruled out the sister. If Connor's vision was even about whoever was leaving notes. The two might not have anything to do with the other. Deacon didn't know enough about his mate's life prior to meeting her. She could have a crazy ex who wasn't ready to let go. Sabrina had mentioned a boyfriend who didn't take it well when she broke things off. Deacon wanted their date to go smoothly, but he needed to know more about her past so he could get to the bottom of this whole stalker business. He would casually ask her about the boyfriend she mentioned. Deacon would also do his best not to kill him if he found out she'd been hurt in any way.

After stopping and purchasing a box of condoms, Deacon drove to the Pen. He wasn't surprised to find Isabelle walking down the hall. After Gabriel's breakdown, she had been called in to help calm her brother.

"How's Gabriel?" Deacon asked.

"Better now, but hearing the name of the man who tortured him and left him for dead brought back memories best left in the past. When we find the doctor, I'm going to torture him far worse than he did my brother." Isabelle's claws and fangs were front and center, so Deacon pulled her into his office and closed the door. Most of the guards were Gargoyles, but there were a few humans who worked at the Pen. It wouldn't do for them to catch sight of an enraged half-blood. He also needed to get her emotions in check from a personal standpoint.

"Sorry," she stammered, dropping into the chair across from his desk.

"I get it. I'd feel the same in your shoes. Have you had any success in deconstructing Evan's blood?"

Somewhat calmer, Isabelle sat up straight, but she didn't loosen her grip on the chair arms. "I'm still running tests, because something about what I found is bothering me. I found Gargoyle blood in Evans system, and it's pure."

"What does that mean?"

"Craven used Gabriel to create the Unholy. He is a half-blood. His Gargoyle half is from an Original line, so his blood was potent but not pure. The sample taken from Evan had traces of pure Gargoyle blood. Whoever Craven got the blood from is not only from an Original bloodline, but both parents are shifters."

"If Craven's working for Drago, he could be getting it from him or one of the other Greeks."

"No, there's something else. The blood of Gargoyles contains no platelets in adolescence. It isn't until after their initial transition that platelets are formed. Also, at that point, the amount of white blood cells multiplies, unlike in humans. The samples from Evan contain the normal human percentage of white cells."

"Are you telling me Craven is using the blood of a Goyle child?"

"It looks that way." Isabelle rubbed her temples.

Deacon leaned back against his desk. "But there are no

151

full-blooded children in the States. Are there?"

"Not according to Nikolas. Unless there are undocumented Goyles."

"Then there's your answer. Drago and the Greeks aren't here to offer loyalty to Rafael. Evan said there were others who had recently joined Drago. We know nothing about them or who they might have brought with them."

"But to sacrifice their own child's well-being?"

"Who's to say it's their own child? Look at all the human children who are sold to traffickers. Money talks, no matter the species."

Isabelle stood. "Gods, this is giving me a headache." It was also making her heart hurt, just as it was Deacon's, only he was feeling everything she was on top of his own emotions. "How are things with Sabrina?"

Deacon smiled thinking about last night. "So far so good. We have a date tonight."

"I hope you have a wonderful time. I'm going to my office for a while before I have my own date tonight with Connor and Amelia. I'll talk to you later." Isabelle patted Deacon's arm before letting herself out of his office.

Thinking about their conversation, Deacon made his way down to where Evan was being held. Deacon opened the door and closed it behind him, locking them both inside. Deacon whispered, "Did you happen to see any children wherever it was Craven took you?"

Evan took the hint and lowered his voice. "Children? No. There were just those of us undergoing the treatment and the doctors."

"Okay, thank you." Deacon inclined his head and turned toward the door.

Evan stopped him. "Is there any way I can go outside? I've cooperated. Done everything y'all asked, but I'm going stir-crazy in here."

Deacon thought about the time of day and where the

inmates were. "Sure. I won't put you out with the others, but there's a side area some of the guards go to get out of the building for a few." Deacon led Evan outside, and the male sat on a bench, his eyes closed, and his head tilted back, enjoying the sunshine. Deacon used the time to think about Sabrina until his cock stirred. Not wanting Evan to see the bulge in his pants, Deacon changed his thoughts to what Isabelle said about a young Gargoyle being used, and that was enough to keep his dick in check. After about an hour, he returned Evan to his room, promising to give him more time outdoors in the days to come.

They still hadn't figured out what to do with Evan long-term. If it were up to Deacon, he'd give the male some money and let him get on with his life. But it wasn't his decision. Deacon couldn't imagine having family who didn't want him. He hadn't seen his parents in a long time, but he knew he'd be welcome if he returned to Africa.

The rest of the day went by quickly, and Deacon went home, stowed the new box of condoms in the nightstand, showered, and put on some of his new clothes. He didn't pack an overnight bag, because he wanted Sabrina back in his home after their date. There was nothing wrong with her house, but he felt safer at his place. Plus, he wanted her to get used to being there so when they completed the bond, it would become her home as well. If he wasn't a Gargoyle, he would think he was moving too fast, but if she agreed to be his, living together was inevitable. The sooner that happened, the better. He'd been skeptical in the beginning about claiming her, but after one night of having her in his bed, he was ready.

MALAKAI WAS WORKING the front desk at Hartley's, waiting

for his women's self-defense class to start. A young man entered the building, looking around. "Welcome to Hartley's. Can I help you?"

"Hey, uh yeah. Is Matthew here?" the man asked with a faint accent. "I was hoping to catch up with him before school started."

"No, I'm afraid not. He's on vacation for a few days."

"Oh. Good for him. We all need a break between high school and college. Who'd he go with? Where'd he go? Somewhere fun, I hope."

The door opened, and several women from the class walked in. Kai's attention was distracted when he answered, "I think they went to the beach. Him and Slade. Not sure. I can give him a message when he gets back if you'd like."

"The beach? Wow, that's great. Is he somewhere on the Atlantic?"

"Yeah. No. I think the Keys," Kai muttered to the kid, not taking his eyes off one of his students. It had been a long time since someone caught his eye, and this particular blonde had caught it, but he couldn't figure out why. Kai couldn't get her off his mind. It was like he was drawn to her, but only mildly. Not like the others when they found their mates. She smiled at him, and everyone else in the room – the kid included – melted away. "Good morning, ladies. If you want to go on back and begin stretching, I'll join you in a few minutes." After they were out of sight, Kai returned his attention to Matt's buddy, but the man was already gone.

154

Chapter Eighteen

SABRINA'S DAY WENT by slowly. Several times Lorenzo approached, asking if she was okay. She needed to get her head out of the clouds and focus. Her patients as well as her colleagues counted on her to be professional, but she couldn't help it when her thoughts turned to Deacon and the mate bond. The notion of giving herself over to someone – a shifter at that – so quickly was irrational. It had only been a few days ago when he approached her for coffee, and now she was considering something permanent with him. It was the equivalent of agreeing to marriage after such a short time, and that should scare the crap out of her. He had said it would be a lifetime commitment. And not just that, but she would stop aging. There was so much to consider, but she'd already made up her mind that morning when she awoke in his home.

By the time Deacon returned, Sabrina was on edge. Not because of her decision. Several times during the day, she'd felt as though she were being watched. She knew Lorenzo was shadowing her, but this was different. More than once, the hair on her arms stood on end. Each time, she'd glanced around, but there hadn't been anyone there who shouldn't have been. Not that she recognized anyway.

When Deacon stepped into her office, Sabrina had to bite back a groan at how hot he looked. Gone were the loose-fitting, ripped-at-the-knee jeans, and in their place were new ones that molded to him like a second skin. The dark denim hugged his thick thighs and wide hips. Deacon's ass was a cliché all its own, and Sabrina could look at it every day for the rest of her life. Grab onto the firm globes while he was thrusting into her.

"If you don't want me to bend you over your desk right here and now, you need to curb whatever it is you're thinking about," Deacon warned, his voice low.

"If you don't want me thinking sexy thoughts, you need to not wear those jeans," she countered.

Deacon gestured down at his pants. "These old things?" he joked. Sabrina laughed out loud, and Deacon grinned. They both knew the jeans were one of the pairs that Brynna had shopped for him. Sabrina needed to call the woman and thank her. "Come on, Pretty Lady. Let's get out of here and onto our date." Deacon held out his hand, and Sabrina took it. She was packed up and ready to go, eager to see what the night brought them.

After walking her to her car, Deacon followed Sabrina home. She parked in the garage, leaving the door up so he could follow her into the house through the side door.

"Hold up." Deacon gripped Sabrina's elbow and was standing so still she wondered if he was breathing.

"What is it?" Sabrina looked around, but nothing was out of place.

Deacon moved his hand down to clench Sabrina's. "Stay close." He led her to the side door where he pushed the button to lower the garage door. "As soon as we get inside, punch in the code and wait there."

Hands shaking, Sabrina did as Deacon asked. Or she was going to, but the alarm had been disabled. "Deacon?"

"What's wrong?"

"The alarm. It wasn't set."

Deacon muttered a "fuck" under his breath while getting his cell phone. Sabrina waited while Deacon made a call.

"Jules, I need a favor. Can you hack into Sabrina's alarm and see when it was disabled?" Deacon put his arm around Sabrina and tugged her close. "Okay. Yes. I have a different idea, but if that changes, I'll let you know. Thanks, Brother."

"What's going on?" Sabrina curled her front against his chest, tucking her arms between them.

"Someone disabled your alarm this morning around nine. They aren't here now, but that doesn't mean nothing was disturbed. I don't hear anything out of the ordinary, so I feel it's safe for us to move about the house."

Sabrina was calm, considering. She attributed it to being with Deacon. He was a shifter, so if someone were in the house, he would keep her safe. Deacon bent down and kissed her softly before taking one of her hands. Together, they walked through her home, looking for anything that had been broken, taken, or otherwise disturbed. After checking every room, including the closets, they returned to the kitchen. It wasn't until she stepped around the island that she noticed something on the floor. "What's that?"

Deacon squatted down and picked up what looked like a patch. "Kennedy," Deacon said, holding the name patch up so Sabrina could see it.

"Is that...?"

"A patch that could belong on your brother's uniform? Looks like it." Deacon stood and showed it to Sabrina. "Look," he pointed to the back of it. Written in black marker were the words "Help the kid."

"I haven't seen or heard from Jerrick in years. Do you think he could be the one leaving these messages?"

"Anything's possible. I was going to wait until later to tell you something, but considering this" – Deacon indicated the patch – "I think now's a good time. I had Julian and Lucy run checks on your brothers. Terrence is still in California, but Jerrick was medically discharged from the Army three years ago. After that, he disappeared."

157

"Why did you have them check out my brothers?" Sabrina wrapped her arms around her waist.

"I was speaking with Tamian, and he made a good point. Whoever is leaving you these messages isn't being malicious. Even though he left roses which you hate, they are still one of the most popular flowers to give someone. Then there was the photo of your siblings, and now, the patch. Tamian thinks it's possible whoever is doing this is someone close to you but afraid to approach you. You've been in contact with Terrence, and I doubt he'd have an issue picking up the phone if he was trying to warn you. That leaves Jerrick."

"But why not Jasmine, too?"

"There's something I haven't told you." Deacon closed his eyes and let out a harsh breath. When he looked at her, his smile was sad. "This isn't the way I wanted our first date to start, but it's par for the course with mates."

"What do you mean?"

"I mean that none of the other Gargoyles who've found their mates have had it easy in the beginning. There were kidnappings, car chases, malicious husbands, attempted murder. I'm not trying to scare you, but the fates haven't made it easy for us to just find our mate and live happily ever after. Not that what you're going through is on par with what the others went through, but I was hoping now that the war was over and Alistair was gone, things would calm down."

"What war? Who's Alistair? And husbands?" Sabrina had a lot to learn about Deacon and his Clan.

"I promise to tell you everything. First, I want you to go pack your things. Until we figure out who's doing this and why, I want you to come stay with me. While you do that, I'm going to send a picture of this off to Julian and Lucy so they can add it to the other messages and see if they can figure out what the hell they mean. After, we'll go to dinner. Eat good food. Drink some wine. Enjoy our first date like we

158

planned. Afterward, we'll go back to my place and have a long conversation."

"Sure." Sabrina went to her car and retrieved her bags. Instead of emptying them, she filled them with more items she would need for at least a week. She had hoped to go back to Deacon's to spend another night, but she hadn't wanted these messages to be the reason. Was it possible Jerrick was behind everything? She thought back to the man she saw in the parking garage and then the one in the hallway. She couldn't see his face because of the hoodie, but that man was larger than Jerrick had been. Then again, she hadn't seen her baby brother in years. He would have filled out in the military. Been trained how to move differently that the regular person. If it was him, why wouldn't he just come up to her and talk to her?

When she returned to the kitchen, Sabrina picked up the patch and ran her fingers across the name. It was hard for her to see Jerrick as anything other than the skinny little kid he'd been before their mom died. He'd been so sweet and loving. She couldn't imagine him as a war-hardened soldier, but she had to face the fact that it was probably what he'd become. Was that why he wouldn't approach her? If it was even him leaving the messages. And this last one – "help the kid." What kid? Deacon said there were things he needed to tell her, so maybe he had an idea of what the messages were about.

"Ready?" Deacon asked as he entered from the back door. He stepped into her space and ran a finger down her cheek.

Sabrina shivered at his touch. She was ready all right. Ready to get back to his house and get comfortable. She knew they had a lot to discuss, but the way he lit her body up from the inside out had her mind on other things. She had changed from her work clothes into something better suited for dinner out, including matching lace lingerie. Keeping her hands to herself, she managed to respond, "Ready."

Instead of going through the garage, Deacon led her out the front door. Sabrina set the alarm. "How do you think the alarm was turned off earlier?"

"I was talking to Julian about that just now. Your system is good enough to deter your average person, but someone with any type of advanced training could bypass it easily. Lucy found out your brother was an ordnance expert during his time in the Army. Not saying he's definitely the one leaving the messages, but he would have the knowledge to bypass a security system like the one you have. I've asked Julian to upgrade your alarm."

"Thank you." Sabrina had no issues with her home being more secure, even if she didn't plan on staying there for much longer. She'd already decided to accept the mate bond, and when that happened, she planned on moving in with Deacon. It was what she'd thought about all day.

"Do you have any idea what the messages mean?" Sabrina asked once they were seated inside Deacon's truck.

"I think so. The one on the photo mentioned Craven. He's a scientist who helped create the Unholy. Now it seems he's found a way to unmake them. That could have been coincidence, but with the last message about the kid, we don't think so. We captured one of the Unholy who went through the reversal process. He has been cooperating, and in doing so, Isabelle took some of his blood to try and figure out what he was given to reverse what was originally used to make him Unholy. She found evidence of an adolescent Gargoyle's DNA in Evan's blood. While it might not be your brother leaving these messages, whoever it is might think because you're a doctor that you can help somehow."

Deacon's phone rang, and he hit the Bluetooth button on the steering wheel. "Jules, you're on speaker."

"Hey, Brother. I wanted to let you know we were able to decipher the message on the card from the flowers."

"Go ahead," Deacon said, glancing at Sabrina before turning his attention back to the road.

"It said, 'I need your help.' That, along with the other two, doesn't sound like someone who means to harm Sabrina."

Sabrina spoke up. "Julian, has Lucy been able to find out anything about Jerrick's whereabouts over the last three years?"

"No, I'm sorry. Like I told Deacon earlier, it's like he disappeared. But Tamian brought up another good point. If whoever this is knows about Craven and the child Isabelle suspects is being held, it's a possibility they are one of the Reborn."

"Reborn?" Sabrina asked.

"It's what Craven and Drago are calling the Unholy who have their conditions reversed."

"Oh, god. Do you think Jerrick could have been an Unholy?" Sabrina covered her mouth with her hand as her eyes burned with unshed tears.

Deacon reached over and took her free hand, lacing their fingers together. "It is a possibility. From what Evan said, Flanagan made joining his army enticing. When men and women come home from war zones, they already have to deal with the lack of support. Being away from their team and those who became their family while serving. A lot of them have PTSD or are depressed from all the things they did and saw. Being accepted, given a job with supposed benefits, doing the same thing they were familiar with, it was too good to turn down. What he didn't tell them was instead of being given an immunization, they were given the Unholy serum.

"I've listened to Evan's story. His family turned their back on him when he enlisted, so he had no one to come home to. And even though he is now one of the Reborn, he still has nowhere to call home other than a warehouse filled

161

with others like him. He has no marketable skills other than fighting. He begged us to kill him instead of sending him back. It broke my heart."

Sabrina choked out a sob. Was that what had become of her little brother?

"Jules, I need to call you back." Deacon disconnected the call, pulled the truck over to the side of the road, and put it in park. He unbuckled Sabrina and tugged her against him. "Shh. It's going to be okay. We'll find Jerrick and make sure he has all the help he needs."

"But what if he's still Unholy? You and your Clan hunt them down and put them in prison."

"If he's the one giving you notes, he is more than likely one of the Reborn. That means he has the ability to think and function at a normal level. Let's focus on finding him first, and then we'll see what kind of help he needs."

"Can we please go to your house? I don't think I can sit in a restaurant and put on a happy face."

"Of course. Tell me what your favorite dish is, and I'll call in a to-go order. Maybe you'll feel like eating once we get home."

Home. That sounded so good to Sabrina. She didn't allow herself to think too hard about how they were moving too quickly. She'd already decided she was going to be with Deacon, so she told him what she wanted to eat. While he called in the order, she closed her eyes and tried to put Jerrick out of her mind.

Chapter Nineteen

DEACON'S HEART WAS breaking for his mate. They weren't sure the stranger leaving notes was Jerrick, but if it was, Deacon was going to find the male and help him any way he could. He had no idea of how to find him, but he had the best person to help in his Clan. While he was waiting to pick up the food he'd called in at Giovanni's, Deacon reached out to Julian. After telling him what he and Sabrina had discussed, Julian promised to make finding Jerrick a priority. There were other things he and Lucy were working on, like finding Craven, but nothing they couldn't tackle together. Julian had already called Nikolas to come in and be an extra set of eyes.

Sabrina was silent as they drove to Deacon's home, and his beast was trying to help push her emotions to the side, but in that moment, Deacon realized he didn't want that. He wanted to share in her pain just as he wanted to feel her happiness. "Would you like to sit outside?" Deacon asked. The weather was warm but not unbearably so.

"Sure." Sabrina grabbed the plates and silverware while Deacon poured the wine. Once seated, Sabrina took a look around. "I really like it here. I guess that's a good thing since I'll be living here."

"Does that mean you've made up your mind about being with me?"

"Yes." Sabrina took a sip of wine before continuing. "It's all I thought about at work today. I hated that for my patients, because they need my complete focus, but this is a life-changing decision. I wrestled with how quickly everything is happening. But then I figured I have no one to answer to except myself. Joseph is putting my name in the running for chief of staff when he retires, but since he's one of your kind – he is a Gargoyle, right?" Deacon nodded, and she said, "Then, I don't see him having a problem with us."

"If anyone understands, it's Joseph. He was one of the first of our kind to mate with a human. Theirs is a story in its own, but let's say the two of them weren't without hardships when they mated. He understands the bond and how quickly these types of relationships move. Once a Gargoyle finds their mate, it becomes nearly impossible to take things slowly." He wasn't going to mention how Tessa refused Gregor for years or how Brynna was keeping Travis in the dark. Tessa had her reasons, those being how she was influenced by Jonas. As for Brynna, she was giving Travis time to mourn his lost girlfriend.

"I know I'm staying here because of whoever is stalking me, but I'd like to use this week as a trial run to make sure we get along. You know all about how the bond affects mates, but it's an idea I'm still trying to wrap my head around. I have no doubt we'll end up making things official, but I'd like to take this week to be sure, if that's okay."

"As I told you, take all the time you need. I'm not going anywhere. We can use these next few days to get to know one another better. I want you to become comfortable in my home and with me."

Sabrina dug into her food, like she was using the movements to give herself time. Whether to think or what, Deacon didn't know. They ate their meal and drank the wine, neither saying anything else. Sabrina wiped her mouth with her napkin and placed it atop her empty plate. Holding the glass in her hand, she swirled the red liquid.

"If we're getting to know one another, there's something

164

I should tell you. I dated a man a few years ago. He is a policeman, and he's built similar to you. Things weren't going the way I wanted in the relationship, and when I told him to pack his things, he got violent."

Deacon growled low in his chest, his fangs popping out. Sabrina's eyes widened, and Deacon took a deep breath, calming the beast. He retracted his fangs, apologizing. "Sorry. I didn't mean to scare you, but the thought of any man putting his hands on you in anger, well, it makes me a little crazy. What's this cop's name?"

Sabrina shook her head. "Oh, no. What happened is in the past. It won't do any good for you to go after him now."

"It'll do me a world of good to punish him. Please tell me you filed charges."

Sabrina briefly dropped her gaze. When she looked back up, she sighed. "No, I didn't. He's a cop, and it was his word against mine. Sure, I had the marks, but I couldn't prove he did it. I stayed home, healed, and then I went back to work. He left me alone afterward."

"So, you lived with this man?"

"Not really. He wanted to move in with me, but I didn't love him enough to make that commitment. After it was over, I realized I didn't love him at all. He brought clothes to spend the night, and more and more of his things found their way into my home. I wouldn't give him a key, and that was one of the things we fought about. You told me you mostly went on first dates, so does that mean you haven't you ever lived with someone?"

"No, I haven't. I've spent my life waiting for my mate. I haven't been celibate for the last four hundred years, but..." Deacon took a deep breath. "The last time I tried dating someone, it didn't go well." Deacon downed the last of his wine and poured another glassful.

"What happened? You have that look in your eye."

"The last time I went out with someone more than once,

165

she tried to trap me. Told me she was pregnant. I knew she was lying. For one thing, I used protection, and besides, Gargoyles can only get their mate pregnant."

"And you knew she wasn't your mate?"

"There was no pull to her. Did I find her attractive? Yes. At first, she was kind. Charming. But if I didn't see her for days on end, it didn't bother me. She wanted more from me than I did her, and she wasn't satisfied with something casual. I never led her to believe we would be serious, because I wouldn't do that to someone. There are Gargoyles who have dated and even married humans while waiting for their mate just because they didn't want to be alone, but that's not me. I ended it with her, and I've been alone since."

"That's kind of sad. I mean, I'm not upset that you haven't really played the field, but weren't you lonely?"

"Were you? Did you miss having someone to come home to?"

"Honestly? No. My ex was all about what I could do for him. Some days, I just want to come home and decompress after dealing with the heartache of what my patients are going through. Instead of being supportive and helpful, he expected me to cook for him. Not once did he offer to help clean the kitchen afterward. Said it was the woman's job. I only dated a couple times after that, but I couldn't bring myself to do anything more than go to dinner. And then I met you, but if it wasn't for the mate pull, I doubt I'd have agreed to going out with you."

"I appreciate your honesty. I happen to like cooking, and I have no problem cleaning the kitchen, whether you or I cook. I've taken care of myself all these years, so I'm happy to continue doing so. Your job is stressful, and I want to help alleviate as much of your stress as possible. Not only is that helping you, but it will help me as well. Being empathic means I want everyone around me happy. I want you to feel comfortable around me and the other Gargoyles as well since they'll become part of your life. If you'd like to meet up with other mates to pick their brains, we can set that up. I think you'll find hearing their stories to be fascinating. You've already seen how accepting Sophia and Katherine were. And Kaya, well, we both know how our Queen was meddling," Deacon said, grinning.

"Queen?"

"Yes. Each territory has a King. Rafael is the King of our Clan here in the Americas, and that makes Kaya our Queen. Tessa's father, Xavier, is King of the Italians. He's ready to step down and pass the crown to Tessa's brother, Tamian. Brynna's brother, Banyan, is King of the Norse Clan. He and Urijah have a home here, and Travis is designing them a new home in Norway."

"Wow. There's a lot I need to learn about your culture. And I would love to spend more time with the other mates. Not that I don't trust you to tell me what I need to know, but I think it will help me navigate the waters of being with a shifter if I can learn from those who are already mated to a Gargoyle."

"You've met Kaya, Sophia, and Katherine. You know Isabelle. She's Joseph's daughter and is a half-blood. She and Dante are mates. Connor is their son. Trevor, Dante's assistant, is mates with Jasper who is a police officer. Trevor is also Travis's brother. We have Sunday dinner at Rafael's manor every week, and you can meet all the mates, or if you'd rather do it here away from the Gargoyles, we can make that happen."

"I know of Isabelle, but we've never met. Can I ask you about Connor?"

"Of course."

"It's just, I met him a couple days ago, and he had the strangest reaction when we shook hands."

Deacon had forgotten about Connor's drawing. "I'm glad you mentioned that. Connor is a very special boy. He is wise beyond his years, is a genius, and is a talented artist. He also has visions. I need to show you something." Deacon pulled up the photo of the drawing and held it out for Sabrina. "This is why he reacted strangely when you shook his hand."

"Oh, my god. This is the man I saw outside my office. But, wait. Why doesn't he have a face?"

"That's a good question. This has never happened before. Connor's drawings are always specific, so we don't know why he couldn't see the man more clearly. You didn't see his face either, so it might have something to do with that."

"Poor child. I would hate to have visions as an adult. I can't imagine what it does to him being so young."

"He has a good support system. Dante and —" Deacon's phone rang, cutting him off. "Speak of the devil. Excuse me, please." He connected the call. "Dante?"

"Hello, Brother. I know you're supposed to be on your date with Sabrina, but Connor had another vision. I was hoping you could stop by here on your way home."

"We got our food to go, so we're already home. We can leave now, if that's convenient."

"If you don't mind. Have you spoken to Sabrina about the first drawing?"

"Yes. Just now, as a matter of fact."

"If it won't disturb her too much, we'd love to see you both. I was going to snap a photo of it, but Isabelle asked if you could see it in person. It has to do with your conversation earlier."

"We'll be right there." They said their goodbyes, and Deacon turned to Sabrina. "I apologize. I should have asked your opinion before I spoke for both of us, but Dante and Isabelle have something to show us. Another drawing. Do you mind going to their house? They don't live far."

"I don't mind. I'd love the chance to visit with one of

the mates, even if she is a half-blood."

"Excellent. Leave the dishes. I'll get them when we get home." Deacon stood and reached out for Sabrina's hand. "I need to get you a helmet so we can ride the bike together."

"I'd like that. What kind of drawing is this one? Does it relate to me?"

"I'm not sure. Dante said it pertained to a conversation Isabelle and I had, and we spoke about an adolescent Gargoyle's DNA. I guess we'll have to wait until we get there to find out for certain."

Five minutes later, Deacon pulled up to Dante's gate, rolled down the window, and spoke into the security box. The gate opened, and he drove slowly down the paved drive. Dante and Isabelle were waiting for them on the front porch. Deacon walked around the truck and helped Sabrina out of the cab. When they stepped onto the porch, Dante said, "Sabrina, good to see you again. I'm not sure if you've met my mate, Isabelle."

Isabelle held out her hand. "We haven't had the pleasure, but I've heard so much about you. Welcome to our home."

Sabrina thanked them both, and when they turned to head inside, she paused. Connor was standing in the doorway. He didn't hesitate to come forward and hold out his hand. "Miss Bailey," he said when she placed her palm against his smaller one. There was no vision this time that Deacon could ascertain. Just a little boy with impeccable manners.

Once they were inside and seated in the living room, Dante said, "Connor had another vision. I wanted you to see the drawing in case you recognize the man." Connor came forward with a piece of paper and held it out to Sabrina.

"Oh, my god. That's Jerrick. That's my brother." Her hands were shaking, and Deacon took the picture from her, placing it on the coffee table so he could pull her into his

169

arms.

"This is a good thing. It means he's most likely the one leaving you the notes."

"How is that good? If what you said was true, he allowed himself to be turned into one of the Unholy."

"Look at the picture. His features are normal. Maybe he was Unholy at one point, but if he knows about Craven and this boy, more than likely he's now one of the Reborn. Your brother might not be exactly as you remember him, but I have a feeling he's trying to do the right thing here. He's asking for help."

"But I don't know how to help him," she whispered.

Dante stepped forward. "No, but we do."

Chapter Twenty

SABRINA COULDN'T STOP shaking. Her baby brother had been an Unholy. How could that have happened? Sure, they were separated when they were younger, but he had to know he could come to her when he got out of the Army instead of turning to the man in charge of the monsters. "I failed him."

"You didn't even know he was home. Let's listen to what Dante found out."

"If you'll look closely at the drawing, Connor was able to see where they were in his vision."

Deacon picked the paper back up and studied it. Sure enough, there was a building in the background with distinct markings on it. "You think this is where Craven is treating the Unholy?"

"I know it is. As soon as Connor showed it to me, I snapped a picture of it and sent it to Remy. He showed it to Evan who confirmed that was where he and the others were taken. I've already spoken to Rafael and Frey. Frey is gathering a team to do recon so they can pick up Craven and rescue the child."

"What about Jerrick?" Sabrina asked. "I don't want him harmed."

"Now that you've identified him as your brother, I'll ask Julian to distribute the photo to all Clan phones. He'll be detained but not harmed. We may have to take him to the Pen for safe keeping, same as Evan, because by now, Drago has to know more than one of his men are missing," Deacon said.

"How are you going to find him, though? He's been hanging around the hospital and my house, not this place," Sabrina said, pointing to the drawing. Dante looked at Deacon, and something passed between them. "What is it?" she asked.

"Brother?" Deacon said.

Isabelle came around the coffee table and sat down next to Sabrina. "We needed you to identify the drawing before we told you what has happened. Jerrick's already been found. Sabrina, it's not good. He was found earlier by some of the Gargoyles who were patrolling. Normally, when they find Unholy who've been injured, they take them to the Pen where Dante or I see to them, but with Jerrick being Reborn, they reached out to my father. Jonas has Jerrick in a private wing of the hospital."

"Jonas? I thought your father was Joseph." Sabrina knew Deacon had told her that.

"You didn't tell her?" Isabelle asked Deacon.

"No. I was going to let Jonas tell her himself."

"Tell me what? You know what? It doesn't matter. I need to get to the hospital and see my brother." Sabrina stood from the sofa and headed for the door.

"We'll be right behind you," Isabelle said.

Sabrina jogged to the truck, but somehow, Deacon got there before she did and had the door open for her. "How did you do that?" she asked when he was seated next to her.

"Shifter speed. We have exceptional eyesight and hearing as well. About Joseph. His real name is Jonas Montague. To remain in New Atlanta for so long, he had to reinvent himself."

"Jonas Montague? As in the scientist who cloned the world's first baby? The man who brought the world to its knees, Jonas Montague?"

"The one and only, but the apocalypse wasn't his fault. A cult who calls themselves the Ministry took credit for that. Jonas is a genius. He came up with prosthetic masks for those who need to hang around a city far longer than their looks allow. The man you know – Joseph Mooneyham – is really a nine-hundred-plus-year-old Gargoyle. When he isn't posing as Joseph, Jonas looks as young as I do."

Sabrina didn't respond. Her thoughts volleyed between that new information about her boss and the fact that her baby brother was in the hospital. Why hadn't she asked Isabelle about his injuries? She said it wasn't good, but how not good was it? Was he critical? In a coma?

What felt like hours later, Deacon parked at the back of the hospital where he led Sabrina into the hallway leading to the morgue. "Why are we going this way?"

"This is where Jonas will have your brother."

Sabrina had never ventured to this level of the building. She never had reason to. After meandering down several corridors, they reached a section of the hospital that appeared abandoned. Deacon knocked on a door, and a few seconds later, Joseph opened it, only sticking his head out. "Dante called ahead. Sabrina, your brother's in bad shape, but with time, he should make a full recovery." He held the door open. It was only then she noticed Dante, Isabelle, and Connor were behind them.

She didn't understand why they were allowing the child to come along, but she wasn't his parent. Her only concern was Jerrick.

"I need to see him."

"Of course. Right this way."

As she followed her boss, she tried to imagine what the older man looked like without his mask. It had to be the work of a genius, because she'd known him for years, and she'd never seen him look any way other than he did now.

The room he led them to was set up like any other

173

patient room with the exception of two large men standing guard. She recognized both from having been in Mr. Holt's room, but they'd never been introduced. As Sabrina reached them, they both placed a fist over their hearts and bowed their heads. "On my honor," they said in unison.

Deacon shook both their hands before escorting Sabrina inside. When she caught sight of Jerrick, her knees threatened to give out, but Deacon was there to support her. Her brother wasn't hooked up to any type of life support nor did he have an IV attached. His face and arms were marred with deep gashes. "Why isn't he hooked up?" Sabrina asked.

"All his wounds are external. He took one hell of a beating, but Mason and Jasper got to him before any internal damage was done."

"Then why isn't he awake?" Sabrina stepped up to the bed and placed her hand on the only patch of skin not split open.

"I gave him a strong sedative to keep him still." It was then she noticed he was strapped down. "Until Dante called, I didn't know he was your brother. The straps were necessary for his safety as well as mine. As soon as he awakens and you assure him he's safe, we will remove his bindings."

"Thank you, Joseph. Or should I say Jonas?"

Her boss gave her a sheepish smile. "Down here, Jonas is fine, but around those who aren't aware of my true identity, I'm afraid Joseph is necessary."

"I understand," she responded, her eyes still on her brother. "Oh, Jerrick, I'm so sorry," she whispered as tears streamed down her face. Deacon stepped behind her, wrapping his arms around her. She leaned against his body for comfort.

When Connor stepped up to the other side of the bed, Sabrina narrowed her eyes at the boy, wondering again why he was there. He placed his small hand on Jerrick's arm and closed his eyes. The boy smiled when he looked at Sabrina. "He started to bring you dandelions, but he figured you would prefer something prettier like roses." Sabrina gasped.

Connor returned to his parents who were standing by the door. If Deacon hadn't already told her the child had special abilities, she would worry his words had been a trick of sorts.

"I take it that means something to you?" Deacon asked against her cheek.

Sabrina nodded. "He would pick dandelions whenever he found them and give them to me. He never saw them as weeds. Just pretty flowers growing wild and free."

"Bree…" Jerrick's voice was weak, and his eyes were closed, but it was the best sound Sabrina had heard in a long time.

"I'm here Jerrick. I'm right here."

Deacon's hands tightened around her waist, and he stepped away from the bed, taking Sabrina with him.

"What are you doing?" she hissed over her shoulder.

"Until he's fully awake, we don't know how he's going to react."

"He would never hurt me." Sabrina struggled to get loose, but Deacon tightened his grip. "Let go of me."

"Pretty Lady, I just—"

"I said let go!"

"Let her go!" Jerrick yelled, struggling against his restraints. All of a sudden, the room was filled with Gargoyles. Fangs and claws bared. Sabrina felt a *whoosh* behind her, and when she turned, Deacon had unfurled his wings. The next thing she knew, she was cocooned within the wings, her face smashed against Deacon's broad chest.

"Deacon, if you don't release me right this second, we're finished!" Sabrina stumbled backwards at being released so abruptly. She glared at Deacon before turning to check on her brother. "Stop it! Jerrick!"

"Bree?" Jerrick stopped fighting against the Gargoyles

and settled back against the pillow.

"I'm here," she cried, rushing to the side of the bed. She placed her hand on his marred cheek as gently as possible. "Oh, Jerrick. What did they do to you?"

"Nothing I didn't deserve," he whispered.

"No. You didn't deserve this. You were trying to help. Weren't you? Get these restraints off him. Now."

Tears welled up in her brother's eyes as he nodded. "Yes, but it was too little too late. I couldn't save the boy."

"What do you mean? I thought you wanted us to help him." When none of the others moved to undo the bands strapped across his body, Sabrina began releasing them herself. Deacon stepped up beside Sabrina, but when he placed his hand on her shoulder, she shrugged it off. They were going to talk about his high-handedness later.

"I'll release him," Deacon said.

Sabrina moved over, giving Deacon room to work. As he released the straps, he asked Jerrick, "Did something happen to the child?"

"While I was getting my ass handed to me, I heard one of Drago's men yelling orders about the boy and Craven. I'm sure they're gone by now. I'm sorry. Bree, I should have just come to you, but I couldn't face you. I was so ashamed."

"Hey, you have nothing to be ashamed of. Yes, you could have come to me instead of leaving clues, but you were trying to help in your own way. This isn't your fault. None of it is. Why don't you let me give you something for pain, and you get some rest? I'll be right here when you wake up."

Jerrick shook his head. "I don't need anything. But what's going to happen to me now? Am I going to jail?"

"No." Sabrina leveled a gaze at Deacon. She remembered what he said about taking Jerrick to the Pen to keep him safe.

"Once you're stable, we may need to keep you

176

somewhere safe while we figure out how to get Drago off your back. I had mentioned keeping you at the penitentiary but not locked in a cell. It's the safest place for you for the time being."

"We'll figure out something else. I promise," Sabrina said, overriding Deacon's decision. She felt him bristle at her side, but she didn't care. If she had to, she would use all her savings and find somewhere far away to take her baby brother. She wouldn't fail him again.

"Deacon, may I speak to you outside?" Dante asked. Deacon inclined his head and followed the ME out the door. Isabelle and the others went with them, leaving Sabrina alone with Jerrick. She didn't have to be psychic to know they were discussing the situation without her.

"Bree, it's okay. If they want to take me to the Pen, that's fine. I'm sure the accommodations will be better than what I'm used to."

"No. I will take you home with me. Deacon's friend promised to upgrade the security, so I'm sure we'll be safe there."

"I won't put you in danger. I would say you have no idea what I'm up against, but seeing as you're surrounded by Gargoyles, I guess you do. You mind telling me why you're with him?"

"I'm his mate." Sabrina pulled the chair closer to the bed and sat down, taking her brother's hand in hers. "One of my patients is the caretaker for one of their kind, and I met Deacon through him. It all sounded ridiculous at first, but seeing is believing. What about you? How did you end up...?" Sabrina couldn't bring herself to say the words.

"Unholy? I was medically released from the Army. Shrapnel from a bomb tore me apart. The doctors put me back together best they could, but I was no longer able to serve in the same capacity I did before. I was lost, Bree. The army had been my whole life, and when I got back stateside,

177

I felt like a loser. I was approached by a man named Gordon Flanagan who promised I could still be of use even if the US government thought otherwise. He offered me a job and a place to live. When I went in for a physical, I was given a shot that was supposed to be some type of immunization in case I'd brought something back with me. It didn't make sense, because I'd spent the last three months in a military hospital."

Jerrick tried to push himself up, but he struggled with his injuries. Sabrina jumped up to help, and carefully, she helped him to sit up, propping pillows behind his head. When he leaned back, he blew out a shaky breath.

"Let me get you something for pain. You need to rest, and when you wake up, you can tell me the rest." Sabrina had heard all she could stomach for the moment. She knew what her brother had endured was going to break her heart more than it already was. Besides that, she needed to have a chat with Deacon.

"Yeah, okay. I'm sorry, Bree. So sorry."

Sabrina bent over and kissed his forehead. "None of that. I've already told you, you have nothing to be sorry for. We're going to figure this out, I promise."

Jerrick nodded, and Sabrina went to find Jonas. When she reached the door, Deacon's words stopped her from stepping into the hallway. "He's a threat, and I'm not going to let him get in the way of having my mate."

Chapter Twenty-One

DEACON KEPT ONE ear on Sabrina's conversation with her brother while he and Dante discussed how to proceed. Isabelle had taken Connor down to the morgue, and Jonas was standing guard at the end of the hallway.

"She's a stubborn one, and if her reaction earlier was any indication, I would say you haven't completed the bond," Dante said.

"No. When you called, we were discussing it, and I promised to give her time to get to know me before we made it official. Now, that might not happen." And if it didn't, Deacon knew he would have to leave town. Being around her without claiming Sabrina was harder than anything he'd ever endured. Now that she was feeling the sadness from what her brother had been through, being near her was close to crippling. His beast was doing its best to help, but it wasn't working.

"Have faith, Brother. It will happen, but you need to tread carefully where Jerrick is concerned. If I can see how badly Sabrina feels she let her brother down, I can't imagine what you're going through. But if you play your cards right, you will have your mate. We have options considering Julian is the best at what he does. We'll need to get Jerrick's opinion, but Julian could easily give the male a new identity. If Drago sent those males to kill Jerrick, the threat isn't over if he thinks Jerrick is still alive."

"I was hoping once Alistair was taken out, the threat to our Clan would be over, at least for a while. I know Rafael has a lot on his plate with Kaya close to giving birth and Jonathan close to the end of his life, but we should be doubling our efforts on finding Drago. He's a threat, and I'm not going to let him get in the way of having my mate."

Dante inclined his head, indicating they should step away from the door. They walked down the hallway, away from where Jonas was. Away from where Sabrina was now talking to her boss. He kept an eye on her until she returned to the room a few minutes later.

"I agree. We need to decide which is better – find what Craven is giving the Unholy to make them Reborn or going up against the Unholy as they are. Having met Evan and Jerrick and hearing their stories makes it harder to want to fight Drago's army and take those men down. If all the Unholy have similar stories, that makes them seem more human. Fighting the Reborn, well, I guess if they're still willing to serve under Drago, then that's their choice."

"But what if it isn't? You see what they did to Jerrick when he decided what was happening wasn't right. He was probably used as an example. If Jasper and Mason hadn't stepped in, Jerrick would probably have been killed. We need to step up our efforts against Drago, but I need to first help Sabrina get Jerrick somewhere safe. I'll talk to them about a new identity. If he agrees, we'll need to find a way to let Drago know the male's 'dead', or else he'll probably come after him again."

Dante clapped Deacon on the shoulder. "You work on that. If he agrees, I have an idea of where you can take him. I'll check on that now."

"Thanks, Brother. I'm going to get back to Jerrick's room and see if I can convince Sabrina to come home."

"Good luck with that." Dante turned and strode down the hallway where he stopped and spoke to Jonas.

180

Before stepping back into the room, Deacon reached out with his senses. Jerrick was calm, but Sabrina was both sad and pissed off. He knew an apology was in order, but he needed to phrase it carefully or she'd be even more upset. Deacon eased in the room, pausing to get Sabrina's eye. When she glanced up at him, her hands were gripping the chair so tight he thought she might break it. Okay, it was worse than he thought. He didn't wait for her to say anything. Instead, Deacon walked around to where she was seated and squatted in front of her.

"I'm sorry for how I reacted. You have to understand that a mate is the most precious gift a Gargoyle can receive. We haven't completed the bond, but I don't count you as less because of it. There is nothing I wouldn't do to protect you. My beast took over when my wings came out. It detected a threat, and when our mate is threatened, the shifter can be hard to control. You have to know, there is nothing I wouldn't do for you. That means there is nothing I wouldn't do for your brother as well. He is now my family, just as the Clan is yours."

Sabrina narrowed her eyes as she stared at him. Was she searching his face to for a sign of deception? Because that was the vibe he was getting from her. "I don't want him going to the prison. He's done nothing wrong, and putting him there won't be good for his mental health."

"Before I left the room, he was agreeable. What changed? Not that anything is definite. Dante and I were discussing the best way to keep him safe from Drago, and we have an idea, but I will need to speak with Jerrick about it."

"Why would Drago still be after him?"

"Because he's not dead," Deacon said honestly. Sabrina flinched, and Deacon reached out for her hand. She pulled away, and his heart shredded. He had to fix this for her. For them. "I'm sorry to put it so bluntly, but Drago was trained under Alistair. From what we've heard, there was no mercy."

"Drago isn't any different," Jerrick muttered. Sabrina stood, going to her brother's side.

"You're supposed to be resting."

"It's kind of hard to with the two of you whispering so loudly about me. But he's right, Bree. Drago is building an army, and you don't win wars by being nice. If he knew I was here, talking to the enemy, he'd find a way to cut me down." Jerrick turned his eyes to Deacon. "Deacon, was it?"

"Yes. In all the chaos, we weren't properly introduced. My name is Deacon Wright. It is a pleasure to meet one of my mate's siblings; I just wish it was under different circumstances. I'm glad you're awake. There's something I need to speak to you about."

"The Pen, right? I already agreed to go with you."

"Jerrick—"

"No, Sabrina. I've already put you in danger by coming around. If I stay in New Atlanta, the Pen is the only place where I'll be safe from Drago's reach, and I can't go anywhere else. When I became Unholy, my information was wiped. At least I was told it would be. It was one of the things I had to agree to when I signed up to join Flanagan."

"That's explains a lot, but that's sort of what I want to talk to you about. One of our Clan is the best when it comes to all things related to computers. He can create a new identity for you as well as a back story to go with it."

"Can he do anything about my face? Because even if I have a new name, there are too many Unholy and Reborn alike who know what I look like. I would still need to disappear."

"I just got you back. Please, Jerrick. I can't lose you again."

"Bree, I love you, but we haven't been together in so long you won't miss me any more than you have these last twenty years."

"That's not true. You can ask Jasmine. Oh, crap. I need

182

to call Jasmine and Terrence. You might not believe it, but we have missed you."

"You should probably wait about that," Deacon said. "Until we figure out the best way to keep Jerrick safe, we need to be cautious of who we talk to about him. His identity might have been stricken from official records, but we don't know what kind of information Drago has at his disposal. If he knows about your siblings, he might go after them to get to Jerrick."

"It really is true when they say no good deed goes unpunished. When I got my mental faculties back, the first thing I thought was to run as far away as possible, but I couldn't do that knowing a child was in danger," Jerrick said.

"I promise we will find a way out of this for you. It might not be what you envisioned when you got out of the service, but even if we have to get one of Jonas's prosthetics for you to wear, we'll make sure you aren't at risk," Deacon said.

"Prosthetics?"

"It's a type of realistic-looking mask which can be worn long term. I've never worn one myself, but I've seen them. Unless you know the person is wearing one, you can't tell it."

Sabrina nodded. "It's true. My bo—"

"How do you feel about dying?" Deacon asked, cutting Sabrina off. He didn't know Jerrick well enough to trust him to keep Jonas's identity safe.

"Dying? I've faced it on many occasions. If it's my time to go, I'm ready."

"I don't mean literally. Dante and I were discussing faking your death. That would go along with the new identity. If we put it out there you were killed in the attack, it would hopefully take Drago off your scent. You could go anywhere. Be anyone."

"While that sounds good in theory, just because I have a new name or face doesn't mean my brain becomes someone else's. I'm still me at my core, and I can't just waltz into a hospital and say I'm a doctor."

"No, but you can go to school if you'd like. As a child, what did you want to be when you grew up?"

Jerrick hesitated before he answered. Sabrina took his hand in hers. "It's okay. You can be honest."

A tear rolled down Jerrick's cheek. "I wanted to be someone else's kid. Don't get me wrong. The Wilsons treated Terrence and me like we were their own grandkids, but money was tight. We weren't much better off than when Momma was alive. I know I sound ungrateful, because we could have gone into the system, and that would have been so much worse. It's... being poor sucked. I'd see other kids at school who didn't wear secondhand clothes. They had a mom who wasn't dead and a dad who wasn't in prison. He died, you know. It was two months before he was set to be released, and instead of keeping his head down, he mouthed off to the wrong inmate. Shivved in the shower."

Sabrina wiped the tears from her cheeks. "Jasmine and Terrence went to college. Was that not what you wanted? Did you want to go into the army?"

"Jasmine was smart, so she was able to get scholarships. Terry went to the community college on grants. Then he met a girl whose father got him a job at his company in California. I figured I'd join the military and have them pay for my education, but one tour turned into two. When I was discharged, I was so screwed in the head there was no way I could think about school."

Deacon bowed his head and called on his beast to help with the heartache. When he looked at Jerrick, he said, "I'm sorry for bringing up such a painful subject. I only want to help you with your future. But don't worry about that now. Let's concentrate on keeping you safe from Drago, and the rest will fall into place."

"How? I have no money. Nowhere to go. I mean, I could get a job at a fast food restaurant, but that's not going to get me an apartment. I'm back where I was when I returned home."

"No, you aren't. When you returned home, you didn't have your sister and me to help get you on your feet. I don't want you worrying about money or a place to stay. If we get you a new identity, I'll help you find a job and a place to live."

"Why would you do that?" Jerrick choked back a sob.

"Because we're family. How much do you know about Gargoyles?"

"Not much. Only what I've seen from Drago and the other Greeks who've come to help take over the Unholy."

"Gargoyles have one mate for life, and Sabrina is mine. My family became hers, and hers mine. We take care of our own, and I will take care of you. However long it takes, whatever you need."

"But you don't know me. Neither one of you do. I've done things…" Jerrick turned his head away, tears flowing down his face.

"Jerrick, as an Unholy, did you harm innocent humans?"

He hesitated then shook his head. "No. At least, not that I recall. Being Unholy was like being in a fog. We ate, slept, and fought whenever we were told to. I didn't sign up to hurt people, and I can't imagine even in my transformed state I would harm innocent people." Jerrick closed his eyes. "I only wanted somewhere to belong."

"If you didn't harm anyone, not counting your time in the military, you and I have no problems. There's another Reborn who told me much the same story of why he agreed to work with Flanagan. He's in the same position as you. He didn't run; we captured him to get answers. But now that he's out of Drago's clutches, he needs the same type of

185

help." Deacon had thought about Evan's situation ever since meeting the male. He'd always wondered why someone would agree to working for Flanagan and allow themselves to be turned into an Unholy. Now he knew their situations, and he wanted to rescue them all.

Dante entered the room after knocking softly. Frey entered the room with him. "Sorry to interrupt, but we need to ask Jerrick a few questions. Jerrick, this is my cousin, Frey Hartley. Frey, Sabrina's brother, Jerrick."

"Can't all this wait? Jerrick needs his rest," Sabrina said gruffly. Deacon didn't know if she was speaking as a doctor or a worried sister.

"It's okay, Bree. And it's nice to meet you, Frey."

Frey crossed his arms over his chest, but quickly uncrossed them when Sabrina shrunk back. Deacon stepped behind her, placing his hands on her shoulders. He expected her to shrug him off, but she didn't. Either her anger at Deacon was waning, or she was really that scared of Frey. He remembered what Sabrina said about her ex being a large man, but she had to know none of the Gargoyles would harm her. Then again, they had been talking about Drago, and he was a Goyle.

Frey stepped back, leaning against the wall. He must have picked up on Sabrina's unease. Dante gave Deacon a knowing look. He pulled his cell phone out and texted someone. When he finished, he said, "This is about the child. We are hoping you can help us find him."

"I already told Deacon, when I was getting my beatdown, I heard someone yelling about Craven and the kid. I'm sure they're long gone."

"You're probably right, but we need a starting point. Can you tell us where this building is?" Dante held up the drawing of Jerrick and the boy.

"What the... Where did you get this?"

"I drew it," Connor said as he strode into the room

holding Amelia's hand. Isabelle and Abbi were behind them.

Abbi went to Frey and nestled into his side, leaning her head against his chest. Isabelle stood next to Dante and laced their fingers together. Deacon had to hand it to the ME. He could read people just as well as Deacon. Having the mates there would hopefully ease Sabrina's mind about being around the large males.

The kids walked over to where Sabrina was standing. "Hi. I'm Amelia. Connor is my best friend. He's really smart. And a good drawer. I draw stick people, but he doesn't laugh at me."

"But you can dance, and I cannot," Connor stated matter-of-factly.

Amelia let go of Connor's hand and did a pirouette before taking a bow. Connor smiled, as did the adults in the room, but it was Jerrick who laughed aloud. Amelia ran to her father who caught her when she jumped and set her on his hip. She placed her hands on his face, smushing it until he looked like a fish, and placed a sloppy kiss there. Deacon glanced over at Sabrina and was pleased to find her smiling. When Dante caught his eye, Deacon inclined his head briefly to say "thank you."

Chapter Twenty-Two

DRAGO GRABBED THE male around the neck, lifting him off the ground. "I should take your head!" His claws dug into the male's neck. What good was spending money on these fuckers if they kept getting away? Granted, the Stone Society was responsible for both abductions, and that was worse. If the two Reborn had simply run away, Drago wouldn't be as concerned. But these males had information Rafael could use against him. If the two Reborn talked, everything Drago was working toward could be ruined. He tossed the male against the wall, where he slid down, landing hard on his ass. The male simply pushed himself off the ground and waited for instructions. This wasn't one of the Reborn. This male was still Unholy.

Maybe Drago had been going about this the wrong way. Did he really need his army to be able to think for themselves? No, he didn't. He needed males who would fight to the death without question. Retracting his claws, Drago stormed off toward his car. He needed to speak with Hagen, who was still living at Drago's place. The young human was no trouble. He was quiet unless spoken to, and he cooked and cleaned without being asked. Drago found he rather liked the young man, so keeping him at his own home not only saved money, it gave him someone to go home to. It didn't hurt the man was handsome as well as useful.

When he walked in the door, all the lights were off

except the one over the stove. Drago knew there would be a plate of food in the microwave. He was too worked up to eat, so he decided to take a shower first. Soft music sounded from the room Hagen was staying in. Drago bypassed the door, continuing down the hallway to his own room where he made quick work of his clothes. He had just stepped into the bathroom when someone gasped behind him. When he turned, Hagen was rushing from the room, muttering apologies. Drago chuckled softly at the young man. Being over six hundred years old, Drago had long since put things like modesty behind him.

Until he met Audrey, he'd also not given much thought to his random sexual encounters. For a brief moment, he'd imagined what it would be like to come home to a mate every night. Someone who was glad to see him. Someone who cooked for him. Cuddled on the sofa when the mood struck. Drago might have been a bastard in most things, but he wasn't one to shy away from affection if the person he was with offered it. Being close to another was soothing to his beast. His mate had been taken from him, so those thoughts of what might have been did him no good. He now had other worries to focus on, like whether or not to continue with the Reborn program.

Ignoring his cock, he showered quickly, and then dressed in sleep pants. He didn't bother with a shirt since he would be going to bed as soon as he ate whatever Hagen had cooked for him. He expected Hagen to be hiding in his bedroom, but the human was waiting for Drago in the kitchen.

"Uh, sorry about barging in on you like that," Hagen said, not meeting Drago's eyes.

"I imagine I don't have anything you haven't seen before, so don't worry about it." Drago headed for the microwave, but Hagen jumped down from the stool.

"Here, let me." Hagen punched in the time and pressed

start. "Would you like your usual beer?"

"Sure." Drago sat at the island, watching Hagen move about the kitchen. The man kept his eyes averted while he poured the beer from the bottle into a chilled pint glass. When the microwave dinged, Hagen placed the plate in front of Drago along with silverware and a napkin. Service with a blush.

"Thank you, Hagen. This looks delicious."

"You're welcome. If you need anything else, I'll be in my room."

Drago stopped him. "Sit, please. I want to run something by you."

Hagen nodded and climbed onto the stool next to Drago. He still wouldn't look at him. Between bites, Drago explained how the two Reborn had been captured by the Stone Society. He then brought up his thoughts on finding more men to turn Unholy to build his army. It wasn't necessarily cheaper. The cost of the Reborn serum was more expensive than that of the Unholy serum, but if they increased their numbers, they would need more housing. "We also have the problem of the two Reborn talking. If Rafael gets hold of Craven, then none of what we're discussing matters."

Hagen lowered himself from the stool and went to the table where his laptop was. He sat down and talked while he worked. "Have you reached out to the doctor? You know, to make sure he hasn't been found?"

"Yes. He assures me he and the child are well hidden."

"Okay then. It sounds to me like the Reborn aren't worth the cost. If you take the money allotted for that program and put it towards Unholy, you could..." Hagen tapped away and concentrated. "There are several warehouses for sale about thirty miles south of here. With the money you were going to give Craven for the Reborn serum, you could buy these warehouses, and that would give you plenty of room for the

190

Unholy you already have plus a couple hundred more if you wanted to house them all together. The money coming in from Florida would provide the funds needed to feed and clothe them plus pay the utilities. They're farther away from downtown, but they offer more privacy than your current location." Hagen looked up, and his cheeks flushed.

Drago smiled at the young man. It was the first time he'd had something to smile about since losing Audrey. "That could work except for two things. One, I've already paid Craven to produce the anti-serum. And two, I'm not exactly a citizen with the credentials to purchase property legally."

"Oh, I forgot to tell you. These came in today." Hagen grabbed an envelope from a pile of mail and handed it to Drago.

"What's this?" he asked, opening the flap and dumping the contents beside his empty plate. Drago shuffled through the papers, and his eyes met Hagen's.

"I started the process for citizenship as soon as Kallisto paid me off in case I needed to get out of Greece. I had to fake all the documentation, because I didn't meet the requirements." Hagen shrugged like fooling the US government was no big deal. "As soon as I arrived here after you called for me, I looked into setting up a company. Everything is in my name, so you don't have to worry about Julian Stone tracking anything back to you. You now have the ability to purchase whatever you need."

"How did you manage this? Where did you get the money?"

"I used some of the funds Kallisto gave me before she sent me away."

"You used your own money for this? For me?"

"Yes, Sir. I figure we are in this together. The better equipped you are at taking over the States from the Stone Society, the more likely we are to succeed. As for the

191

money, Arden has been more than successful in moving women. I'll add the money I have left to it for the warehouses. Call Craven, and have him switch from the antiserum to the original Unholy serum."

Something shifted inside Drago. The human had taken it upon himself to move things forward. No one had ever been so thoughtful where Drago was concerned. If he hadn't met Audrey and felt the mate bond, he might have considered this human to be his intended, even though there was no burning desire to get physical. Drago had never excluded men from his bed when wanting to scratch an itch. Pleasure was pleasure, no matter whether the body was soft curves or hardened muscles. Most everyone Drago knew wanted something in return, but it sounded like this man only wanted to help Drago in his plans to take over the throne. Before he could ponder this new situation further, Hagen brought up the project Drago had tasked him with earlier. When he told Drago what he'd found out, it was all Drago could do not to kiss the man.

DEACON HAD TO be lying, but if he was, the rest of the people in the room were in on the deception. Sabrina knew what she heard. Deacon was threatened by Jerrick, and he would do anything to mate with her. Did that mean coming up with a ruse so plausible she fell for it? She didn't know the Gargoyles and their mates. But she knew her boss. Didn't she? No, she didn't. Not really. The man she'd called boss and friend all these years had deceived her, so why wouldn't the others do so as well? She hadn't missed Dante sending a text, and soon after the two women and children had shown up. That was for Sabrina's benefit. It was to set her mind at ease. That or to lull her into a false sense of security. But she

192

did feel secure. Safe. She didn't want to believe Deacon was lying to her. What if she was jumping to conclusions? She hadn't heard the whole conversation. Still, it was up to her to protect Jerrick. She would play along until she had proof one way or another.

"Connor's drawings are from visions he has. In this one, he saw you and the child. Can you tell us where this building is?" Dante asked Jerrick.

"Yeah. It's about three blocks from the bus terminal. West, I think? I don't remember getting there, but when we left, we were ushered into an SUV and taken back to the warehouse."

"I'll call Julian," Frey said, leaving the room still holding Amelia in one arm.

Dante stepped closer to the bed. "How do you feel about a vacation in New Orleans?"

"I've never been, but it's just as good a place as any, I guess."

"My brother's mate has a house there. Julian is already working on a new identity for you. If you were to head down there for a while, you wouldn't have to worry about anyone recognizing you."

Sabrina spoke up before Jerrick could comment. "Jerrick, I don't like the thought of you going off to a strange city alone."

Jerrick rolled his eyes. "I'm not a kid anymore. I'm a trained soldier. But if you feel the need to babysit, then by all means, come with me."

"I can't. I have patients. Look, I know you're an adult, but I think it would be better if you stay here with me. You won't know anyone down there." Sabrina was being ridiculous as well as selfish. Jerrick had been to war, yes. But he'd also been Unholy, and she didn't know how much of that mentality was left over.

"My sister lives in the French Quarter. She's mated to

the leader of our Clan in that area. Lilly and Dominic would be willing to keep an eye on him," Isabelle said.

"You all have an answer for everything. This is my brother's life you're playing Russian roulette with." Sabrina wrapped her arms around her waist and blinked back the tears. Was she being unreasonable? She didn't think so.

"Sabrina, we all want what's best for Jerrick. We're not going to make him go anywhere he doesn't want to. We aren't going to force him to change his name or wear a prosthetic. He's free to do what he wants. We're just giving him options to keep him safe from Drago," Deacon said.

"Can I talk to my sister alone?" Jerrick asked.

"Of course," Deacon said. He grabbed Sabrina's hand and squeezed it before walking off. The electric spark between them was still there. The need to be close to him hadn't dissipated. If anything, it was getting stronger, and that was messing with her brain. She needed a clear head to think about her brother, not about hauling Deacon back to his house and sealing the bond the way she'd wanted to earlier. Had that only been a couple hours ago?

"Sabrina, you need to stop," Jerrick said.

"Stop what?"

"Trying to mother me. I appreciate your concern, but I got myself into this mess, and I'll get myself out of it."

"I'm not—"

"You are. You took care of us even when Momma was alive, but I'm grown now. It sounds like you have a good family with Deacon and the others. I know they're looking out for me because of you, and it feels good. They have every right to toss me in the Pen, and not in a room, but in a cell."

"I'm not so sure that's not what they have planned. I overheard Deacon talking with Dante, and he said you're a threat."

"No, he said Drago is a threat. You must have only

194

heard part of the conversation."

"How do you know what they were talking about?"

"Because I can hear exceptionally well. I have been able to since I became Unholy. I guess that's one of the side effects, but I heard every word the two of them said. Well, most every word. I was trying to pay attention to you at the same time. I know Deacon loves you. I can see it in the way he looks at you."

"He can't love me. We haven't known each other long enough. It's what they call the mate bond."

"So, are you saying Frey doesn't love his mate, or Dante doesn't love Isabelle? Because Deacon looks at you the same way they look at their mates. And if it isn't love, it's at least a deep devotion. They don't have to help me, but they are, and it's because of you. You don't see them offering the man in the Pen the chance to vacation in New Orleans. I know who they're talking about. Evan is his name. We are both ex-military. We both saw and did things while serving our country that most people would think unforgivable, but when it's at the government's discretion, it's considered a duty. Neither he nor I ever harmed a human after becoming Unholy. We're basically the same, so why do I get special treatment and he doesn't?"

"Maybe they'll let this Evan go with you to New Orleans. I'd feel better if you had someone with you that you know."

"I don't have the right to ask that of them."

"No, but I do."

"And you're willing to ask that of Deacon even though you don't trust him?"

"I don't… God, I can't wrap my head around all this."

"Cut yourself some slack. I can't imagine what I put you through acting like a stalker. I'm so sorry I didn't trust you enough to come to you."

"And I can't imagine what you've been through. Being

195

Unholy? What was that even like?"

Jerrick shook his head. "You really don't want to know. I'm just glad Drago chose me to become one of the Reborn, or I might have never gotten away from him."

"Are you sure you want to go to New Orleans?"

"Definitely if Evan can go with me. If not, I'll need to think about it."

"Okay, I'll talk to Deacon. If he meant what he said, he would give me anything." Sabrina was a fool for ever doubting Deacon. She prayed she hadn't screwed everything up with him.

Chapter Twenty-Three

"YOU'RE RIGHT. I will give you anything that I can possibly give," Deacon said, walking back into Jerrick's room. Dante and Frey had taken their families home since it was getting late. Deacon had remained in the hallway, but he had eavesdropped on their conversation. He hadn't been aware the Unholy had exceptional hearing, but it didn't surprise him. They had been created from Original Gargoyle blood. His own exceptional hearing had caught every word of their conversation, and it broke Deacon's heart to hear Sabrina's doubt.

"I can't promise I will be able to convince the others to allow Evan to travel to New Orleans with you, but I promise I will try. I had already been thinking of how to help the male, and I believe this would be a good opportunity, but only if it's what you wish. I've heard Sabrina's argument against it, and as her mate, I want her to be happy. Therefore, I'm torn. I want you to think it over tonight. Sabrina is right in that you need to rest. There are two Gargoyles standing guard outside your room. If either of you need anything, just let them know."

"What do you mean either of us?" Sabrina asked.

"I assumed you would stay here with your brother. Was I wrong?"

Sabrina blinked back unshed tears. Her sorrow was as great as his, and they had a long way to go before they would complete the bond. She didn't trust him, and he, well, he didn't know how he felt other than like his heart was going to split in two.

"Go home, Bree. I'm going to be asleep, so there's no need in you trying to rest on that crappy chair."

"Are you sure?"

"Yes. Come back in the morning, and I'll have my answer."

Sabrina leaned over and kissed her brother on the forehead. The sigh Jerrick released was loud in the otherwise quiet room. Deacon waited for Sabrina to precede him out the door. He stopped and said a few words to Lorenzo and Paxton, thanking them for watching over Jerrick.

They walked without speaking to Deacon's truck. He held open the door then helped her inside. Once he was seated, he put the key in the ignition, but he didn't turn it. Closing his eyes, he begged his beast for help.

She is as conflicted as you are. Remember, this is new to her, and she's only human.

I know. Doesn't make it hurt any less.

"Deacon?"

"Sorry." He started the truck and headed toward his house.

"So, I'm guessing by your silence you overheard my conversation with Jerrick." She wasn't accusing, just stating a fact.

"Yeah, but I don't blame you for doubting my sincerity. You don't know me." Deacon barely got the words out without crying. As much pain as he'd felt in his long life, nothing compared to what he was going through now.

"I'm sorry. I shouldn't have doubted you. You haven't given me reason to. You have been nothing but honest since we met, and I... Please forgive me."

Deacon didn't have to think about it. "I forgive you." Nothing else was said until Deacon pulled down the

198

driveway. When he didn't pull into the garage, Sabrina squirmed in her seat. He didn't have to check her mood, because her body was broadcasting it loudly. He had planned to take her back to her house since the threat of the stalker was over, but it seemed she had other things on her mind.

Take her inside and claim her.

It's too soon. Still, he opened the garage door and parked inside. If she had sex on her mind, she probably wasn't going to ask to go back home. Sabrina didn't wait for Deacon to come around to help her out. She met him on the driver's side, grabbed his hand, and pulled him toward the door. Once inside, she continued upstairs to his bedroom. She released his hand and began undressing.

Deacon was frozen. He stood numbly as she revealed every inch of her smooth skin. Deacon's dick was already hard, but the more skin he saw, the harder he became. Sabrina stepped closer and released the button from his jeans after he pulled his shirt over his head, dropping it on top of her clothes. Slowly, she lowered his zipper. When it was all the way down, Sabrina hooked her thumbs inside his jeans, pushing them down his hips.

"What are you doing?"

Sabrina stilled her hands. "I thought... Do you not want me?"

"With every breath I take. But I have to tell you, I don't think this is a good idea. I'm too close to losing control, and you shouldn't give your body to me when your mind is unclear."

"My mind is clear. I realized I was being an idiot. You may be the empath, but I felt your sorrow wrap around me like a vise. That is something I hope to never feel again, especially by my own doing. So, Deacon Wright, mate of mine, will you make love to me and complete the bond?"

Deacon was speechless. Just minutes ago, he thought he had no chance with his beautiful female, and now she was

199

giving him the most precious words he ever hoped to hear.

"Did you change your mind?" she asked.

"Never." Deacon pulled Sabrina to him and pressed their lips together. He poured every ounce of love he had into the kiss. The mate bond was strong, but he was in love with his doctor. His beast was clawing to be released, and Deacon growled, "Wait your turn."

Sabrina pulled back, her eyes wide. "Excuse me?"

"Sorry. My beast is being impatient."

"Your beast? What does it have to do with this?"

"When I complete the bond, my shifter will push to the front. I will still be in control, and I promise not to hurt you, but I will bite your neck to claim you. From what I've heard, you will only experience bliss when it happens." Deacon searched Sabrina's eyes for any hesitation, but he found none.

"I can handle bliss," she muttered against his lips, taking control. Sabrina pushed Deacon's jeans down far enough to get her hands on his ass. She kneaded the globes, moaning into his mouth as their tongues danced.

Placing his hands on her shoulders, Deacon pushed Sabrina back to ask, "Are you certain?" She nodded, biting her bottom lip. "Words, Pretty Lady. I need your words."

"I'm certain. Make me yours."

Deacon picked his mate up and laid her in the middle of the bed. He scanned her body as he removed his clothes. When he brought the box of condoms out of the drawer, Sabrina took the box and placed it in the nightstand. "We don't need those. I stopped by my doctor today at lunch and got a shot. It's good for six months. I want to feel you. All of you."

That was all Deacon needed to hear. He climbed on the bed, settling between Sabrina's legs. He pushed one knee toward her chest and slid inside her slick opening in one thrust. "I promise I'll make love to you soon, but my beast is

200

too close to the surface. This is going to be quick, because I can't wait to make you mine."

Sabrina wrapped her other leg around his hip, digging her heel in to bring him closer. "I'm ready."

Deacon took her at her word and thrust hard and quick. Sabrina closed her eyes and threw her head back as he hit something deep inside that had her writhing against him. His fangs dropped and his wings unfurled behind him. He begged the beast to keep the claws from popping out because he had his hands wrapped under her shoulders. "Open your eyes," he demanded. When she did as commanded, Sabrina gasped when she caught sight of his wings. Reaching out, she ran her fingers along the rigid edge of one, and Deacon's beast took over. Deacon roared loud enough to rattle the windows just before he lowered his mouth to the delicate skin of her neck and sank his fangs in. Sabrina cried out as her orgasm pulsed around his dick. Deacon's release pulsed into her body as he experienced the most intense orgasm of his life. He finally remembered to retract his fangs, and he licked at the two insertion points. Sabrina continued to moan and writhe beneath him.

"I... wish... I... had fangs," she whimpered.

Deacon stilled his movements, catching his breath. He kissed everywhere he could reach on her face, her neck, her shoulders, as Sabrina rubbed every inch of skin she could reach with her hands.

"Bliss doesn't even come close," she murmured as she pulled his mouth to hers. When they came up for air, she said, "My turn." Pushing against his shoulder, Sabrina urged Deacon onto his back. Straddling his legs, she sank down on his cock that was hard and ready to go again. Deacon was mesmerized as his mate rode his cock like she owned it. She did. She owned every part of him, inside and out. Reaching for his hands, Sabrina pushed against his grip for leverage as she used her thigh muscles to raise and lower herself.

201

"That's it. Take what you want," Deacon encouraged as he fought the urge to come again. He was close, but he gritted his teeth. Now that they were mated, he vowed silently to always be a giving lover, allowing his mate to find her release first.

"Deacon," Sabrina husked. "I... Baby, you feel too good. If I had fangs, they'd be digging into your neck every time we did this." Her eyes stayed on his, and he could have sworn he saw love there. He felt it, but there was no way he would tell her while they were having sex. He wanted her to know he was sincere, not just throwing out words in the heat of passion. But he wouldn't wait too long. Not only would he tell her he loved her, Deacon would show her every day how he felt. Prove to her she made the right choice.

SABRINA KNEW SEX with Deacon would be spectacular, but she didn't know just how close she would feel to him. It had never been so explosive. He'd warned her the bite would enhance her orgasm, but she had a feeling every time would be just as intense. It wasn't just the way their bodies moved together. It was the look in his eyes as he watched her ride him. As she told him before, she didn't have to be empathic to know what he was feeling, because his face was so expressive, and in that moment, he was telling her he loved her. She loved him, too. It didn't matter that it was quick or that she could blame it on the mate bond. She felt a connection to Deacon. An invisible tether joining their souls. Why she ever doubted him was beyond her grasp.

"I'm so close," she whispered, her thighs burning from exertion. She was slowing down, but she didn't want to stop.

"Let me back on top, Love. Your legs have to be on fire," he offered. Sabrina nodded, and in a move she didn't see coming, Deacon rolled them without pulling out. True to his word, Deacon made love to her. His movements were reminiscent of the dance he'd performed, only there was no music save the beating of their hearts, their heavy breathing, and the moans she couldn't help from releasing. Never had she been vocal while having sex, and now she knew why. It was because she'd never been with a lover who catered to her body. Deacon rolled his hips, grinding against her clit, ensuring she found her release. He was gritting his teeth, so that let her know he was holding back for her.

Her inner walls clamped down around his cock once again, and she cried out as she came, just as hard as the last time. Deacon followed quickly, pumping in and out in short bursts, his eyes squeezed tightly. The muscles in his neck strained as he let loose another cry, not quite as loud as the first. Chest heaving, Deacon hung his head, grinning.

"I can't believe I get to do that every day for the rest of my life," Sabrina said.

"At least for the first fifty years. We might slow down after that." Deacon nipped her nose with his teeth before pulling out of her body, taking their mixed release with him. Sabrina didn't care. It was proof of their joining. Their mating. She was a mate. She would live a long life with this male, and she couldn't be happier. Okay, that was a lie. She could be happier if things with Jerrick weren't up in the air.

"What just happened?" Deacon asked. "You were ecstatic, and all of a sudden your mood dropped. Did I do something wrong? Are you regretting mating with me?"

"No, nothing like that." Sabrina pushed Deacon's shoulder to move him off her. When he was lying on his side, she turned to face him. She placed her hand on his cheek, rubbing at the stubble. "I will never regret mating with you. I was thinking how I couldn't be happier, then Jerrick popped in my head."

"You'll learn our Clan is all about family. That includes

Jerrick. We will make sure he's safe away from Drago, whether it's here, or New Orleans, or somewhere in California with your other brother. Money isn't an object, so really, he can go anywhere he wants and be whomever he wants to be."

"I know I'm being selfish, but I kind of want him to stay here. I just got him back."

"If he decides to hang out at Tessa's house in New Orleans, we can always go visit. It's less than seven hours, and it would make a good road trip on the bike. And he's only going to be there until we make sure the heat is off."

"Unless he falls in love with the city and decides to stay. But again, I'm being selfish. I missed so much of his life after our mom died. I hate to say this out loud, but I was jealous. Even though I had my own grandmother, I wanted to go with my siblings. I wouldn't have cared how poor they were. Heck, we were already poor, so it wouldn't have been anything new. I think Jerrick resents me because I had my own grandmother and didn't have to share her. I would have shared her in a heartbeat."

"Let's get cleaned up and get some rest. I'm sure you'll want to be back at the hospital early enough to see Jerrick before you start your rounds."

"You're right." Sabrina rolled to sit up, but before she stood, she looked at Deacon. "Thank you."

"For what?"

"For being my everything."

Chapter Twenty-Four

NOW THAT SABRINA'S "stalker" had been identified, there was no need for her to have a shadow. Deacon drove her to the hospital after an early morning of lovemaking followed by breakfast on the patio. They entered through the back door by the morgue and stopped to say good morning to Trevor who was dancing to music coming through his earbuds. When he noticed Deacon and Sabrina, Trevor's face morphed into a grin.

"Good morning, Deacon," Trevor said, removing the earbuds. Holding out his hand, he said to Sabrina, "Good morning, My Lady. Trevor McKenzie at your service." When Sabrina placed her hand in Trevor's, he bent low and kissed the back of her knuckles. Deacon growled, even though he knew Trevor was no threat. "Easy, Big Guy. You know I only have eyes for a sexy redhead. So, what brings you to my lair?"

"Just passing through. We're on our way to see Sabrina's brother."

"Ah, yes. The mythical Reborn in the flesh. Jasper was telling me about how he and Mason saved Jerrick from the Unholy. I must say, I'm a little intrigued how a man can go from human to monster to human again. That shit has to take its toll on the psyche. But I know Jerrick is in good hands having such an excellent doctor for a sister. And if the way you two are clinging to each other is any indication, the mate bond has been forged, and therefore, Jerrick has you in his corner as well. Am I right?"

"You are correct. We need to speak with Jerrick so Sabrina can get to work. Maybe you and Jasper can come by soon for a cookout?"

"We would be honored. I can't wait to spend a little time with your mate. Tell her my story and hear all about hers."

"I would like that," Sabrina said. "It was a pleasure to meet you."

"And you as well, My Fair Lady." Trevor bowed deep. When he rose, he returned the earbuds to his ears and danced away from them before pulling open a drawer housing a dead body.

"He's different," Sabrina said, laughing as they were walking down the hallway.

"He is, but he's a great guy. He and Jasper went through hell before they became mates, but I'll wait and let him tell you all about it."

Hand-in-hand, they made their way to the private area where Jerrick was. When they got to the room, Dante and Gregor were outside the door. "Good morning," Deacon said.

Both males fisted their hearts and bowed their heads to Sabrina before shaking Deacon's hand.

"Dante called me last night, and we had a conference call with Rafael. We're all in agreement that Evan should be allowed to accompany Jerrick to New Orleans if that is his wish. I've spoken to Evan at length, and I don't believe he should be held accountable any more than Jerrick for what they've been through. If the two of them can spend some time together, I think it will go a long way to helping them both heal," Gregor said. Laughter sounded from Jerrick's room, and Gregor smiled. "I also thought if Jerrick could talk to Evan, he'd heal from his injuries better. Shall we?"

Evan was sitting in the chair beside Jerrick's bed. They

both looked up when Deacon and the others entered the room. "Hello, Evan. It's good to see you again. This is Sabrina Bailey, Jerrick's sister."

Evan stood and held out his hand. "It's my pleasure, Ma'am."

Sabrina blushed. "Thank you, Evan. I appreciate you coming to talk with Jerrick."

"He and I have a lot in common." Evan shyly glanced over at Jerrick. The vibe coming from the male was more than friendship. Deacon had never thought about either male's sexual preference, but the way they kept stealing looks told him a lot. Maybe there would be more than healing going on in New Orleans.

"How are you feeling?" Sabrina asked her brother.

"Better. My wounds are fading faster than I thought possible, but I guess that has something to do with whatever I was given to reverse the Unholiness." Everyone chuckled at his phrase.

Dante stepped up to the bed. "Julian has already started the process of getting you both new identities. You don't have to use them if you don't want to, but we think it would be wise for the time being."

"What do you think? Want to become someone new?" Evan asked Jerrick.

"Definitely. The more we can do to keep Drago off our tail, the better."

"Okay, then. Let's do it. Uh, how are we getting to New Orleans? I don't have a car," Evan said.

"Don't worry about anything," Gregor said. "Tessa and I will take you down there and get you settled. She's been itching to go see Lilly. With Remy helping out at the Pen, I can take a few days off to show you around. With your new identities, Julian will set up bank accounts in both your names, and we'll leave the car with you so you don't have to rely on public transportation."

"Why are you being so kind?" Evan asked, his voice choking over the words. Jerrick reached out and took Evan's hand.

Gregor smiled. "Let's just call it trying to right the wrongs of others. Gordon Flanagan thought he was my mate's father, and when her mother disappeared with her, Flanagan lost his mind. Even though it wasn't Tessa's fault, she hates having any part of the Unholy being created. More than one of our family was affected by Flanagan. That's the short of it."

"What about the other Reborn? What's going to happen to them?" Jerrick asked.

Dante answered, "We'll do everything we can to get them away from Drago. Those who want help will have it. Those who don't will end up in the Pen if they break the law. With the information Evan has given us, we're better equipped to go after Drago and the other Greeks before their army of Unholy gets much larger. My brother Sinclair has seen an uprising of Unholy in California, so we're working hard to battle them on both coasts."

While Deacon had been claiming his mate, the other Goyles had been working to keep Jerrick safe. He thought he'd have to argue Evan's case to get him out of the Pen, but his Clan had been on the same wavelength. It was one less thing he had to worry about in regard to Jerrick. With that settled, Sabrina told her brother she'd check in with him around lunchtime, and Deacon escorted her to her office.

As soon as they were inside, Sabrina grabbed Deacon around the neck and pulled him down for a kiss. It got heated quickly, and Deacon grabbed Sabrina's thighs, lifting her so she had to wrap her legs around him. "I'm never going to get enough of you," he muttered against her mouth.

"I don't think this is the way the future chief of staff should behave," a voice said behind them.

Deacon lowered Sabrina to the floor, putting himself

between her and whomever the voice belonged to. The man had his phone out. Using his shifter speed, Deacon grabbed it out of his hand.

"Hey, give that back," the man said, lunging toward Deacon.

Deacon growled low in his chest, and Sabrina stepped up beside him, looking at the phone.

"Paul, if you're so hard up for pictures, I suggest you go home and watch porn."

Deacon smirked at his mate. He knew she had fire underneath her professional exterior, but it still surprised him. He deleted the photo and handed the phone back.

"You think you're untouchable, but you're not," Paul snarled.

Sabrina pushed the man, closing the door in his face. She leaned against the door, grinning.

"Who was that?" Deacon asked.

"Paul Blankenship, Chief of Pediatrics," she answered, laughter in her eyes.

"I thought pediatrics was on the third floor. What was he doing up here?"

"Ever since Joseph mentioned retiring, names have been tossed around for his replacement. Paul thinks he should get the job." Sabrina shrugged. "It's nothing other than office politics. It's probably a good thing he's a pain in my ass, or we might have taken things too far."

"You're probably right. I need to get out of here so you can get to work. I'll be back around five." Deacon bent down and gave her a chaste kiss. Leaving Sabrina was even harder now since they'd completed the bond, but they both had jobs to do.

Deacon figured this thing with Paul was more than office politics. Sabrina was an alluring, successful woman, and he had a feeling Dr. Blankenship had something on his mind other than a job. That was too bad for the human, because Sabrina was Deacon's. Deacon reached out with his senses, searching for Paul. Sabrina didn't seem worried about the other doctor, but Deacon didn't like his attitude or the tension in his body as he'd spoken to Sabrina. He followed the man's scent to the stairwell. Deacon strode down to the third floor, but his scent continued downward. When Deacon reached the second floor, he opened the door and headed toward Jonas's office. A loud, familiar voice carried down the hallway.

"I want to know who the Neanderthal is," Paul demanded.

Jonas's response was softer, but it still carried the weight of a shifter. "I don't see how that is any of your business. What were you doing on the fifth floor anyway?"

"I... I was going to ask Sabrina if I could take her to dinner," Paul responded, his voice defeated. Deacon had been right. Well, too damn bad.

"A word of advice, Paul. Forget about Sabrina. Her heart fully belongs to the man who was kissing her."

"He wasn't kissing her. They were practically having sex in her office!"

Jonas chuckled. "Ah, I remember when my Caroline and I first got together. We couldn't keep our hands to ourselves either." Paul sputtered, but Jonas kept going. "New love is like that. My suggestion is you mind your own business. I'll talk to Sabrina."

"And warn her away from the loser?"

"What? Of course not. I'll remind her to close her office door for privacy."

Deacon had just enough time to duck into the office next to Jonas's when Paul stormed down the hallway, cursing under his breath. Looking around, Deacon was glad the office was empty, or he'd have to explain to whomever it belonged to why he was hiding in there. When the coast was clear, Deacon strode to Jonas's door and knocked. When the male looked up, he grinned.

"I take it you heard?"

"Yes, and I apologize. It won't happen again."

"Nonsense. I wasn't lying when I said I remember how it was in the beginning. And I'll let you in on a little secret. Two and a half centuries later, and that need hasn't dissipated one bit. If you're mauling one of my doctors in her office, I take it things are going well?"

"We completed the bond last night."

Jonas's eyebrows shot up. "I'm surprised you left the house this morning."

"It was difficult, but we both have jobs to do, and Sabrina wanted to check on Jerrick."

"How is he this morning? I haven't had a chance to stop by there."

"Doing well. Whatever is in the serum that he was given is healing him pretty fast. His wounds were barely visible."

Jonas leaned back in his chair and steepled his fingers beneath his chin. "Interesting."

"I know that look. What are you thinking?" Deacon had a feeling it had something to do with Gabriel.

"I was thinking of my son. If Isabelle can synthesize Evan's blood properly, I'd like to recreate the serum and see if it has any effect on Gabriel."

"We're going to do our best to find Dr. Craven. If that happens, it's possible we can get our hands on the serum itself. If we do, I'll let you know."

"I would appreciate that. Isabelle isn't the most forthcoming with regards to my wishes. Anyway." Jonas waved Deacon off. "Congratulations on your mating. Sabrina is a welcome addition to the family."

Deacon said goodbye, and as he was walking toward the staircase, his phone pinged. He stopped to check his text, and it was a videoconference request from Rafael. If he hurried, Deacon could make it to the Pen before the meeting started.

Twenty minutes later, Deacon walked into the back door with five minutes to spare. Gregor and Remy were in Gregor's office, and Gregor called Deacon in. "Just in time."

"Do you know what he wants to talk about?" Deacon asked.

"Yes. We're going after Craven and the child. With Jerrick's help, Julian was able to pin down the location of the building where the Unholy were taken for their reversal." Gregor set his laptop on the conference table and the two of them sat together while Remy went to answer a call from one of the guards.

Rafael's face popped up, and he greeted them as he always did, "Good morning, my Brothers."

"Good morning, Our King," Deacon and Gregor responded in unison, as did everyone else on the call.

"Julian was able to locate the building where Dr. Craven has been turning the Unholy. I sent last night's patrol to check it out, but there was no sign of the doctor or the child. Just a few minutes ago, Connor had another vision. In this one, the child was alone in a dark room, crying. With no discernable features, Connor wasn't able to give any details as to the location of the room."

"Brother, excuse me," Dante said.

"Go ahead, Dante."

"When Isabelle called to tell me Connor had another vision, I rushed home. He was quite distraught at not being able to give us any details. I had him meditate to help calm him. Rafe, Connor did more than that. He reached out to the other child, and he actually made contact. I don't know how it's possible, but I'm learning that there's much more to Connor's abilities than we know."

"Was he able to get a location?"

"No, but he has a better description of where Craven took the child. I'm sending everything to Julian as we speak."

212

"Excellent. Frey, choose a team. As soon as Julian has the information, be ready to move out. I want that child found today."

"I'll take Paxton, Jasper, Lorenzo, and Deacon. Everyone, bring your swords just in case. We'll meet at the gym as soon as we finish on this call. I want to be ready to roll out as soon as Julian has any information," Frey instructed.

Deacon was torn between doing his duty and being home with Sabrina, but she was his mate, and as such, she would need to become accustomed to his duties to the Clan.

"With that settled, I'll let those of you know who aren't aware, I've agreed to release Evan. He and Sabrina's brother Jerrick have decided to stay at Tessa's house in New Orleans until we get a handle on Drago. Gregor and Tessa will be escorting them as soon as Jerrick is well enough to travel. Deacon, congratulations, Brother. I just got off the phone with Kaya. Sabrina told her you bonded last night."

"Thank you, and yes, we did. I take it Kaya's at the hospital with Jonathan?"

"Yes. He wanted to talk to her about Priscilla."

"How is Priscilla?" Deacon asked. He had purposefully stayed away from the manor because the woman's grief was too much.

"She's not well. Not even Kaya's pregnancy can pull her out of her despair. Honestly, I'm afraid we'll lose her from a broken heart once Jonathan passes away."

"We'll all rally together and make sure that doesn't happen. If nothing else, Tessa and I can take her on a vacation somewhere to get her mind off things," Gregor offered.

"I appreciate that, Brother. Frey, how is Slade and Matthew's vacation? Have you heard from either of them?"

"I haven't, but I didn't expect to. Let's hope no news is good news," Frey said.

213

"If there's nothing else, we'll wait for Julian to figure out where the child is, and we'll go get him. Thank you all. Be well."

"Be well, our King." Gregor shut the connection to the video feed and leaned back, scrubbing a hand down his face. "Connor's amazing, and I couldn't be prouder to be his uncle, but I hope any children I have with Tessa don't have special abilities."

"I hope I don't have children, period," Deacon admitted.

"Really? I thought you liked kids. You're great with Amelia and Connor."

"I love kids, but then I watch what Dante has to go through with Connor. He can do his best to protect him from outside forces, but how can he protect him from the horrors he sees in his mind? I don't envy him at all."

"Truth, but it's no different with adults. All you can do is love them and be there when they hurt."

Deacon didn't disagree.

"Gregor, Deacon, we could use some help in the Basement," Remy called over the radio.

"Never a dull moment," Gregor said. Deacon didn't disagree with that, either.

Chapter Twenty-Five

SABRINA STOPPED BY Jonathan's room to say hello and found Kaya visiting. Kaya took one look at Sabrina and grinned. "Congratulations."

"For?" Sabrina did her best not to blush, but Kaya was a mate, and she would know what the afterglow of having incredible sex with her mate looked like.

"You know what. You and Deacon mated," Kaya whispered. Jonathan was resting, and it didn't look like he was resting peacefully if the harsh rise and fall of his chest was any indication.

"Yes, we did. I had every intention of waiting. Spending time with Deacon to make sure it was what I wanted it, but last night... Well, something happened. I hurt his feelings pretty badly, and I knew when I saw the pain in his eyes that I never wanted to put that look on his face again. It made me realize I didn't want to wait."

"Good. That means we'll be seeing you every Sunday," Kaya said.

"Sundays? You mean family day at your manor, right? Deacon mentioned that."

"Yes. It started off as the males getting together in the afternoon, playing video games or shooting pool. Something to get them together and relax. When they started finding their mates, we moved it to breakfast, and everyone typically hangs out most of the day unless there's something

215

pressing."

"Sounds fun. What do I need to bring?" Sabrina asked. She was excited about meeting the rest of the mates and hearing their stories. She didn't have an exciting story to share. Not really. Everyone already knew who she was from being Jonathan's doctor.

"Just you and that handsome male of yours. Priscilla has all the food covered. We worried she'd slack off with Jonathan in the hospital, but it gives her something to keep her mind occupied. Cooking for such a large crowd takes a while."

"Well, if I need to pitch in in anyway, just let me know."

"I will. Thank you."

"Okay, I'm going to get Jonathan's discharge papers ready." Since the man had opted to stop taking treatments, he was ready to move back home. He had wanted Kaya's advice on whether or not that was advisable. His other option was to move in with one of the other Clan members, but that wasn't what he wanted. His wish was to pass on at his home. Kaya assured him they would handle Priscilla. If the woman got to be too much for him, they would deal with it when it happened.

Sabrina stopped at the nurses' station and made the necessary arrangements for Jonathan's release. Deacon had texted earlier asking how her day was, and she responded honestly. She wished they were back in his bed. He corrected her: *our bed.* Which got her to thinking. Now they were mated, she could go ahead and move into his house. She would need to either put hers up for sale or rent it out, and she didn't think she wanted to be a landlord. She put it on the back burner for the time being until she could speak to Deacon about it and get his opinion. It felt good to have someone to help make decisions.

By the time she got back to the secure area where Jerrick was, his wounds had all healed, and he and Evan were sitting

216

up playing cards.

"Hey, Bree. "

"You're looking amazingly healed." Sabrina smiled and wrapped her arms around her brother's shoulders. He returned her embrace, smiling back.

"I am. Gregor and Tessa have gone shopping for Evan and me some clothes since everything we had is at the warehouse. Then we're headed out."

"I'm proud of you. Both of you," Sabrina said, smiling at Evan too. Deacon had told her how Evan's family wanted nothing to do with him. "I've got vacation time coming up, and if Deacon is agreeable, we'll come visit soon. I've always wanted to see New Orleans."

"I'd like that. It feels good having at least one of my siblings back in my life. Maybe someday, the four of us can get together."

"That sounds wonderful. As much as I would love to stay and chat, I need to head back upstairs, but I wanted to stop in and tell you I love you, and I hope you have a great trip."

"I love you, too." They hugged each other again, and when Sabrina released Jerrick, she pulled Evan into her arms for a quick embrace. Sabrina left the room quickly before the threatening tears fell. She wanted more time with Jerrick, but she had to be realistic. His life, if he remained in New Atlanta, was in danger. She understood the concept of war, but she'd never given much thought to the intrinsic nuances. There were people in power and others wanted that power. It wasn't only pitting one army against another. Pawns were created and used. Lives were considered nonconsequential in the larger scheme.

Now, she was in the middle of one, or at least on the fringes. Sabrina didn't doubt things between Gargoyles were just as serious and complicated as human wars. If this Drago was willing to use a child to further his army, there was no telling what he would do to Jerrick. *He already tried to kill him, so there's your answer.*

Deacon showed up not long after she said goodbye to her brother and explained he and several others were going to look for the boy. He gave her a key to his house, telling her to text Julian when she arrived so he could override the code. When she told him she'd just go back to her place until he was finished, he shook his head. "I'd prefer you stay at our home. My security is much better."

"Why are you worried about my security? Jerrick was the one leaving the messages."

"We don't know if Drago is aware of your connection. I'd rather err on the side of caution. Besides, my house is now yours, as is everything I own, and I would prefer to come home to my mate."

"I'm okay with that, except I don't have my car."

Deacon handed her his keys. "Take the truck. It's parked in your spot. I'll get one of the others to drop me off later. We don't expect the rescue to take too long, but I will text or call you to keep you posted." Deacon closed the door to her office before kissing her long and hard. Her body reacted to his touch, fire burning low in her belly, traveling farther south the longer they kissed. Sabrina gasped for air when Deacon broke the kiss.

"Stay safe, my love. I'll be home as soon as possible."

Sabrina nodded, touching her fingers to her lips, which were still tingling. Smiling, she got back to work. The rest of her day passed by in a blur. Jerrick was on his way to New Orleans. Jonathan had been checked out and was back home at the manor. She stumbled her way through the staff meeting with her department, but if anyone noticed she was off her game, no one said anything. If that wasn't bad enough, a child had been brought into the pediatric ward, and none of the other doctors had been available to consult. Paul had remained professional if not distant.

Instead of heading directly to Deacon's home – her home – she stopped by her house and began packing. There was no use in putting off moving in considering they were mated. Sabrina tried to wrap her head around the fact that a week ago, heck even a few days ago, she'd been single, and now she was practically married. Some of the others had referred to their mates as their wives, and she wondered if she and Deacon would get married too. He told her everything of his was now hers, so maybe things were different in the Gargoyle world. Sabrina snorted. Of course things were different. She never would have allowed herself to move so quickly with a human. He'd called her his love. Was it possible he did love her so soon after getting together? Her feelings for him were intense, and she thought about how badly she wanted to spend every waking moment with him. She felt lust, definitely. But love? If it wasn't love, it was close to it.

She looked around at her furniture and tried to imagine it mixing in with Deacon's. She loved his house. It was furnished perfectly as far as she was concerned, so her things could be sold or donated. Other than her clothes, there was very little she wanted to take with her. That was a sad statement to how bland her life had been up until that point. She was thirty-six, yet her home wasn't filled with mementos of a life well lived. Sabrina had been merely existing. She was ready to start enjoying her nights. Spending her free time with the gorgeous male who had claimed her.

Sabrina found a leather jacket in the back of her closet. It took her a minute to remember when or where she bought it. Seeing the coat reminded her of Deacon's Harley. Sabrina dug her phone out of her purse then opened the search engine for the nearest motorcycle shop. There was one not too far out of the way from the route that took her to her new home, and they were open for another couple hours. Abandoning her clothes, Sabrina took what she'd already packed and tossed it in the back seat of the truck and then made her way to the bike store. Less than an hour later, she walked out with a shiny, black helmet, a couple pairs of jeans, and some riding boots.

Pulling up to the gate, she texted the number Deacon had given her for Julian and told him she was there. A few seconds later, the gate opened, and Sabrina pulled through. As she eased down the long driveway, she took her time so she could get a good look at her surroundings. All this land was now hers. Sabrina had never taken the time to enjoy activities like hiking, but she could envision walking with Deacon through the trees, enjoying nature in its purest form. Movement caught her eye, and for a second, Sabrina was scared someone was out there watching her. When she finally caught sight of what startled her, she laughed, joy infusing her soul. A doe and two fawns were bounding through the brush, the mom's white tail a flag as it moved away. Yes, she could definitely get used to this.

IT HAD TAKEN a couple hours of Julian and Lucy working together, but they finally figured out where the building was Connor had seen in his vision. It turned out to be one of many abandoned churches in an area formerly known as Little Five Points. The small section of northeast New Atlanta had once been a thriving, artistic and eclectic area but now was nothing but shattered windows, broken sidewalks, and a haven for the homeless. That was one of the reasons it had taken so long to find the building. In his vision, Connor had seen it as it looked now, but in searching online, the building had been depicted with its flourishing façade from thirty years prior.

Stealth was not on their side. Five large males dressed in black battle gear with swords strapped to their backs drew attention from even the most strung-out person. Waiting until the cover of night would have been preferable, but they didn't want to risk the child being moved. They had agreed on a cover story. If anyone asked, they were working on a film set. New Atlanta had become one of the premier cities for shooting movies, and a studio was set up a few blocks south of where the church was. An action movie currently being filmed in the area helped with their story. Dane had been advised of where they were going and for what reason. Paxton, being a cop, would be able to smooth things over if any other officers saw them and questioned what they were doing, as long as they didn't inspect the swords too closely.

The five males separated, surrounding the old building. Deacon, not being a believer in the human God, had never stepped foot in a church. That didn't mean he couldn't appreciate a beautiful structure for its architecture, the ornate wooden pillars rising from floor to ceiling, or what once had been artistic stained-glass windows. As he silently made his way along the side aisle leading from the front of the church to a doorway which opened into a dark, dank stairway, Deacon kept his senses open for anything which didn't belong. This particular church had a floor beneath the sanctuary. The upstairs was one open cavern with the exception of a couple rooms behind the choir section. Lorenzo and Paxton had been tasked with searching there, while Deacon, Frey, and Jasper moved about the lower section. He felt the other Goyles' tension as each one surveyed their own space within the building.

The lower level housed classrooms which at one time had been filled with adults and children learning lessons that helped them live a pious life. Offices now abandoned had been used by the men who were supposed to have a deeper knowledge of what the Christian Bible taught. Since said

Bible had been translated many times over the centuries, Deacon wondered how much of the original text had lost its true meaning.

Pausing outside a closed door, Deacon searched the interior for any emotion or the subtlest heartbeat coming from within. The others were doing the same in their section of the massive structure. They had agreed on radio silence unless they found something. After reaching the last door, Deacon was ready to call it a bust. He ran his hand over his short hair, and a sigh caught in his throat when he felt it – fear. Holding up a closed fist so the others remained still, Deacon closed his eyes and concentrated. The faint sound of breathing came from somewhere below. "Do you hear that?" he whispered knowing the others would understand his words.

Frey responded, "It's coming from below our feet. Julian, is there anything on the blueprints showing rooms underneath where we are now?"

Julian and Lucy were monitoring the comms. Tapping sounded through the earpiece as they waited for Julian to do his thing. "There isn't another level to the church, but there is a tunnel which is left over from the old viaducts. It was supposedly closed off back in the early 1900s. The church was built on top of a stretch of abandoned railway property when the city diverted the traffic closer to downtown. It's possible there is a covered trapdoor leading underneath, but I'm sorry. There's nothing—"

"Wait. I've got something," Lucy inserted. "Frey, I found an old article from the Prohibition Era. It says many buildings in that area were built on top of the old tunnels and were used by bootleggers. The church you're in was originally a speakeasy and much smaller. Julian, look at this..."

Deacon and the others waited while Julian and Lucy chatted excitedly in their ears. "If what we're looking at is

222

correct, there's a hidden door underneath the middle room on the west side of the floor you're on," Julian relayed.

Deacon, Frey, and Jasper moved quickly to the middle room and searched the floor. "Look," Frey said, pointing. Several pieces of the hardwood were a darker color. Deacon dropped to his knees and extended his claws, inserting them between the seams of two boards. They came away with little effort, and after prying up the other discolored planks, he found a round, metal hasp.

Frey put a hand on his shoulder, halting his progress. "Lor, Pax, we found the trap door. Remain upstairs just in case Drago and his men come back for the child. We are going down."

"Copy that," Lorenzo replied.

Frey nodded, and Deacon pulled the handle. A heavy, iron door swung upward, and Deacon peered down into the dark hole. The sound of breathing hastened, and the fear he felt earlier intensified. "He's scared," Deacon said. "Frey, you should go first. You have a child, and you're better equipped at dealing with one."

Frey didn't argue. He lowered himself into the tunnel below, and Deacon and Jasper followed. The three moved silently down the tunnel until they came upon a small boy who was lying in the fetal position with his arms over his head. The smell of urine was strong, and Deacon had to calm his beast. It was ready to find Drago and take his head.

Frey put a hand to the boy's shoulder, and the child whimpered. "Shh, it's okay. You're safe now. My name is Frey. This is Deacon and Jasper, and we've come to take you home."

Red-rimmed eyes turned to look at them, and Deacon's heart broke. "I don't have a home," the child whispered with an accent.

"You do now," Frey assured him. "I have a large family, and now so do you. Let's get you out of here, okay?"

The child's eyes were filled with fear and distrust. "Look." Frey pulled out his phone, flipping to the photos. "I have a daughter about your age. And my nephew, Connor? He's the one who told us where you were."

"Connor? I thought he was a dream," the boy said.

"No. He might have been in your mind, but I promise, he's real, and I can take you to see him. See? This is him with my daughter." As the boy looked at the photo, Frey asked, "What's your name?"

"I was born Rainier – Rain, but my uncle calls me Pima."

"Why Pima?"

Rain hesitated before whispering, "It stands for pain in my arse."

"Well, Rain, you will never be called that again. I promise." Frey held out his large hand, and the child shuffled to his knees. When Rain took his hand, Frey lifted the boy into his arms. When Rain caught sight of Deacon and Jasper, he buried his face in Frey's neck.

"We have company," Paxton said over the comms, the sound of steel against leather loud as he pulled his sword from its sheath.

"How many?" Frey asked.

"Ten. Two Goyles, seven Unholy, and one human."

"Are the Goyles armed?"

"Yes, and they're on us."

"Grab the human, but take care of the others," Frey instructed. The sound of fighting came through after that.

"Stay here with the boy. We'll go assist," Deacon said.

Frey nodded. "Let me know if you need help."

Deacon returned to the opening, bent his knees, and jumped to the floor above with Jasper right behind him.

Chapter Twenty-Six

DEACON AND JASPER ran down the hallway and up the stairs to the sanctuary. Lor was battling the males single-handedly. The Unholy didn't stand a chance against his sword, but Lorenzo was having a hard time against two armed Gargoyles. They had Lor boxed in, but when Deacon and Jasper stepped in, the two opposing males couldn't hold off the three of them working together. The sound of metal clashing echoed in the cavernous sanctuary. The two they were fighting must have been Greeks leftover from Alistair's army. Their fighting skills were fresh.

Deacon was glad their Clan had trained with swords over the last year, if not happy for the reason. As a Gargoyle, wielding a sword was something taught as soon as their initial transition kicked in, but for most, war was something they didn't think about. Their kind rarely fought each other. Their duties were to keep humans safe and live peaceful lives. Fighting against others of their kind wasn't quick. It wasn't easy. Their stamina was on equal footing, and the only reason they were able to get the upper hand was because they outnumbered their opponents.

The fighting continued for what seemed like hours when a roar sounded, and Paxton charged down the middle aisle. With Paxton adding his sword, they were at a two-to-one advantage. When one of the males turned his attention to Paxton, Deacon swung his sword against his opponent's

225

neck. Beside him, Lorenzo waited until Jasper clashed with his opponent and took the challenger's head from behind. It wasn't a fair fight, but the end result had been inevitable. Blood spilled across the dirty floor as the two Gargoyles fell, their heads landing beside their lifeless bodies.

"Fuck!" Paxton yelled. "I lost the human. There was an SUV waiting, and I couldn't use my shifter speed to catch them. There were too many people watching," he said as he bent at the waist. He wasn't winded, just pissed. Deacon felt the other male's disappointment wash over him. As Lorenzo tried to calm the cop down, Deacon reached out to Julian on his comm.

"It's over. Frey has the child, and we're going to need cleanup."

"Remy is already en route."

"Jules, please call Dante and tell him I'm bringing the child to his house. There's no way we can take him to the hospital," Frey said. "Please tell him we need clothes. Rain is about a size eight."

"On it, Brother."

"Thank you. Deacon, is there a way out of there without me walking through the sanctuary?"

Paxton answered, "Yes. When you come up the steps, there's a door that leads behind the choir, and there's an exit out the back. I'll go get the car and pull it around so we can get the hell out of here."

Deacon and the others sheathed their swords before heading to the door where Frey would come out with Rain. Before they got to the back exit, Remy and Kai walked inside with Caleb and Aldredge, two guards from the Pen who helped with cleanup when necessary.

"Daddy?" Rain cried out. All the males turned to see who the boy was talking to.

"Rainier? Oh, Gods. Rain? My son!" Remy cried, dragging the boy out of Frey's arms, hugging him close.

226

Rain's little arms closed around Remy's neck as the two held on for all they were worth.

"Wait. I thought Isabelle said the child had Original blood," Deacon muttered.

With tears streaking down his face, Remy said, "Yes. He does. His mother, my mate, she was from an Original line out of Australia. She went back to visit last year. Her brother and I don't get along, so I told her to take Rain and go for a holiday. I got a call…" Remy choked up. "Her brother called and told me there'd been an accident. Said…"

Frey put his hand on Remy's shoulder. "It's okay, Brother. We get it. But Rain told us he didn't have a home."

Remy looked at his son, frowning. "Let's go get you cleaned up and we'll talk, yeah?" Rain nodded then laid his head back down on his father's shoulder.

"Come on. We'll take him to Dante so he and Isabelle can check him over. They should have clothes for him by the time we get there." Frey gestured toward the back door.

"Thanks, Brother," Remy said, his smile speaking of the joy at finding his son alive.

"I'll stay here and help with cleanup," Paxton, who was back inside, offered.

Lorenzo looked around at the mess. "I'll help as well. The sooner these bodies are out of here, the better."

Once outside, Frey and Jasper climbed into the front of the SUV after Deacon helped Remy and Rain get settled into the backseat. Deacon sat in the back with them. He couldn't take his eyes off the boy. He never believed in miracles before that moment, but seeing Remy and his son reunited was nothing short of something supernatural.

The mood on the ride was joyous all around. Rain still emitted fear, but not nearly as much as he had when Deacon first encountered the boy. As much as he wanted to get home to Sabrina, Deacon's need to make sure the child was okay was greater. Dante and Isabelle were waiting outside their home when Frey parked in the driveway. Even though it was late, Connor was standing with them.

Remy carried Rain, and the others followed them into the house. Isabelle directed Remy to follow her to Connor's bedroom where he would be comfortable while she checked him over. Deacon and the others waited downstairs to give them privacy. Connor sat on Dante's lap, his young face fraught with worry.

"Thanks to you, Rain is safe," Dante told his son.

"I'm glad, Da. I'll be his friend. He needs one," Connor replied.

Dante hugged Connor, a proud smile gracing his usually stoic face.

They waited in silence until Isabelle returned downstairs. "Connor, will you please join Rain and his father in your bathroom?"

"Yes, Ma'am." When Connor reached the staircase, he turned back to his mother. "Is he okay?"

Isabelle forced a smile. "He will be."

When Connor was up the stairs, Isabelle's face was twisted in fury as she walked to Dante and sat down on his lap. "I'll need to run bloodwork, but physically, he's okay. Remy wants to wait until the morning so Rain can get some sleep. Dante, when you all capture Craven, I want a go at him before anyone else. No one, but especially not a child, should be used in such a way."

"Did he say anything about how he ended up with Craven?"

"Just that one day his uncle took him for a ride to get ice cream, but instead, he handed him over to a stranger. Remy was getting upset, which was in turn upsetting Rain, so I suggested he get Rain a bath and offered for them to stay the night."

"We'll get to the bottom of it on Remy and Rain's time. When Remy's ready, we'll go after the uncle," Frey said.

Deacon already knew the male was a dead man. Nobody messed with the Clan, but when it came to children? Deacon shook his head. It was another mark in the negative column of why he shouldn't have kids.

He stood, as did Jasper and Frey. After saying their goodbyes, the three walked out to the porch. "Come on. I'll drop you at your homes," Frey said.

"I think I'll fly," Jasper countered. Deacon didn't have to look at the sky to know it was the perfect night for it. Both their houses were close by, so he agreed to fly with him. Before they removed their shirts and unfurled their wings, they texted their mates to let them know they were on their way.

SABRINA WAS SITTING on the back patio sipping a glass of wine when she heard a car pull up. Thinking it was Deacon, she hurried to the front door. When she opened it, Trevor was walking up the steps. His grin was sheepish. "I should have called first, but I don't have your number." He held up a bottle of wine. "I brought a peace offering."

"How did you get in the gate?" she asked, holding the door open so he could enter.

"Oh. All the gates are programmed so family can get in. I hope I'm not bothering you; it's just when Jasper and I first got together, I remember how lonely it was when he went on patrols or had to do Clan stuff, and I didn't like sitting home alone. Since he's off with Deacon and the others, I thought I'd keep you company and answer any questions you have about being a mate. Well, not any question, because I'm a guy, and I don't get some of the hetero stuff, but anything else…" He shrugged, and Sabrina couldn't help but laugh.

"You're not bothering me, and I would love to chat. I

was sitting on the patio enjoying the peacefulness of the evening."

"Oh, then you probably don't want me here, because I'm anything but peaceful. I tend to ramble, but you probably already know that."

"I do want you here. Can I get you a glass?" She took the bottle of offered wine and inspected the label, wondering if it was a brand Deacon had stashed in his wine room.

"I'd prefer a beer, if you have it."

"One beer, coming up." Sabrina put the wine on the counter and grabbed a bottle of ale out of the refrigerator, handing it over to the colorful young man. Trevor followed her outside and sat down next to her, popping the cap.

"Ahh, that's good," he said after taking a long pull. "I love what Deacon's done with his yard. He's very domesticated with all the flowers. I love the hummingbirds, too." Several swooped around the feeders, diving in and out before chasing each other off. "I'm sort of surprised they show up. Most critters won't come around the Gargoyles. Except for Tamian. He's like the animal whisperer or something. We're neighbors, if you didn't know. Not like next door or anything, but next acre? Next property?" Trevor pointed to the trees, and said, "About one hundred acres that way. You can either walk through the woods, or Deacon could fly you."

"Fly me?"

"Oh, yes. It's exhilarating. You have to try it sometime."

"I haven't seen Deacon fly. I've only seen his wings a couple times. And here I thought riding on his bike was going to be an experience. Anyway, tell me about yourself." Sabrina lifted her glass and took a sip, watching Trevor over the rim.

"Let's see. I think you met my brother, Travis. I'm his clone. He had a heart condition when he was born, and I was created in case he needed a spare one. You already know I

230

work in the morgue, and I'm studying to become a doctor so I can take over for Dante one day. I figure it'll take me about ten years since I'm in no hurry, but now that I'm mated to a Goyle, time really isn't the same as it was before. That still blows my mind. That whole living hundreds of years thing. Anyway, our start was rough. Has Deacon told you about Alistair?"

"Some of it. We really haven't talked about much," Sabrina admitted, blushing.

"No, I get that. The bond is intense. It was one reason our start was so rough. I had this need to be around Jasper, but there was so much of his past getting in the way." Trevor went on to tell Sabrina how both Craig and Theron, two of Jasper's exes, came into their lives, and how Trevor hadn't known about Gargoyles until Dante explained it to him while he was on the outs with Jasper. The story had Sabrina enraptured if not mortified. She thought having a stalker was bad, but her experience was nothing compared to what Trevor had been through. Trevor spent the next half hour talking about Alistair and what he'd put the other mates through, and how the Goyles had flown to Greece and battled the male who'd made their lives hell.

"Everyone thought with Alistair out of the picture our lives would find some sense of normalcy, but now that Drago's here in New Atlanta, we're still looking over our shoulders. October can't get here soon enough."

"Why's that?"

"Jasper and I are getting married. Then we're going on our honeymoon, and I'm ready to get away from all this for a while. Don't get me wrong. I love the Clan, and I'd do anything for any one of them, but things have been intense for a while. I'm looking to get away and relax without surprises popping up at every corner. I know the others feel the same way. With Kaya about ready to push out Sebastian, we just want our little part of the world to be a safe place.

231

What about you? You and Deacon gonna add little Goyles to the mix anytime soon?"

Sabrina smiled at Trevor's bluntness. Instead of being annoying, it was refreshing. "No. I'm not going to say never, but I doubt it will be anytime soon, if ever. Things are already moving too quickly. I mean, yes, I have seen Deacon in Jonathan's room for a while now, but we only actually met this week. We were supposed to go on our first date last night, and now we're mated. If anyone had told me I'd be in a committed relationship and moving into his home after less than a week, I'd have sent them to see a colleague of mine who's a psychiatrist. Hell, I still think it's crazy, but I couldn't deny the pull to be with him."

"Believe me, I understand. Not to make you feel bad, but I do think yours is the fastest mating out of all the rest. Most everyone had some type of ordeal to get through to be together, though. I'm not saying that to make you feel bad or worse or… I think you should count yourself lucky you got to where you are so quickly. It means you didn't go through all the crap the rest of us did. As bad as my story is, some of the others are worse. You'll get to hear them Sunday when we go to the manor for family day."

"I would say I'm looking forward to it, but if what happened to them is worse, I'm not so sure I want them to tell me. Yes, I'm curious, but I don't want any of them to relive that pain."

"You're a peach, and I'm glad you're one of us." Their phones pinged at the nearly the same time. "Ah, the boys must have saved the day. I'll see myself out so you can get ready to welcome Deacon home." Trevor stood then took Sabrina's hand and kissed her knuckles. "Until Sunday, My Lady."

Sabrina grinned at Trevor's antics as she opened her text.

Deacon: *On my way. Wait for me on the back patio*

Sabrina replied simply: *Okay*

She leaned back in the chair with her wine, crossing her legs. Why would he want her to wait out there? She had just taken a sip when something large floated down, landing in the yard. When she realized what it was, Sabrina dropped her glass, wine splashing her ankle. Thankfully, the glass didn't break. She jumped to her feet and ran into the yard where her Gargoyle was waiting, wings spread wide, looking like something out of a fantasy. Yeah, her fantasy.

DRAGO THREW THE glass against the wall, crystal shards spraying in all directions as the whiskey stained the paint. He ignored Hagen's footsteps. "I don't care about the kid. Find the godsdamned doctor!" he shouted at Trexon before disconnecting. Hagen didn't look at Drago as he began cleaning up the glass. "Leave it. I made the mess; I'll clean it up," Drago said, surprising himself. Usually he was all for delegating tasks to those he felt were lesser, but with Hagen, he genuinely appreciated the human. The more time he spent with his assistant, the more he liked him. Drago imagined their relationship to be what he would have had with Audrey, minus the sex.

"Why don't you fix yourself another drink and tell me what happened while I clean this up?" Hagen continued picking up the glass.

"Somehow, the Stone Society found out where the boy was. Craven assured me no one could find him, but they did. Now, Craven is gone, and I want him returned to me."

"Craven or the boy?"

"Craven. He has my money, but I don't have the serum. Since we decided to abort the Reborn program, the child is no longer necessary."

"And if he talks?"

"It doesn't matter. With two of the Reborn already missing, it's more than likely the Stone Society already knows Craven is the one helping me. And that is another reason I need him found. If they get their hands on him before I do, not only will I have to find another doctor capable and willing to help with the Unholy, but all the money I paid him will be for nothing."

"What can I do?" Hagen asked as he dumped the glass into the garbage can.

"Get into Craven's accounts and figure out where he's going." And when he was found, Drago would make him wish he'd never run.

Chapter Twenty-Seven

SABRINA ROLLED HER eyes when Deacon asked her for the tenth time if she was sure about leaving her furniture. They were packing up the rest of the things she wanted to take with her, and when he realized how little it was, he frowned.

"But this is your stuff, Pretty Lady."

"Stuff being the operative word, Handsome Male." Deacon huffed out a laugh at her endearment. "What? Would you rather I call you baby? Stud-muffin? Wait, what's your middle name?"

"I don't have one. I had a hard enough time choosing a first and last name when I recreated myself."

"What do you mean?" Sabrina leaned against the arm of the sofa, giving Deacon her undivided attention.

"As I told you, Gargoyles sometimes need to move around and create new identities because we never age. I kept my birth name until I moved to the States, and then I chose a more modern name."

"What is your birth name?"

"Oba Abara." Deacon sat down on the sofa and pulled Sabrina onto his lap.

"Oba... I like it. What does it mean?"

"King. My father wanted to name me Prince, but my

mother forbade it. I thanked her for that almost every day of my young life." Deacon grinned, leaning in for a kiss.

Sabrina wrapped her arms around his neck, pulling him closer. Seeing Deacon with his shirt off and wings spread out behind him had lit a fire in her the night before. They hadn't made it inside before she divested him of his jeans and gave him a blowjob in the backyard. Deacon then carried her inside to the kitchen counter where he made her come on his fingers with his mouth torturing her clit. After that, he made love to her on the sofa, and then took her hard against the wall. She rode him as he sat on the stairs, and they made love again when they finally made it to the bed. She'd woken him up around three a.m. with another blowjob, and he woke her at nine by taking her from behind while spooning.

When he told her to get a shower while he cooked breakfast, she convinced him conserving water was the responsible thing to do. Considering how long they spent getting each other off, she had no doubt they used more water than if they had showered separately. Afterward, they cooked breakfast together and ate it on the patio.

"There's so much I don't know about you," Sabrina said against Deacon's mouth.

He pulled back to look into her eyes. "Are you having doubts? I know this was quick, but—"

Sabrina cut him off with a kiss. "No. No doubts. I was merely stating a fact. Like I don't know your birthday. Or your favorite music when you're alone. Whether you like nuts on your ice cream sundae. Your favorite movie. I know we have all the time in the world to learn about one another, but you have to admit, this was probably the fastest mating in the history of matings."

"My birthday is June first. I listen to all types of music depending on my mood, but more often than not, I prefer jazz. I like extra walnuts on a double chocolate sundae, but no cherries. My favorite movie changes all the time, because there are so many good ones. As far as the fastest mating, my parents have us beat by a long shot. I knew you were my mate the first time I saw you in Jonathan's room, and that was months ago. My parents met on a Saturday and were mated the next day. They only waited because my father was mourning his father's passing. My parents met while my father was tending to his parents' estate, and my mother refused to complete the bond that day stating it would be disrespectful."

"If you knew I was your mate, why did you wait?"

Deacon hugged her tighter and ducked his head into the space between her neck and shoulder. "I didn't think I was good enough for you."

"Thankfully, you got your head out of your spectacular ass."

Deacon jerked his head back, grinning. "You think my ass is spectacular?"

"Meh." Sabrina smirked and tapped his nose. "Let's get the rest of this stuff packed up so we can get home. I have a surprise for you."

"I like surprises."

"See? Something else I learned about you."

They packed what she wanted to keep and put it in the truck. That morning in bed between bouts of love making, Sabrina asked what Deacon thought about her keeping her house in case Jerrick wanted to come back to New Atlanta at some point. He thought it was a wonderful idea. If Jerrick decided he didn't want to come back, they could sell it then. Deacon admitted he had paid the mortgage off, but he did it when he was balls-deep and she couldn't think straight. Sabrina brought the topic back up during breakfast, and it was then Deacon admitted how much money he had. Sabrina had nearly choked on the bagel she was swallowing at the time. When he made sure she didn't actually need the Heimlich, he told her if she ever wanted to quit her job and stay home, he wouldn't be opposed.

Sabrina held his hand, smiling, but she told him truthfully, "I appreciate that, but I like my job. What I do is important to me, as is the hospital. I want the chief of staff position if it's offered to me."

"Then you should take it. I only want you to be happy, Pretty Lady."

Deacon made Sabrina happy, and she told him as much. She had to admit she was thankful for the mate bond. Without it, she might not have given him a chance because of her past. When they arrived home, Deacon unloaded the few boxes, putting them in one of the spare bedrooms for Sabrina to go through later. While he was doing that, she went to their closet and pulled out the helmet and boots she had hidden. She changed clothes into something appropriate for riding, slid her feet into the boots, and found Deacon in the kitchen drinking a glass of water.

She slid the helmet on her head without fastening the strap, since she didn't know how, and said, "Ta-da. Surprise."

Deacon's eyes darkened, and after putting the glass in the sink, he strode the short distance to her. "Oh, Pretty Lady. That is sexy."

"I have a jacket, too, but it's too hot for it now," she said with her hands splayed on his chest.

Fingering the strap, Deacon said, "Not if we go for a midnight ride."

"Well, it's only two. What should we do until then?"

Deacon removed the helmet, setting it on the island, and picked her up, tossing her over his shoulder. Sabrina laughed, smacking his ass as he carried her up the stairs. "Spectacular," she mumbled.

DEACON THANKED THE fates about once an hour for bringing Sabrina into his life. His mate was perfect. Her outer beauty was outshone by the light from within. When he first met her, he thought her to be abrasive, but he learned that was her defense mechanism. He had given her the option of quitting her job, but she'd declined. What she did mattered, and he couldn't be prouder.

Their day together had been one of the best Deacon could remember. On the way to pack up her old house, they had stopped by Dante's to check on Remy and Rain. The child was doing well considering what he had been through. It helped that Connor, although younger, took Rain under his wing and offered his friendship. Frey had brought Amelia to play with them, adding another friend to the mix. Remy was only supposed to be in New Atlanta temporarily, but Deacon had a feeling the male might make the move east after getting the California prison set up. Remy had only been in California a few months after moving there from France. He had been lost after losing his mate and son, but now that he had Rain back in his life, Remy had something he hadn't felt in a while – hope. After Rain told his father what happened in Australia, Remy asked Julian to do some digging into his mate's death. Deacon and the others were ready if and when Remy confronted his mate's brother.

After making love several times the night before, Deacon told Sabrina about rescuing the child. He didn't omit having to fight the other Gargoyles. He never wanted to lie to her or keep things from her. He wanted her to always be prepared for whatever might happen. Sabrina shared that Trevor came by to keep her company while Deacon and Jasper had been doing their Gargoyle duties. Deacon appreciated Trevor for taking the time to visit Sabrina and bring her into the mate fold. Sophia and the others had done the same for Trevor when he first mated with Jasper. The

239

mates were as loyal and fierce of each other as they were with their Gargoyles. Sabrina was strong, but according to her, she'd never had a solid group of friends she spent any time with. Deacon knew that was a thing of the past. He couldn't wait to see her flourish with the help of the others.

Deacon never would have taken Sabrina for the adventurous type, so seeing her with a helmet and boots had definitely been a surprise. She looked cute standing in the kitchen with the strap hanging down. When he told her it was sexy, it hadn't been the helmet he was referring to. It had been the fact that she'd taken it upon herself to go shopping for something that would make him happy. In all the years he'd been riding, he had never had a female on his bike. It was one of many firsts he looked forward to sharing with his mate.

Deacon had never been the type to experiment with a female. He had sex to sate a need, but his mate brought out the beast. Literally. When they shed their clothes, Sabrina didn't hold back. Deacon hadn't been with anyone who put his needs first. It wasn't that she tried to dominate their lovemaking, but she didn't allow him to do all the pleasuring. When they reached the bedroom, they didn't waste time when removing their clothes. The need to be one was too great to slowly strip. Deacon took her hard and fast, and after that, they explored each other's body. Soft caresses were mixed with teasing strokes. Chaste kisses turned into licks and nips down her neck to her breasts. He loved Sabrina's breasts. Her nipples were sensitive, and each time he put his mouth to them, she arched her back, begging for more.

He gave her more.

She gave him everything.

Sabrina was a generous lover. By the moans and sexy words she unleashed, as well as the wetness between her legs, Deacon didn't have to use his Gargoyle senses to determine whether or not she was enjoying herself. The heat in her eyes as she wrapped her lips around his cock let him know she liked sucking him. When he warned her he was close to coming, she didn't shy away from doubling her efforts to make him come down her throat. The taste of his release on her tongue when she kissed him afterward made Deacon want to tie her to the bed and never let her go. When he told her as much, she asked if he had any rope, and he nearly came again from her tempting words.

Sated for the time being, they showered together, and after, they cooked together, moving around the kitchen as if they'd done it hundreds of times before. As was becoming habit, they dined on the patio, enjoying the peacefulness of Deacon's property. Their property. They talked about Sabrina's siblings, and Deacon didn't miss the longing in her voice to see Jasmine and Terrence. He suggested visiting Jerrick in New Orleans and asking the others to join them there. He wanted Sabrina to be happy in all aspects of her life, and after talking to her, he knew that was the one thing missing, whether she admitted it or not.

After the dishes were washed and put away, Deacon suggested they take a ride. He gave Sabrina a quick tutorial on how to hold on and lean with him in the curves. His mate was a natural. Snuggled against his back with her arms around his waist, he took her on back roads to the Talladega forest in Alabama. Sabrina had worn her leather jacket, but it wasn't enough to keep her warm in the higher elevation of the Cheaha Mountain, so he kept to the lower route. The roundtrip ride was almost five hours, but it was the perfect amount of time for her to enjoy the wind on her face and the exhilaration that came with being on two wheels.

They arrived back home a little after midnight. Deacon could have ridden all night, but he knew Sabrina's butt and back would be tired. When he pulled into the garage and parked, Sabrina's legs were wobbly when she slid off the

241

bike. He turned to grab her in case she fell, but she waved his hand off. Grinning, she said, "That was the best."

"Yeah?"

"Yes. Now I know why so many people ride. I would catch myself smiling, but then I'd close my lips so I didn't get bugs in my teeth."

Deacon leaned his head back, laughing loudly. He snaked an arm around Sabrina's waist and pulled her close, planting a solid kiss on her lips. It turned heated quickly. He had been hard since they left home hours ago, having his mate plastered to his back and her hands exploring his stomach as they rode. "Inside, now," he snarled against her mouth.

"Or, we could do it right here." Sabrina stepped back and began removing her clothes, starting with the leather jacket.

Deacon pushed off the bike and unfastened his jeans. If she was serious about having sex in the garage, Deacon was ready to live out a fantasy he'd had ever since meeting Sabrina. When she was completely naked, he growled, "Hands on the seat and spread your legs."

Sabrina bit her bottom lip and did as instructed. With her hands braced against the bike, she arched her back and pushed her ass higher. Deacon had to bend his knees since he was so tall, but he was going to make this position work for both of them. He stroked his hard cock several times over her wet entrance before sliding in. He placed his hands on her hips and held her steady as he rocked back and forth, dipping his knees then rising up again. Sabrina threw her head back and groaned.

"Deacon, oh... Yes... Ungh, harder," she cried. Sabrina held onto the seat with one hand while the other snaked between her legs, rubbing her clit while he stroked her core.

"Gods, you make me so hard," Deacon ground out as his thrusts got faster. "You're so tight around my cock."

242

"Deacon, I need you" – Sabrina gasped – "to bite me."

Deacon's fangs slid down from his gums, and when he felt her pussy clamp down around his cock with her release, he sank his sharp teeth into her shoulder. Sabrina yelled at the sting as she spasmed around his dick.

"Hold on," he warned. Sabrina slapped both hands down onto the bike as Deacon lifted her feet off the ground, pounding into her soaked passage. His orgasm rolled through his body, starting at the base of his spine, through his balls, until he was erupting inside his mate. He came with a roar, rattling the windows of his truck. He banded one arm around her stomach, holding her to him as he came down from the high. He twisted Sabrina around, placing her ass on the edge of the seat and knelt down between her legs. He lapped at their mixed releases, cleaning the inside of her thigh as well as her swollen lips. When he touched his tongue to her clit, she cried out, grabbing his head with one hand while balancing on the bike with the other.

Never had Deacon tasted anything as exotic. Never had he been so fulfilled. So sated. So in love. He kissed his way up her stomach and her chest until he got to her lips. Sabrina didn't hesitate to open for him and taste their combined essence as she'd done before. The kiss turned lazy, and he ended it with a soft nip to her bottom lip.

Standing straight, Deacon tucked himself back into his jeans but didn't bother fastening them. It was a moot point because he was taking his mate to bed. He grabbed beneath her ass and lifted. When Sabrina wrapped her arms and legs around Deacon, he looked her in the eyes. "I love you, Pretty Lady. Thank you for being my mate."

"I love you, too, my Oba."

Sweeter words had never been spoken.

Chapter Twenty-Eight

SABRINA WAS LOOKING forward to family day at the manor. After spending time with Trevor, she was ready to meet the other mates. She'd met a few of them, but she hadn't been able to hear their stories and really get to know them. She was looking forward to checking in on Jonathan as well. While it was an ideal day to ride the bike, she was sore from all the sex they'd had on top of last night's ride. She thought she would be embarrassed when she told Deacon as much, but he had run her a bath and pampered her so sweetly.

When they arrived, Sabrina wasn't surprised at the number of vehicles in the driveway. Deacon had already told her what to expect so she wouldn't be overwhelmed. She had met many of the males while they visited and watched over Jonathan. What did surprise her was Priscilla's mood when they entered the kitchen. The older lady was in her element, bustling around the kitchen.

"Oh, Dr. Bailey. It's so good to see you again. Welcome to the family," Priscilla said, hugging Sabrina tightly.

"Please, call me Sabrina. Is there anything I can do to help?" she asked.

"Oh, thank you, but I've got this. You go on in the den and mingle. Breakfast will be ready shortly."

Deacon bent down and kissed Priscilla on the cheek, and the older woman placed both her hands on Deacon's face. "I'm so happy for you," she whispered.

Deacon closed his eyes for a second, and Sabrina could tell he was enjoying the woman's affection. Now she understood what he meant when he told her Priscilla was like a mother to them all. He led Sabrina into a large room where couples were sitting together while single males stood drinking coffee. Dante's son, Connor, was sitting with a little boy Sabrina didn't recognize, while Frey's daughter, Amelia, danced around in a pink tutu.

Rafael, who held a very pregnant Kaya on his lap, called out to her. "Sabrina, welcome to our home and our family. Deacon, I'll let you make the introductions. We would get up, but Kaya's been having contractions, and I don't want her to move any more than necessary." Kaya rolled her eyes at his words, but she remained nestled against his chest.

"I'm so glad you're here, Sabrina," Kaya said.

"I'm glad to be here."

The room got quiet. Even Amelia stopped dancing so Deacon could go around the room and introduce Sabrina to everyone. Each male who was seated stood as Deacon presented her as his mate. And each one, including those who had already been standing, fisted their hand over their heart and said, "On my honor." Sabrina now knew what the gesture symbolized. It warmed her heart to have the loyalty of each member of their Clan, but it was the women who brought tears to her eyes. Each one, with the exception of Kaya, stood and hugged her, welcoming her to the family.

Sabrina had never felt so accepted, and it wasn't because she had been Jonathan's doctor. It was because she was one of them. As they talked a little about themselves, Sabrina expected there to be at least a little bit of cattiness or jealousy, but there was none. These women – and Trevor – loved one another. Trevor had explained how the mates had a bond of their own, but she hadn't expected to be included into their circle so easily. They accepted her because she was Deacon's mate. Her station in life and the color of her skin had no bearing on how they treated her. Each mate was different. They all had a story to tell, and they promised to do so after breakfast.

Priscilla called them to the dining room where an elaborate buffet was set up. She excused herself, telling Rafael she was going to go sit with Jonathan. Sabrina wanted to see her former patient, but she had time for that after breakfast. The food was delicious, and talk was loud, boisterous, and what Sabrina had dreamed of all her life. When she sat looking at all those gathered around the table, Deacon leaned over and whispered, "Are you okay?"

She smiled up at him. "I'm great. Thank you for giving me not only your love but this family." Deacon kissed her cheek and went back to eating. When she glanced across the table, Abbi smiled at her.

"Well, shit," Kaya said from her seat beside Rafael. "Either I peed myself, or my water just broke."

"What? It's too early!" Rafael cried, jumping from his chair, which fell over with a thud.

"Obviously, your son thinks it's the perfect time. Besides, we have three doctors here. Oh!" Kaya shouted, grabbing her stomach. "I think he's really ready. Rafe, I think he's coming now!"

"Somebody find Priscilla," Rafael instructed.

"I'll go. I can sit with Jonathan," Sabrina offered.

"But we might need you," Rafael said.

Sabrina smiled and shook her head. "Kaya is in good hands with Isabelle and Dante. Please, point me to Priscilla?"

"They're in the garden. Deacon, show her where that is." Rafael appeared to calm down as Kaya clutched his arm, but Sabrina saw the worried look in his eyes.

Deacon hurried Sabrina out the back door and down the steps to the entrance to a breathtaking area. A concrete path meandered through all types of plants, flowers, bushes, and trees, until they came to a bench where Priscilla was seated

246

next to her brother.

"Kaya's in labor, and they have requested your presence, Priscilla," Sabrina said.

When Priscilla turned to Jonathan, he patted her on the arm. "They need you. Go."

"I'll sit with him," Sabrina said.

Priscilla hesitated, but Jonathan nodded to her. "Thank you," Priscilla said then took off back to the house. Sabrina took the seat beside Jonathan, leaning gently against the older man's shoulder, and Deacon stood sentry beside the bench.

KAYA HAD RAFAEL'S hand in an iron grip while Priscilla dabbed Kaya's forehead with a damp cloth. All her plans to deliver Sebastian at the hospital had flown out the window when her son decided he was going to be born at home. Rafael managed to keep a level head once the initial shock had worn off. He carried Kaya to their bedroom. Dante might be a doctor as well as Rafael's brother, but they all knew Rafael would lose his shit if Dante was anywhere near a half-naked Kaya while Isabelle examined her.

Dante called for an ambulance and then Kaya's obstetrician, while the others sat with the kids. Frey was doing his best to get in touch with Matthew and Slade, but Kaya told him to let them enjoy their vacation. There would be enough Clan wanting their hands on the Prince once Sebastian was born. When Priscilla finally made her way into the house, Kaya hadn't missed the tear-stained cheeks of her dear friend. The woman had been spending every moment she could with her brother while he was still with them, but Kaya knew Priscilla didn't want to miss being there when Sebastian was born.

Everything Kaya had been told about giving birth didn't prepare her for the pain or the fear. She wasn't due for another few weeks, but Isabelle assured her Sebastian was strong. He was his father's child, after all. The ambulance was almost there, but Kaya wasn't sure it would get there in time.

"I know you want to push, but we need to wait for the paramedics if at all possible. They have the necessary supplies to keep both you and Sebastian safe," Isabelle said.

Rafael took Kaya's hand in his and kissed her knuckles. "My Queen," he whispered. "You probably hate me right now, but please know I would take your pain if I could. You are about to give me the most precious gift imaginable, and I am in awe of you. You are the strongest female I've ever known, and it humbles me to be your mate. I love you more than I ever thought possible, and my love grows for you daily."

Kaya reached up and placed her hand on Rafael's damp cheek. "I could never hate you. Yes, I want our son out of my body, but what kind of Queen would I be if I allowed you to carry my pain? Love is aaaaaaaaaggggggghhhhh!" Another contraction hit, and Kaya gripped Rafael's hand as hard as she could as she breathed through it. When it subsided, Priscilla wiped the sweat from Kaya's forehead again.

Rafael and Priscilla helped Kaya the best they could through the next few contractions, but finally, Isabelle told her they couldn't wait any longer. Sebastian was coming. At the top of the next contraction, she told Kaya to tuck her chin to her chest and push. Kaya grunted and strained. When Isabelle told her to stop, Kaya leaned back against Rafael's chest.

"The ambulance is here," Dante announced from outside the room. Before the paramedics could get inside, Kaya pushed twice more. When a male and female strode into the

248

room carrying supplies, Rafael growled, and Kaya shushed him. The man ignored Rafael, but he let the female take lead when Isabelle moved out of the way.

"Okay, Mrs. Stone, I need you to give me one more good push," the female said. Kaya did, and after what seemed like an eternity, the sweetest sound she'd ever heard filled the air. "Congratulations on your son," the medic said.

"We have a son," Rafael whispered, kissing Kaya softly, while the manor erupted in cheers.

SABRINA STUDIED JONATHAN'S face. He was smiling at her in a way she'd never seen before.

"How are you feeling, Mr. Holt?"

"Oh, stop with that Mister stuff. We're family now, Sabrina. Is it true? Is Kaya about to give birth?"

"It seems that way. Did you want to go inside?"

"No. This is perfect." Jonathan reached out and took Sabrina's hand in his. "One life ends as another begins." Jonathan closed his eyes and turned his face to the warm summer sunshine. Sabrina wanted to argue, but she couldn't. She knew Jonathan's time was drawing to a close, but it didn't make it easier. She did her best to keep things professional between herself and her patients, but she'd become attached to this man. He had brought Deacon to her. Without him, she might never have found such profound love and the family he brought with him.

Deacon placed his hands on her shoulders, offering silent strength. As intense as their lovemaking was, it was the quiet times like this she cherished the most where their connection didn't need words. Deacon's hands tensed, and Sabrina looked up at him.

"The baby's coming," Deacon told them. "They've

called for an ambulance, but I'm not sure if Kaya can hold out that long." They sat in companionable silence while they waited. The siren's wail rent the air, louder as it neared the driveway, and once it entered the grounds, the sound cut off, bathing them in solitude once more.

After a few minutes, Jonathan muttered, "I can hear him," and both Sabrina and Deacon looked at the man.

"Hear who?" Sabrina asked.

"Sebastian," Jonathan replied, smiling. His tight grip on Sabrina's hand grew lax.

"Jonathan?" Sabrina turned to face him, but she knew in her heart he was finally at peace.

"He's gone," Deacon whispered. "Kaya just gave birth, and Jonathan has passed on."

Sabrina reached over to check his pulse, because the doctor in her told her to, but Deacon was right. Sabrina wrapped her arm around Jonathan's shoulder and kissed his cheek. "Until we meet again."

DEACON LIFTED JONATHAN'S body, and with Sabrina holding the man's hand, he carried him back to the house. Sabrina held the door for Deacon. Inside, everyone was celebrating the birth of their Prince. When they caught sight of Deacon with Jonathan in his arms, a hush fell over the room. Deacon continued down the hallway that led to Jonathan's bedroom. He laid the human on his bed, placing his hands on his stomach. Deacon kissed Jonathan on the temple and led Sabrina back to the den. He didn't want to put a damper on Rafael and Kaya's big day, but there was no way to keep the news from them.

Gregor was closest to Rafael, but he and Tessa were still in New Orleans, so Deacon got Dante's attention. He led him away from where Priscilla was hovering next to Kaya. When they were out of earshot, he explained what happened.

"I'll handle it," Dante assured him, but Rafael rounded the corner.

"Is it true?" he asked.

"Yes. I put him on his bed," Deacon said only loud enough for the shifters to hear.

Rafael closed his eyes for a few seconds, but when he opened them, he was smiling. "He's at peace now. Sebastian was with him in those last few moments, and now, we will all carry Jonathan forward in our hearts. I need to get back to Kaya and my son, but do me a favor. In Jonathan's room, there's an envelope in the drawer by his bed. Bring it to me, please."

Deacon inclined his head then strode down the hall to retrieve the envelope. He carried it with him into the den where Sabrina was waiting with the others. While the ambulance was loading Kaya and Sebastian for the ride to the hospital, Rafael came into the den and passed out cigars to anyone who wanted them. Deacon handed the envelope to Rafael. "Thank you, Brother. Thank you both for being there with him when he passed."

Rafael then turned to everyone else. "It is a day for celebration. Sebastian is going to need special care since he decided to grace us with his presence a little early, so I'll ask that you all give Kaya and me some space at the hospital. It's not that I don't want you there, but there's no need in you all sitting on uncomfortable chairs when you can sit here or at your own homes in comfort." Priscilla came into the room, and Rafael pulled her to him. "We're all going to need your help over the coming days, so I thank you in advance."

Rafael gave the envelope to Dante and asked him and Isabelle to stay with Priscilla while she read it before allowing her to see her brother. Rafael then rushed outside to ride in the ambulance with his mate and new son.

251

Deacon didn't want to wait around for Dante and Isabelle to break the news to Priscilla. It had been a good day up until that point, and Priscilla's pain would hit him hard. When he realized how selfish he was being, Deacon mentally slapped himself. If Priscilla could endure the pain of her brother's passing, so could he.

Chapter Twenty-Nine

PRISCILLA UNDERSTOOD WHY Rafael asked everyone to remain at the manor, but she didn't understand why Deacon and Sabrina were inside. "Who's sitting with Jonathan?" she asked. When she turned to go to his room, Dante stopped her.

"Jonathan asked that you have this. If you'd rather be alone to read it, we can all give you some privacy."

She knew. In that moment, Priscilla knew her love was gone. She took the letter from Dante and moved to sit down on the sofa. "I'd like you all to stay, please," she whispered. She needed the strength of her family to get through the next few hours. Dante sat to her right, and Isabelle took the space to her left. She pulled the letter out, and with trembling hands, she attempted to read the words. The tears were so thick, she couldn't see the letters. Priscilla handed the paper to Isabelle and asked if she would read it out loud.

Isabelle nodded. She cleared her throat a couple times then read to Priscilla the words her love wanted her to hear.

"My darling Ruby,

I love you beyond measure, and I will love you beyond this life as well. You have been my rock, my best friend, my everything, for as long as I can remember. I need you to continue doing that for me

253

now. Sebastian is going to need a grandmother's love, and Kaya needs your ever-present mother's guiding hand. I need you to be strong, not only for me, but for Rafael as well. You are and always have been the glue holding our family together. Carry my love and the memories we've shared over the years in your heart. Know I am watching over you always.

Share with our precious Sebastian the stories of his father, his uncles, and all the Clan who will one day be under his rule. Teach him the same way you taught those who have come before him. Show him what it means to love. Remind him to be kind and fair. And when he's old enough, tell him where to find the cookies you've hidden from Rafael.

And when it's time, pass the same love, knowledge, and lessons on to his cousins and any siblings he might have. Never let Sebastian forget I have loved him from the beginning, and I will love him forever more, as I will you.

You are the most giving person I know, and I have to selfishly ask you to once again put my wishes above your own. Your sacrifice has been too great. Knowing this, I still ask that you do not mourn me. Instead, celebrate my life. Our life. Honor me this one last time without tears but with laughter. I know you will, because I know how much you love me. Our secret is now yours to share, if you so desire.

You made my life complete, and I can pass on to the next part of my journey knowing you are strong enough for both of us. I will be waiting for you when you take your last breath. Until then, know I am with you. You are my heart and my soul.

Now and forever yours, Jon"

Priscilla wiped her tears and smiled as Isabelle handed her the letter. "By the way you're all looking at me, I know you are confused. Those words do not sound like a brother's dying letter to his sister." Priscilla pressed her hands down her thighs to smooth out the nonexistent wrinkles. "The Holt family has been looking after Di Pietros for many generations. For most of their family, it was an honor to do so. But for Jonathan's sister, it was a burden she refused to bear. His sister fell in love, and because the man she loved wasn't from one of the families who had been sworn to secrecy, their marriage was forbidden.

"But Jonathan loved his sister deeply. She was his twin, and as such, theirs was a bond unlike most siblings. My family also held the secrets of the Gargoyles, and I grew up with Jonathan and his sister from diapers. When he told me of his sister's plight, we came up with a plan only he, his sister, and I knew about. Jonathan took his place with the Di Pietros, and his sister joined him. Only instead of it being the real Priscilla Holt, it was me pretending to be her. By this time, both my parents had passed on, so I had no one to answer to. While Jon and I lived together as siblings, Priscilla ran away with her beloved, and they are still together, living in the South of France.

"Jonathan and I fell in love when we were in our teens. We never married, but our lives were spent together as if we were. My real name is Ruby, but I've portrayed Priscilla for so long, that's who I've become. Eventually, his other siblings found out, but by that time, their parents were dead, and his siblings didn't care. I love Kaya and Rafael as if they were my own children. I feel the same about all of you in this room. But my only regret is not being there with Jonathan when he took his last breath. I would like to see him now so I can tell him goodbye."

255

"I'll take you to him," Deacon said. He held out his hand, and Priscilla took it. Deacon led her down the hallway to their wing of the manor. When he pushed open Jonathan's bedroom door, her knees weakened, but Deacon caught her. He helped her walk to the bed, where Priscilla kicked off her shoes and climbed up to lie down beside him.

When Deacon closed the door giving her privacy, Priscilla curled up next to Jonathan and placed her hand over his cold one. She did as he asked and put a smile on her face. Lying next to her beloved, Priscilla sang his favorite song with all the love she'd ever felt for the man who had been her life.

THE MOOD IN the room was somber until Connor stood, looked at his father, and said, "Da, Jonathan wanted us to celebrate, so we should. Please put on some music."

Dante smiled at his son and did as he asked. Connor grabbed Amelia's hand, and the two of them started dancing. Deacon held out his hand for Sabrina. "Care to dance, Pretty Lady?" Soon everyone joined in, and the Clan honored the human who had come to mean so much to them all. Even Rain joined in. He had been through quite an ordeal, but he was reunited with his father, and that in itself was cause for celebration.

Priscilla eventually left Jonathan's side. While she didn't dance, she did what made her happiest, and that was cook. The mates had already cleaned up the breakfast dishes, and they all pitched in setting up the tables outside while Dante and Trevor went to get one of the buses from the morgue and took Jonathan's body to a local funeral home. It had been his wish to be cremated and his ashes spread throughout the garden. Rafael and Kaya had already said their goodbyes to their friend, not knowing if he would wake up each morning.

Father and mother stayed at the hospital with Sebastian until they were able to bring him home. Priscilla visited every day, and with a smile on her face, she kept her promise to the love of her life.

Deacon was rarely without his own smile as he and Sabrina settled into their new normal. They woke each morning to make love before eating breakfast, and then they headed to work. When they came home at night, they shared about their days. Some nights they cooked together, but on those occasions Sabrina had a difficult day at work, Deacon sent her upstairs to relax in a bath with a glass of wine while he cooked for her. The other mates invited Sabrina to their homes, where over time, she heard all their stories.

When Deacon asked for time off to take Sabrina to New Orleans, Gregor surprised him and asked if he and Tessa could tag along. Remy was doing well handling the Pen, and Rain was enjoying spending time with Connor and Amelia. The boy still had nightmares, but for the most part, he was a happy child.

Jerrick and Evan were technically still hiding, and for the time being, they decided to remain in The Big Easy. The two males, while showing no signs of being romantically involved, had become close. Gladys, Tessa's next-door neighbor, cooked for them and doted on them as if they were her own sons.

Instead of driving, the four of them took the Clan jet. Deacon had a feeling if he and Sabrina hadn't been with them, Tessa and Gregor would have made use of the bedroom. The thought crossed Deacon's mind more than once. Instead, they sat in the luxurious leather seats while Tessa told Sabrina stories about Jonas. It was fascinating to hear about Sabrina's boss as something other than chief of staff of the hospital. All the Clan knew Jonas's background, but Tessa knew the man who had cloned her and helped raise her.

With Tessa as their tour guide, Sabrina fell in love with New Orleans. Deacon saw it through new eyes as they strolled the streets of the French Quarter, window-shopped the quaint businesses, and tasted all the local cuisine. Sabrina's true love was the Garden District, and even though Deacon preferred to live somewhere without neighbors, it made sense to purchase a home since Jerrick had decided to remain there.

Tessa introduced them to Dominic and Lilly, and the three couples were walking around, taking in the architecture. When Deacon pointed out a house for sale close to the one Tessa owned, Sabrina shook her head. "Oba, we can't just buy a house."

"But we can, Pretty Lady. Jerrick and Evan need somewhere to live, and we need somewhere to stay when we visit. Think of it as an investment."

Tessa said to Sabrina, "You should know by now the Goyles always get their way. There's no arguing with them."

Gregor laughed, pulling Tessa to him. "No arguing, Red? Seriously?"

Tessa elbowed him in the stomach. "Shut up, Stone."

Everyone laughed along with them, except for Lilly. She was staring at the house.

"What is it, My Love?" Dominic asked.

Lilly winked at her mate before turning to Sabrina and taking her hand. "I have a good feeling about this one. I think you should check it out." Lilly had given Sabrina a tarot reading the night before. While Sabrina had been skeptical, Deacon had been enthralled. According to the cards, big things were going to happen for Sabrina in both her personal and professional lives. Lilly's words had been vague at first, but she had written down exact details, telling Sabrina not to read the note until a specific date.

"What do you say? Want to take a look inside?" Deacon asked.

Sabrina knew money wasn't an issue, so when she grinned and said yes, Deacon wasn't surprised. She tried to be the voice of reason whenever they talked about spending money. Deacon knew it stemmed from her childhood. The realtor was able to meet with them that afternoon, so after lunch at an Irish Pub which belonged to friends of Tessa's, they toured the three-story house.

Deacon didn't need the witch to tell him the outcome of their visit. His mate's excitement was tangible as soon as she stepped out the back door and into the private yard. The previous owners had built a breathtaking garden off the covered patio. The older house had been updated with modern appliances while the structural integrity had been maintained throughout. Dominic knew the previous owner who happened to be one of the Clan. The male had recently found his mate while on vacation in the Keys and decided to move to one of the small islands where his mate had a veterinarian practice she loved.

After looking at every room, each nook and cranny, Sabrina grinned. "What do you think, Oba?"

Deacon loved hearing his birth name fall from her lips. Even if it hadn't been his idea, he would have sold his soul to give Sabrina what she wanted.

"I think we have a new home."

He kissed her deeply, not caring if the others were standing there.

"Get a room," Tessa teased.

Deacon looked around. "I think we'll get them all."

After putting in an offer with the realtor, the six of them headed back to Tessa's to tell Jerrick and Evan the good news. Since the guys were going to be living there, Deacon suggested taking them back to see the house.

Jerrick and Evan were sitting next to each other on the

sofa. Evan hadn't said a lot since Deacon and the others arrived. He mostly deferred to Jerrick's opinion on most subjects. On the outside, the male seemed to be doing well, but his heart was still hurting for some reason. Deacon chalked it up to what he'd gone through since leaving the military. From being unwanted by his family, to becoming Unholy, and then to become a Reborn, the male needed someone to talk to. There were few Gargoyle psychologists, and Deacon was going to recommend one to both Evan and Jerrick.

"Were you planning on buying a house when you came to visit?" Jerrick asked.

"No. When we stopped in front of the one for sale, Lilly had a good feeling about it," Sabrina said. She invited Lilly to tell Jerrick why she thought the house would be a good one. Tessa was arguing with Dominic about his choice of rum, and Gregor was grinning like a fool.

Deacon stood back, listening to the various conversations. He was enjoying being around the other two couples. Lilly was soft-spoken and one of the most genuine beings Deacon had ever met. His beast had never been at such peace as it was around the blonde. And Deacon had to admit, he was a believer. The more time he spent around the witch, the more he thought there was more to her than a tarot readings and mixing potions. She had a true gift. And Dominic... The male with his long, black hair, leather pants and boots, and flowing, white shirt didn't just dress the part of a pirate because he liked the clothing; he had been one. His French accent hadn't abated over the years, and Deacon could admit it was intriguing. Deacon thought about all the different personalities of the males and their mates in their Clan. They were a diverse bunch, and he thanked the gods he and Sabrina had found a home among them.

Deacon had always gotten along with his boss, but now he considered Gregor to be something other than the hardass warden. And Tessa was a hoot. He admired her willingness to jump in and help in whatever Gregor got up to. He wasn't surprised that Gregor allowed it. They were a team. At least they were now. For a while, the two had been in a rough spot, but they seemed to have worked it out.

He knew relationships were hard work, even with the mate bond, but he prayed he and Sabrina were never at odds with one another. He figured if he gave her everything she wanted and then some, he had it made.

After showing Jerrick and Evan the new house, the group went out to celebrate. Dominic called a friend who owned a restaurant down by the river. The man put them in a private room where they were treated like royalty. The food was excellent, and the company was even better. Deacon felt his mate's eyes on him, and when he looked at her, she smiled and whispered, "I love you." Even if she never gave him the words, Deacon felt Sabrina's love in every look, every touch.

"Are you happy, Pretty Lady?"

"I am. I never dreamed my life would be so full. For the longest time, all I had was my career. But now I have my new family, and I have my brother. But mostly, I have you. You're my everything, Oba. Thank you."

"You're welcome, and if you didn't know it, I love you too." Deacon knew there was one thing missing from Sabrina's life, and he vowed to give it to her. Somehow, some way. He would make her life complete. But for the time being, he sat back and relished the laughter and love flowing around the room.

Epilogue

2050

SABRINA DIDN'T UNDERSTAND why Deacon was so nervous about celebrating Thanksgiving at home. Her mate was running around like the proverbial chicken, decorating and cooking more food than Priscilla usually prepared for family day. In the past, they had spent every holiday at the manor with the Clan and then visited Jerrick and Evan after the fact, celebrating with them separately. Today, the boys, as Sabrina lovingly called Jerrick and Evan, were coming to their home in the woods. And, for the first time, Jasmine and Terrence were visiting as well. Terrence was bringing his wife and two sons. Deacon tried to get Sabrina to relax in the tub, but there was no way she was leaving him to do all the work by himself.

Deacon made it his mission to reunite all the siblings. He hadn't managed to make it happen until now. Schedules never coincided for all four of them to be together at the same time. After purchasing their house in New Orleans, Jerrick and Evan moved in, and as in most things they did, together they made it a home. Sabrina had turned them loose with decorating, and they filled the house with local artwork. Their most prized piece was one Lilly had painted. About four months after they furnished the new house, they had a housewarming party, and Jasmine was able to attend.

262

Terrence already had a business trip planned. Then, several months later, Terrence's schedule was free, but Jasmine couldn't get away.

When the doorbell rang, Deacon cursed from the kitchen, and Sabrina chuckled. "Come on, Oba. Let's welcome our guests together."

Deacon looked around the spotless kitchen. Food was either in the refrigerator, the oven, or in rows on the counter. "I think I forgot something," he said, wiping his hands down his jeans.

"Yes, you did. You forgot to breathe. Now, come on." Taking him by the arm, Sabrina led her mate to the front door. Terrence, his wife Dorian, and their two sons, James and Thomas, greeted them both with hugs. Sabrina had been pleasantly surprised to find out her brother was a hugger. When they'd met up in New Orleans, he'd thanked her for taking care of them as kids, and he credited her for his life turning out as well as it had. She didn't believe it for a second. The Wilsons were the ones who raised him, and it was their selflessness that rubbed off on him. Dorian was a lovely woman who taught high school math. James and Thomas were well-mannered teens.

Jerrick and Evan arrived next. Dominic and Lilly had flown to New Atlanta on one of the Clan's jets and brought the boys with them. Dominic had given them both jobs, and Lilly had taken them under her wing as an older sister. The four hung out often, and Sabrina was grateful for it.

When Jasmine finally arrived, she was holding hands with the cutest little boy Sabrina had ever seen, and she was struggling with her bag and a booster seat. "Sorry I'm late. Placement for Scotty fell through at the last minute, and I had to bring him with me. I hope you don't mind." Sabrina fell in love the second she looked into his wonder-filled brown eyes.

"Of course not." Sabrina bent over so she was closer to

263

his level. "Hello, Scotty." The little boy hid behind Jasmine's legs, peeking around then darting back. The adults laughed, and when they remembered why they were there, chaos ensued with everyone holding on to each other, crying and laughing as they became reacquainted. Dorian tried to get Scotty to sit with her on the sofa, but it was Deacon the child homed in on. When Scotty pulled away from Jasmine, the siblings got quiet when the boy walked to Deacon, this large male, and held up his arms. Deacon picked him up, placing him on his hip and smiled.

"Hi, Scotty. I'm Deacon."

Scotty grinned and wrapped his little arm around Deacon's neck. Dorian and Deacon, with Scotty in tow, poured drinks for the adults and sodas for the teens. Scotty had juice in a sippy cup, which he offered more than once to Deacon. Deacon pretended to drink, making *num num* sounds, and Scotty giggled. That made Deacon laugh, and that made Sabrina want to drag Deacon upstairs and have her way with him. There was something sexy about a virile man making a child happy.

As glad as Sabrina was to have her family all together, it was her mate and the little boy she couldn't take her eyes off. When Deacon needed his hands free to finish getting the food ready, Sabrina held Scotty and stayed close to the kitchen. Then, when they all sat down at the large dining table together, Scotty reached for Deacon instead of sitting with Jasmine. Deacon placed the boy's booster chair in the seat next to his and helped him with his food.

Sabrina and her siblings talked while eating, getting reacquainted. The teens joined in the conversation, but Deacon was quiet for the most part. Everyone complimented Deacon on his cooking more than once. The party moved to the living room where they continued talking and letting their food settle. The only topic off-limits was what happened to Jerrick and Evan after they left the service.

Terrence and Jasmine were aware of what their brother had been through. Jerrick left it up to Terrence to tell his wife and sons, and if they knew, they didn't ask.

Deacon relaxed in a recliner with Scotty on his lap, playing with a stuffed bear. The teens talked to Deacon about working at the Pen, and he asked them about school and their futures. Sabrina caught her mate's eye several times, letting him silently know with her smile how thankful she was for bringing her family together.

"I've never seen him so smitten with anyone," Jasmine whispered to Sabrina when they were dishing up dessert. "The couple who was supposed to take him changed their mind at the last minute. Decided they weren't ready for a child with developmental issues."

"What?" Deacon, who had followed them to get Scotty more juice, rounded on Jasmine. He looked down at the child, and in that moment, Sabrina felt more love for her mate than she had in the past two years. He might be the empath, but his eyes betrayed every emotion Deacon felt. She'd grown to know when he was overwhelmed, and she'd learned to get him away from situations that brought on those feelings as quickly as possible. Now, his eyes were filled with love and compassion for a child he'd only met a couple hours earlier.

"What type of issues?" Sabrina asked while filling the coffee machine with water.

"His mother was a junkie. Scotty was born three months premature and addicted to more drugs than most people can name. They didn't think he would make it, and he's only still with us because this little boy is a fighter. His speech has been delayed as has his growth. Mentally, he's bright, but he has issues with his lungs, and sometimes his coordination is off. It's going to take a strong family to love someone who needs so much time and attention."

The two of them hadn't spoken of having kids since

before they were mated. Sabrina continued getting the birth control shot. She figured if Deacon wanted children, he would bring it up. As much as she wanted to keep Scotty, she didn't see how they could take the child in and give him the time and attention he needed. Not with both of them working long hours.

"I need to talk to you," Deacon said to Sabrina. "Scotty, I'll be back in just a few minutes," he said, handing the boy over to Jasmine. Deacon grabbed Sabrina by the hand and led her outside.

"Pretty Lady…" Deacon pulled her hands to his mouth and kissed her knuckles. "I know I said I wasn't sure about having children, but I think we would be the perfect parents for Scotty."

"Oba, you heard Jasmine. He needs lots of time and attention. You and I both work long hours."

"I know you love the hospital, so I'll quit the Pen. We don't need the money, but that little boy needs us."

Sabrina wrapped her arms around Deacon's neck and pulled him down for a kiss. "You are the best male I know, Deacon Wright. Are you sure about this?"

"I've never been surer. Well, other than when I knew you were my mate."

"Then yes, let's do this."

"There's something else. Something I was going to do anyway, a surprise. Now you're going to think I'm doing it for the wrong reason, but I'm not. It's just the timing—"

"Oba, whatever it is, spit it out."

Deacon pulled her hands from around his neck and dragged her back inside. "Can I have your attention?" When everyone was quiet, Deacon dropped to one knee. "I promise, this is for the right reason. Sabrina Michelle Bailey, you have already made me the happiest male in the universe by being with me these last two years. We both know we don't need a piece of paper telling us we're in this for the

266

long haul, but I would still be honored if you would be my wife. Will you marry me?" Deacon reached in his pocket and pulled out an elegant ring. Sabrina would have to count the diamonds later. When she could see without tears crowding her eyes.

"Yes, Oba, I'll marry you." Deacon rose to his feet and kissed her breathless as her family cheered.

Scotty was clapping and laughing along with everyone else. "Dede," he said, stretching toward Deacon.

"Did you hear that? He said Deacon!" The joy on her mate's face was contagious. Sabrina was hugging them both when Deacon whispered, "You have a text message." Other than Jerrick, her siblings didn't know about Deacon being a Gargoyle. Jerrick explaining to his family about being Unholy then Reborn had been hard for him, but the Unholy weren't a secret. Sabrina found her phone in the kitchen and smiled when she saw who it was from.

Lilly: *Happy Thanksgiving. Do you remember what today is?*

Sabrina: *Happy Thanksgiving to you. And yes, today's the day I read your note*

Lilly: *Well?*

Sabrina: *Ha! I'll go read it now.*

Sabrina had kept the note from Lilly in her underwear drawer ever since she'd given it to her. Never once had she opened it. She kept it with her panties so she would see it every day, and on the date in question – today – she wouldn't forget. She had planned on reading it after everyone went to sleep, but she supposed now was as good a time as any. Taking the envelope to the living room where Deacon was playing on the floor with Scotty, she sat down next to him. The others were watching football, drinking coffee, or vegging out.

"You ready to see what Lilly had to say?"

Deacon nodded. It was almost as if he was holding his

breath. Sabrina opened the flap and pulled out the note. When she read Lilly's neat printing, she couldn't believe it.

February 28, 2049 – you will become chief of staff
November 24, 2050 – Deacon will propose, and your family will grow by one

"That's…" Deacon shook his head.

"That's amazing is what it is," Sabrina said.

And amazing was how Sabrina felt when she and Deacon told Jasmine they wanted to adopt Scotty. The process took a while, but while they waited for the paperwork to go through, Deacon talked with Gregor who gave his blessing on Deacon retiring from his job. Remy, who had returned to New Atlanta, stepped into Deacon's position seamlessly. Deacon spent the first few days of his retirement getting Scotty's room ready, and they both visited him every weekend until they could bring him home.

On February 28, 2051, two years after becoming chief of staff, Sabrina married the love of her life with their son in their arms.

A Note from the Author

Thank you for waiting patiently for Deacon's book. Matthew and Slade will get their story (a novella as of now, but that could change when I begin writing), and in it, you'll find out a little more about Remy and Rain. Kai is slated to be the next novel, so stay tuned for that one as well.

As in Frey's story, a song had a big part in Deacon's book. From the moment Sebastian came into being in the first book, I always knew the moment he was born would be the same moment Jonathan passed away. "Lightning Crashes" by Live is a song I've heard many times over the years, but when I was writing Rafael, I happened to hear it, and the scene clicked. Even knowing it was coming didn't make it any easier to write.

Next up will be Mav's story in the Hounds of Zeus. If you haven't read book 1, check out Waging War, where you meet Lucy's father, Warryck, and his female, Kerrigan.

Coming Soon

Double the Mayhem – Hounds of Zeus MC Book 2

Slade – A Stone Society Novella

ABOUT THE AUTHOR

Multi-genre author Faith Gibson began writing in high school, and through the years, penned many stories and poems. As her dreams continued getting crazier than the one before, she decided to keep a dream journal. Many of these nighttime escapades have led to a line, a chapter, or even a complete story.

"Love is love, and there's not enough love in the world." This belief she holds strongly, and it's the prevailing theme in her works, all of which come with a happy ending.

Faith believes her purpose in life is to entertain the masses, even if it's one person at a time. Living just outside of Nashville, Tennessee, with the love of her life and her pit bull pup, when she's not hard at work writing her next adventure, she can often be found playing trivia while enjoying craft beer, listening to live music, or off on an adventure of her own.

Connect with Faith via the following social media sites:

https://www.facebook.com/faithgibsonauthor

https://www.twitter.com/authorfgibson

Sign up for her newsletter:

http://faithgibsonauthor.com/newsletter/

www.ingramcontent.com/pod-product-compliance
Lightning Source LLC
Chambersburg PA
CBHW071234260626
47161CB00003BA/855